Dear Reader,

On my grandmother's side I have family ties going back generations in Texas. I had the pleasure of living a short time in Dallas, which not only has one of the most beautiful and exciting skylines I've ever seen, but the friendliest people, too. Even though my time in Texas was short, the glorious cities and charming small towns, the movers and shakers, and the down-home country folk made a deep impact on me. *Double Vision* was my first Intrigue title for Harlequin, and the first of several stories set in Dallas and in the Hill Country near Austin. I hope you find the people and places as wonderful as I do.

Enjoy,

Sheryl Lynn

GREATEST TEXAS LOVE STORIES OF ALL TIME

GREATEST
TEXAS LOVE STORIES
OF ALL TIME

DOUBLE VISION
Sheryl Lynn

Trouble in Texas

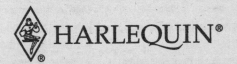

HARLEQUIN®

TORONTO • NEW YORK • LONDON
AMSTERDAM • PARIS • SYDNEY • HAMBURG
STOCKHOLM • ATHENS • TOKYO • MILAN • MADRID
PRAGUE • WARSAW • BUDAPEST • AUCKLAND

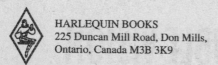 HARLEQUIN BOOKS
225 Duncan Mill Road, Don Mills,
Ontario, Canada M3B 3K9

ISBN 0-373-65248-8

DOUBLE VISION

Copyright © 1992 by Jaye W. Manus

Visit us at www.eHarlequin.com

Printed in U.S.A.

SHERYL LYNN

lives in Colorado with her husband and a pack of excessively furry dogs and cats. When she isn't writing novels of love and suspense, she is tending to a passel of teenaged foster daughters and indulging her passion for creating beaded jewelry.

Chapter One

Collin County courtroom number three was hot and sticky. Reporters scratched pencils against humidity-softened notepads. The screeing squeak of felt-tipped painting pens made a backdrop of noise as the courtroom artists sketched the judge, defendant, attorneys and witness. Spectators packed the gallery, dividing their attention between the defendant, William Abernathy and the State's primary witness, Kerry Byfield. No one wanted to miss a word about one of the most shocking murders to ever strike Plano, Texas.

Photographs blown up into two-by-three-foot posters were tagged as evidence and mounted on easels. One depicted murder victim Louise Abernathy. A once beautiful socialite, she was bathed in blood, her face obliterated by a shotgun blast. There were close-ups of blood spatters on silky papered walls and a close-up of a maimed hand with a diamond ring that glittered in the camera's flash. The photos stood behind the evidence table like come-on's for an obscene splatter movie.

Kerry Byfield wilted on the witness stand, looking smaller than her five-foot-seven, one-hundred-thirty-pound frame. Her light brown hair hung lankly. Purplish smudges marred the flesh under her eyes. Her large, green eyes were wary, haunted and exhausted.

The district attorney had promised her this was an open-and-shut case. All Kerry had to do was tell what she had seen on the night of June 5 at the Abernathy house. Her first day of testimony had been simple. Mr. Marsh, the prosecutor, asked her what she had seen. She told the jury.

Everything was nice and simple until the defense attorney, Mr. Quintas, had started his cross-examination. It seemed as though he would never quit. Quintas called Kerry a liar, ripped apart her testimony and tried to trick her into inconsistencies. She felt under siege, as though she was no longer merely telling the truth, but engaged in a battle in which her integrity was the prize.

Kerry gave up trying to dry her hands by rubbing them against her skirt. Remembering what Mr. Marsh said about not gesturing when she spoke, she forced her hands to rest on her lap. She couldn't stop the trembling of her knees as defense attorney Geoffrey Quintas prepared for another attack.

Quintas shuffled papers on the long defense table. He was a short, compact man. His misshapen nose and bulldog face made him look like a boxer. His charcoal-colored suit, even though expensive, looked out of sync with his sloping shoulders and ravaged face. He had a booming voice and aggressive manner. Kerry suspected the jurors enjoyed his theatrics. She tensed. *How much more can he ask?* she thought wearily.

"Miss Byfield," Quintas said in a friendly voice. "You don't date very much do you?" His brown eyes were fierce.

The question took her aback. She glanced at Mr.

Marsh. He frowned at Quintas. Kerry leaned toward the microphone and said, "No, sir."

"Why is that?"

Marsh stood. "I object, your honor! Miss Byfield's social life has nothing to do with this case—"

"But it does," Quintas interrupted.

Judge MacElroy, a round-faced, no-nonsense Texan whom Kerry hadn't seen smile once during her three days of testimony, rested his cheek on his hand.

"I can show this line of questioning has relevance to the case, your honor, if you'll allow me to continue," Quintas said.

Judge MacElroy glanced at his watch. "Approach the bench, counselors." He covered his microphone with a hand. "You have had this young woman on the stand for three days. Mr. Quintas, your line of questioning has ranged from matters of her mental health to how she likes her eggs cooked for breakfast. What all that has to do with her seeing your client exit the murder scene is beyond me. I'm certain it is confusing for the jury, as well. I do not appreciate theatrics or histrionics, and certainly not nonsense in my court."

"Your honor, I assure you, this line of questioning is relevant. If you will allow."

"Last warning, Mr. Quintas. No more nonsense." The judge looked at his watch again. "It's almost four o'clock. I don't want to see this young lady on the stand a fourth day. Do you understand? Make your point and let this trial continue."

"Your honor, sir, I have every reason to doubt this witness's credibility. A man's life is at stake here," Quintas said.

Marsh objected, "You can't prove one instance of

perjury against the witness, nor has she displayed hostility.''

"Just as you can't prove my client murdered his wife. All you have is that woman's say-so and some trumped-up evidence that any first-year law student can see is phony!'' Quintas's voice dropped. "I can't believe this travesty got past the grand jury. This trial is a joke.''

"That is for the jury to decide,'' the judge said. "Continue, Mr. Quintas.''

Quintas paced before the witness box. "You were engaged to be married at one time, weren't you, Miss Byfield?''

Kerry's head jerked upward. The question came from so far out in left field, it wasn't even in the ballpark. "Yes, sir.''

"To one Michael Hammond, formerly of Carrollton, Texas?''

She struggled to regain her composure, her weary mind trying frantically to conjure up Mike and make a connection between him and what was happening in the courtroom. Aside from exchanging Christmas cards, she and Mike hadn't had contact in years. She looked to Mr. Marsh for assistance. He was busily riffling through papers and whispering intently to his associates. Then Marsh glanced up. He looked angry, not at Quintas, but at her. She focused on the mesh-covered microphone. "Yes, sir.''

"Have you dated since your broken engagement?''

"A few times.''

"How many times? Once? Twice? Four times?''

"I don't know. Not often. Maybe three or four men. I don't know.''

"Can you describe Mr. Hammond for the jury?''

Kerry blinked in confusion and looked at Marsh

again. He looked disgusted. His anger was clearly directed at her. She said, ''He's twenty-six, about five foot ten, of average build. Light hair, blue eyes—''

''In other words, he looks very much like William Abernathy.''

''Sort of, but not—''

''Does he or does he not look similar to William Abernathy?''

''He—''

''Light hair, blue eyes, average build. With your own words, you just described William Abernathy.''

''No, I didn't—''

''Objection, your honor!'' Marsh shouted. ''This is irrelevant.''

''Mr. Quintas?'' the judge asked.

''Your honor, I have reason to believe that Miss Byfield's so-called eyewitness account is, in reality, a grudge match. She placed my client on the scene not because she saw him, but because he looks like the man who broke her heart.''

''Mike didn't break my heart!'' Kerry cried.

A soft snicker came from the jury box. Open laughter came from the gallery. Kerry saw a pair of reporters bend head to head. They whispered and pointed at her. She closed her eyes and wondered if they would throw her into jail if she stomped off the stand and out of the courtroom forever.

''Objection sustained,'' the judge growled. ''This line of questioning is pure conjecture and unsubstantiated. I told you to stick to the point. Do so.''

Quintas stalked back to the defense table. Kerry looked at her hands rather than at Abernathy. Looking at him made her want to cry; sympathy crying was her major weakness. She cried at sentimental movies, when friends cried and when animals were hurt. Marsh had warned her to resist weeping on the stand. That was easy for him to say. It didn't matter to him that William Abernathy wore the shocked, hurt expression of an accident victim. It wasn't fair, Kerry thought. A murderer should look brutish and cruel and cunning. He wasn't supposed to be a pleasant-looking man with grieving eyes and a habit of prayerfully folding his hands.

The defense attorney rested against the table, half sitting, half standing. He crossed his arms and graced Kerry with a sharklike smile. "Do you wear glasses, Miss Byfield?"

"No."

"Contact lenses?"

"No."

"When was the last time you had your eyes examined by a doctor?"

Kerry's mind went blank. She shook her head and said testily, "I don't know. They've never been—"

"So you don't know what type of vision you have?"

"Your honor, I object," Marsh said. "This is a ridiculous line of questioning."

"Unfortunately, sir, it is not. Objection overruled."

Quintas bristled. "With respect, I object to your use of the word unfortunately, your honor. It shows favoritism to the prosecution."

The judge glowered, but instructed the court recorder to strike the word *unfortunately*.

Quintas picked up a booklet printed on glossy paper. He waved it at Kerry. "You work with computers, don't you?"

"Yes."

"Can you approximate how many hours a day you use a CRT?" He half turned to the jury. "For those of you unfamiliar with the term, a CRT is a cathode ray tube, the screen of a computer. It's very similar to a television set. Miss Byfield?''

Kerry thought about it. "I suppose about six hours a day, but that's a rough estimate. Some—''

"Thank you. Now I have here a United States government booklet regarding the safety of CRTs. It says, on page nine, 'Extended use of a CRT is suspected as a contributing cause of cataracts, eye strain and of worsening existing vision problems such as astigmatism.' Have you ever read this booklet, Miss Byfield?''

"No, sir.''

"Have you ever experienced problems with your vision after extended use of a CRT?''

"I get a little tired. Sometimes a headache—''

"Blurred vision? Double vision?" He turned a page in the booklet. "Reduced night vision?''

"I don't think so.''

"Yes or no, please.''

"Yes. Not often, but let me explain—''

"Thank you. So it is possible that your vision is not always perfect, despite the fact that you do not wear corrective lenses?''

She waited a beat for Mr. Marsh to object. He rolled his eyes. She said firmly, "My vision is fine.''

"Even after six hours before a CRT, which the United States government suspects is a cause of poor vision?''

"I know what I saw.''

Quintas picked up a yellow legal pad and a black marker. The pen squeaked as he wrote swiftly in sweeping strokes. He held the paper up at an angle, away from the jury, one hand over the letters. He said, "I made the letters about two inches high and thick. Between us is a distance of approximately fifteen feet. You should, if your vision is good, be able to read what I've written.''

Kerry stiffened in apprehension.

Quintas uncovered the letters. ''Please read, Miss Byfield.''

She leaned forward to better see the messy writing. Concentrating, fearing error, she read the large block letters. ''I CANNOT SEE.'' Too late, she realized he'd tricked her. Impotent fury worsened the nervous knot in her stomach.

''I object!'' Marsh shouted.

The press corps erupted in a rumbling mutter. Spectators in the gallery whispered loudly. A few laughed.

The judge slammed his gavel on the bench. He said, ''Objection sustained. Mr. Quintas, that is the last of your foolery in my court.'' He turned to the jury. ''You will disregard that.''

Quintas smirked as he crumpled the piece of paper. ''I have no more questions, your honor.''

Judge MacElroy invited the prosecution to reexamine. Marsh rose calmly. ''Miss Byfield, on the day in question, did you work on your computer?''

''Yes, sir.''

''Can you estimate the length of time?''

Kerry considered the question, wanting to tell the truth. ''About two hours.''

''Two hours?''

''Yes, sir. Most of the day, I was either finishing the layout for a newsletter, running the copy machines or folding newsletters.''

Mr. Marsh smiled. ''And when you saw William Abernathy—''

''Objection!'' Quintas yelled.

"Overruled," the judge said.

"When you saw the defendant exiting the murder scene, were you suffering vision problems?"

"No, sir."

"Did you see him clearly?"

"Yes, sir. There was light in the foyer and the outside of the house was well lit. When he opened the door, I recognized him immediately." She glanced at the defense table. William Abernathy had his eyes closed and was shaking his head slowly from side to side. She quickly looked away.

"No further questions, your honor," Marsh said. He sat down.

The judge looked to the defense. "Mr. Quintas?"

Quintas shook his head. "I have no more use for this witness, your honor."

Judge MacElroy looked sympathetic as he gave Kerry permission to step down. She stared straight ahead as she walked across the courtroom. The reporters were treating this case like some sort of juicy tabloid circus; Kerry hoped they didn't notice her trembling hands or shaky legs. Next to her father's death, this was the worst experience of her life. Now she missed her father more than ever. He'd taught her to always do the right thing, no matter what it cost or how painful it might be. If only he were here to reassure her.

The judge called a recess until the following morning, and the reporters followed Kerry into the hallway. Mr. Marsh had instructed her to make no comments, so she averted her face and pretended not to hear the questions. Spotting her mother, she hurried down the hall. Angela Byfield was a welcome sight in her perfectly cut white linen suit. Thanks to the wonders of plastic surgery and a strict regimen that kept her model slim, Angela looked twenty years younger than her fifty-two years.

"I think it's over for me, Mom," Kerry said. She noticed her mother's wistful gaze at the reporters and their cameras. Angela's quirky ability to completely ignore reality offered Kerry a measure of relief. Worlds could collide and the sky could turn upside down, but Angela would always be Angela.

"Oh, baby, poor darling. You look terrible. That awful Mr. Quintas is certainly no gentleman." Angela bustled her daughter into the ladies' room.

Longing to soak in a bubble bath, Kerry washed her sweaty face. She allowed her mother to fuss and pet her, and even let her dab lotion on her face and neck. The pampering felt good. Kerry felt better when she reentered the hallway. The reporters surrounded Quintas. He demonstrated no shyness about discussing his client's innocence.

"Kerry," Marsh called as she pushed open an exit door.

Angela whispered, "Did you find out if he's married, baby? He's very nice-looking. I saw his car. A Ferrari. Definitely not a family car."

"No." Kerry grinned. *Mom, ever the irrepressible matchmaker.*

Robert Marsh was thirty-five and had an athletic build and just a touch of becoming gray at his temples. He'd taught Kerry the little tricks of making testimony easier: to keep her hands in her lap, to concentrate on the microphone rather than on the examining attorney and most importantly, to keep her answers short. Still, Kerry didn't like him. He had a cavalier attitude, as if this murder trial was a game and the victim and the accused were mere pieces on the board.

"You did a terrific job, Kerry," Marsh said. "It threw me a little when he asked about your engagement. I didn't know about that."

She shrugged. "We broke up almost three years ago and it was fairly friendly. Quintas caught me off guard, too. Is it over? Do I have to go back?"

"Quintas couldn't find any inconsistencies. I doubt he'll risk alienating the jury by recalling you." Marsh patted her shoulder and she stepped away from his hand. "You did fine. You're a tough lady."

"I told the truth." Kerry hugged her elbows. "I can't face Quintas again. He makes me feel so stupid."

"But he didn't make you change your mind. He's doing his job, but trust me, you did your job, too." Marsh's smile revealed very white teeth that seemed to glow under the fluorescent lighting. "Can I buy you a drink?"

Kerry forced a smile; it felt as phony as his looked. "I don't drink, Mr. Marsh. No, thank you."

Angela clutched Kerry's elbow and gave her one of *those* looks. "You deserve a little pampering, darling. You shouldn't be rude."

"I understand, Mrs. Byfield," Marsh said.

"Excuse me, Mr. Marsh. I want to go home, Mom."

"I don't think you ought to be alone. Come to the house and spend the night."

"I won't be alone—I have the cats. Goodbye, Mr. Marsh." Kerry smiled wanly. "If you need me, you know where to find me." With that, Kerry hustled Angela down the stairs.

"Honestly, Kerry," Angela said. "How are you ever going to get married if you don't make an effort? Mr. Marsh is interested. I can tell." She tugged at her suit lapels with hasty little jerks.

Kerry counted silently to ten, then kept going until she reached twenty and could trust her temper. She wondered how it was possible to love her mother so much when she drove her so crazy. The worst part was that no matter how sensible, reasonable and mature she tried to act, conversations with her mother always made her feel like a sullen thirteen-year-old. "He's probably interested in you. You look fabulous, as usual."

"You could look fabulous, too. If you'd take better care—"

"Trust me, Mom, the last thing I want is further company with a lawyer."

"Lawyers are rich, darling."

"Not assistant district attorneys. You know government employees make lousy salaries." Kerry hadn't the faintest idea how much money district attorneys made, but the little lie would serve to get her mother off the subject of Mr. Marsh. She pushed open another door.

"Oh." Angela frowned as she mulled over that information.

They stepped into the blistering heat of the late-afternoon sunshine. Kerry's skin felt greasy with sweat. She wondered how Angela managed to look so cool and perfectly groomed when the humidity hovered at a miserable ninety-four percent.

"Lighten your hair to a golden blond," Angela said, unlocking the door of her dark blue Jaguar.

Kerry glowered. "I like the way I look, Mother. I don't want to be a blonde. Please, I'm tired. I'm sick of lawyers and trials...I'm sick of people in general. Please drive me home."

Angela made that sniffing sound that always grated

on Kerry's nerves. "My daughter, the old maid," she said haughtily. "Fine. I'm too young to be a grand-mother, anyway."

ROBERT MARSH CLOSED his office door, unlocked the center drawer of his desk and withdrew a thick manila envelope. He fingered the ten thousand dollars in cash it contained. It didn't seem enough. This affair was put-ting a bad taste in his mouth. It wasn't the first time he'd crossed the line between legal and illegal. A little bribery, a little tampering with evidence, some creative scheduling of trials...but that was harmless finagling. Everyone did it, even those stiffnecks who pretended to feel deep disgust at the sight of corruption. This went far beyond any of that. He couldn't fool himself that this was creative maneuvering. This was criminal, and he was in deep. He dropped the envelope into the drawer and slammed it shut.

He dialed a telephone number. A woman answered. "Kerry Byfield finished her testimony."

"And?"

Marsh wished the woman would continue to talk. She had the coolest, softest, most elegant voice he'd ever heard. He suspected her cultured tones were as fake as the knockoff of a Rolex watch on his wrist, but the sound of her voice raised visions of luxurious sensual-ity. "Quintas angered the judge and amused the jury, but like you said, Miss Byfield is perfect."

"I told you so. Now goodbye. It isn't smart for you to call me here. Or anywhere for that matter."

He sighed, listening to the dial tone. It was always business with her. Still, he couldn't help wondering what making love to her would feel like. He remem-bered their first meeting. They'd made eye contact across the sultry confines of a lounge—two sharks recognizing each other. There wasn't an ounce of passion in her perfect body. Yet, for Marsh, that made her more attractive.

Ah, well, he thought philosophically. Business was business. He picked up a copy of the telephone company's records that showed the calls William Abernathy had made from his cellular phone on the night of the murder. He knew the defense relied on the records to establish an alibi. He began checking his notes to see if there was any argument Quintas might make for which the prosecution needed a counterargument. He smiled. Quintas was thorough and tenacious, but Marsh was better. William Abernathy didn't stand a chance.

FOR THE NEXT FEW WEEKS Kerry felt like a fugitive. She flinched each time the phone rang or someone entered Copy Copy, the shop where she worked. The thought of going back on the stand made her so edgy that she lost sleep and weight. She avoided news accounts and refused to discuss the trial with any of her friends.

Sometimes she had nightmares of herself handcuffed to William Abernathy. She tried and tried to make him understand that she was doing the right thing. She'd seen him running out of his house after the murder, and she'd had no choice except to testify. William Abernathy pleaded his innocence again, breaking her heart. Sometimes she woke with tears in her eyes.

One afternoon, Robert Marsh called her at Copy Copy. The sound of his voice made her sweat despite the air conditioning.

"It's over," he said. "Thank you."

"Over?"

"Second degree murder, unanimous verdict."

Flooded through with relief, Kerry closed her eyes.

"Quintas has put in for a mistrial, but it's a formality. He'll appeal, too, but he won't get that, either. Despite his efforts, this case was open and shut. Finis." His voice held celebration. "We couldn't have done it without you, Kerry. I thank you from the deepest regions of my heart."

"Just knowing it's finally over is thanks enough, Mr. Marsh."

"Call me Robert. I'd like to take you to dinner. It would be a way of showing my appreciation for the perfect witness." He paused. "We could go to Wellington's. It's a new place. All the best people go there."

Despite the good news, Kerry still disliked him. His hearty pip-pip-good-show attitude seemed inappropriate. Mr. Abernathy was going to prison, and even though he deserved it, it seemed more sad than anything. Lives had been ruined.

"It isn't necessary, Mr.—Robert. No offense, but I'd like to forget everything."

"You aren't holding our encounter with Quintas against me, are you?"

"Thanks for the offer, but no thanks. I'd like to get back to my life. I appreciate your calling."

After Kerry hung up, she stood for a few moments with her hand on the phone. Over. Finished. There was no chance she'd be called back to the stand for Quintas to get another crack at her integrity. She clapped her hands, and whispered, "Yes!" A couple strolled past the shop's big windows. The people eyed the interior with its imposing copiers and glowing computer screens, prompting Kerry to get back to work. She fussed with a stack of sample papers on the counter.

"Kerry! I need the billing invoice for Old & New," her boss called from his office.

She popped her head through the doorway. "Guess who just called, Mr. Piver? That was Robert Marsh. The trial is over."

Piver tightened his grip on his pencil. The wood snapped.

"William Abernathy was convicted. I don't have to worry about being recalled to the stand. Isn't that a relief?"

"Convicted?"

"It's finally over." She gave him a thumbs up. "I've been nearly sick, worrying that I'd have to go back to court. I'm so glad."

"Wonderful."

While she searched a file cabinet for the invoice, she realized that Nolan Piver hadn't seemed at all pleased with the news. It struck her oddly. He'd been very generous during her days of testimony, even paying her salary for the days she'd missed. That had been more than generous, really, since he groused about paying sick leave and insisted Copy Copy was too small to afford paid vacations for its employees. *Oh, well,* she thought, *he's an odd duck anyway.* A person could go nuts trying to figure out what was going on in his head.

She was taking the invoice to his office when the phone rang. "Copy Copy, may I help you?" Kerry answered.

"Nolan Piver, please," a cool, feminine voice said.

Kerry didn't need to ask who was calling. She cupped her hand over the mouthpiece and said, "Mr. Piver, your lady friend." Kerry waited until she heard him pick up the extension. Annoyance pricked her. It was bad enough that he was too cheap to install a second phone line, but his personal calls were growing longer and more frequent. Sometimes he tied up the line for hours. God only knew how much business they lost because of it.

Kerry went into his office and handed him the invoice. Into the phone, he said, ''I heard.''

Kerry didn't understand the look he gave her. His eyes, for a scant second, took on a glassy, predatory glare. He looked as if she'd just murdered ten nuns with an ax. The short hairs raised on the nape of her neck. She smiled wanly as she backed out of his office and quietly shut the door.

Chapter Two

"It's supposed to be over!" Nolan Piver hissed into the phone. "Damn it, it's over." To hear that a private investigator was snooping into the Abernathy murder gave him heart palpitations.

"This is a minor problem," the woman said calmly.

Piver fumbled in his breast pocket for the roll of antacids. He popped two into his mouth. Their minty chalkiness clung to his dry tongue and made him gag.

"Smith is asking questions, but that doesn't mean he's finding answers. You are not to speak to him. Do you understand? Nolan? Do you understand?"

Piver touched the velvet jewelry box, smoothing the nap with a finger. Once they were married, he could trust her. Then, unwanted, came a nagging inner voice. *Very merry, very wealthy widow...* He thrust the box away. "I won't talk to him."

"I don't think it's a good idea for him to speak to Kerry, either."

Piver caught the dangerous note under the gentle words. He ate another antacid. "She did what she was supposed to..."

"She's expendable. Remember that. There's too much at stake for us to make any errors now."

"Expendable?" He stared at his fingernails. Was their color normal or did it seem blue? "No, listen and listen hard. You aren't going to hurt her. She doesn't know anything."

"As long it remains that way, she'll be fine. It's Smith I'm worried about. He's smart and he's nosy." The woman laughed softly, lightly, as if everything were a joke. "Everything is for the best, darling. You and me, the perfect couple. We aren't going to let a stupid little twerp like Kerry stand in our way, are we?"

"No."

"Of course not. Now, about those joint accounts. I want—"

"I told you, marriage first. I can't put your name on the accounts until we're married and all the details are taken care of. I'm trying my damnedest to square the tax angle, you know. Do you want the IRS to trip us up?" He opened the jewelry box. Two and a half carats of brilliant white diamond winked and flashed fire. *Merry widow...*

"I need some cash. Small bills."

The edge in her voice caused his mouth to fill with unpleasant wetness. "That's me, your little banker," he joked weakly. "How much?"

She told him and he closed his eyes, not wanting to know why she needed the cash. He didn't trust her. He *couldn't* trust her, but he was in too deep. A private investigator? Kerry expendable? What about him? How expendable was he? A nasty little volcano bubbled in his belly. He chewed another antacid.

He blurted out, "Let's go to Mexico. A vacation. The two of us on the beach, drinking margaritas. Let's—"

She cut him off with a laugh. "Leave Dallas? Don't

be absurd. I'm going to own this town someday. I'm never leaving.''

After he hung up, Piver felt his pulse and thought about heart attacks. His fingernails definitely looked blue. He was primed for a big one. He was forty-two years old, twenty pounds overweight, a type A personality and under stress. A lot of stress.

He shut the jewelry box and stuck it in a desk drawer. The sound of the shop's doorbell made him freeze. He heard Kerry's cheerful greeting and a customer's reply. *Expendable,* he thought miserably, knowing without doubt that the woman he was involved with was evil. If Kerry stood in her way, Kerry died. It was a simple fact, and there wasn't anything he could do to stop it.

KERRY HUMMED, SMILING despite her exasperation. Hank Pinchot had just called, wanting his advertisement reworded. She muttered, "Serves you right, Byfield. You tell them making changes is easy on the computer. They believe you every time."

Still, she decided, nothing was going to spoil her day. It was a beautiful October afternoon, crisp and blue skied. Her favorite holidays, Thanksgiving and Christmas, loomed within thinking distance. Business was good, and customers were reasonable. If her luck held, Piver would prove reasonable, too, when she asked him about hiring a replacement for Jack, who'd quit months earlier.

At the tinkling bell, Kerry looked up from the computer screen. "May I help you?" she asked, rising. She smoothed her plum-colored skirt.

A man looked around the shop. His gaze settled for

a moment on the big Savin high speed copier, then he looked at her computer. Then he looked at her.

Kerry fussed with her collar, inexplicably flustered by his smile. Her first thought was, *Watch out hormones.*

He was tall, on the right side of skinny and dressed in a plaid Western shirt and blue jeans. His chestnut brown hair gleamed with red under the bright shop lighting. He looked as though he'd stepped off a billboard ad for a Montana ranch resort. He wasn't the usual sort of customer for Copy Copy. It was definitely a pleasant change of pace. "May I help you?" she asked again, moving behind the counter.

His gaze followed her legs; one of his eyebrows cocked appreciatively. Aware of the way he was looking at her, she was embarrassed, but in a nice way.

He leaned on the counter. The cuffs of his shirt were rolled back, revealing sun-browned, muscular forearms. He had big, well-used hands and a disarming smile. His eyes met hers and held. For a moment he looked surprised, then questioning, then unmistakably interested. Kerry stared back, her mind whirling inanely with thoughts of thunderbolts, waves crashing on the sand and resounding Tchaikovsky music. It was dumb and she knew it, but she couldn't stop staring. His was the nicest face she'd seen in a long time.

"Miss Kerry Byfield?"

Surprised and pleased, she asked, "Do I know you?" She couldn't imagine forgetting him.

"Tarkington Smith. Friends call me T.K." He held out his right hand. She took it. His clasp was strong; his skin was warm, tough and callused. She felt her smile turn goofy, but since he didn't seem to mind, neither did she. She withdrew her hand reluctantly.

"You have a boyfriend, Miss Byfield?"

Romantic fantasies aside, that sounded more like a pick-up line than pleasant conversation. She took a quick step backward and ran into the Canon color copier. The collating trays rattled. "I don't think that's any of your business."

He chuckled. "I don't mean anything. I just want to buy you a cup of coffee and don't want to offend anyone while I'm doing it."

"Who *are* you?"

In response, he put a plain, black-on-white business card on the counter. "'Tarkington Smith—Private Investigations,'" she read. A phone number had been penned across the bottom.

An alarm went off in her head. A few days before, Robert Marsh had called. He'd said someone was making a stink about the Abernathy murder and that it was in Kerry's best interests to refuse any contact with the man.

She pushed the card back to him. "This has to do with the Abernathy trial?"

The man nodded.

She shook her head. "No offense, Mr. Smith, but I'm not going to talk about it."

He gazed at her steadily.

She fussed with a display card. "I'm sorry. I just want to forget it. I'm terribly sorry."

He turned the card in his fingers. "Just talk. Thirty minutes. Can't hurt."

She placed both hands on the countertop and gave him what she hoped was a forceful expression. "I saw him leave the scene of the murder. I spent three days in that courtroom while Abernathy's attorney ripped me apart. By the time he got through with me, he knew more about me than my mother knows. Now it's over. Abernathy is in jail. It's done.''

''William Abernathy is innocent.''

''Take my word for it. I saw him there the night his wife was murdered. Please leave.''

''Thirty minutes.''

''I'm very sorry, no.''

Inhaling deeply, he pulled away from the counter. He flicked the card at her. It landed lengthwise, pointing like an accusing finger.

''I need your help, Miss Byfield. Call me if you change your mind.'' He opened the door, then held it, watching her. Newspaper photographs had not done her justice. They'd shown a tired girl with droopy shoulders and a stubborn jaw. In the flesh, her clear skin had a glow of its own. Those big, green eyes revealed a core of pure steel. Her voice was soft and careful, with a hint of deferential hesitancy, but a determined voice nonetheless. She was a real lady, and only a fool would mistake that sweet softness for weakness. He felt no surprise she'd stood up so well to Quintas.

She continued to glare at him, her head high and her mouth set in a prim line. T.K. regretted shaking her up and wished there was another way to do what he had to do. He left the shop, but looked back once and grinned. Kerry Byfield wasn't the only one shaken up around here. He had a hunch he was going to see that pretty lady again, murder case or no murder case. His hunches never steered him wrong.

Kerry watched him until he was out of sight. Only then did she realize she'd been holding her breath. She shuddered, hugging her elbows. ''I will not think about it,'' she muttered, and went back to her computer. She stared at the screen, forcing her attention on the extra wording Hank Pinchot wanted in his ad.

Not thinking about the trial proved impossible. Quintas, his face as ugly as a pit bull terrier's, still seemed to mock her. *Did you really see my client June 5, or do you just think you saw him? How many times were you at the Abernathy house? Once? Are you certain?* She remembered Quintas shoving an eight-by-ten color glossy of the blood-drenched dining room in her face. *Have you ever seen this room before?*

Kerry breathed deeply, staring with bemused detachment at her shaking hands. The perfect witness, she thought wryly. In truth, she had just been an innocent bystander, in the wrong place at the wrong time. She glanced at the windows. She dreaded seeing that private investigator. *Why now? Let it drop. Don't make me remember William Abernathy and his shell-shocked eyes. It isn't my fault he murdered his wife.*

Kerry focused on the computer screen, reading the same words over and again until she was finally absorbed by her work. She was wondering how to fit too many words into too small a place when Nolan Piver arrived, swinging his briefcase. She smiled at him as she typed a print command on the keyboard. The laser printer revved like a miniature jet engine. The words "On-line Processing" appeared on its tiny screen.

Piver was a big man, the kind who looked great in a three-piece suit. He looked as if he should wear a pocket watch on a gold fob. Kerry wavered between liking and disliking him. He paid her well, but treated her like a slave. After nearly two years as his employee—and usually his only employee—she still couldn't bring herself to call him Nolan.

"Anybody in this afternoon?" he asked, glancing at

the cash register. He picked up the card Smith had left behind.

"No," she said. "Quiet as can be. Midmonth, you know. Everyone will be in next week wanting everything last week. Any luck with Grady's?"

"You've got an order for their menus, order forms, sales tickets and stubs for their Saturday-night band dances."

His lackluster attitude annoyed her. He'd been after Grady's, the biggest pizza parlor in the Dallas–Fort Worth area, for months. He'd finally gotten their printing business but he wasn't excited. Then again, in the past few weeks, he'd been edgy and distracted. It was almost as if he were waiting for something to happen. He'd picked up weird habits, too. He never answered the phone, even when Kerry was up to her elbows in customers or office work. And he always locked his office door. Kerry thought that was silly. She never snooped.

Still, she decided, since he was never in a good mood anymore, now was as good a time as any. She asked, "Have you thought some more about hiring someone else? I'll be glad to place the ad and conduct the interviews. All you have to do is give the final okay."

He shot her an exasperated look.

"I don't mean to bother you, Mr. Piver, but I've been swamped since Jack left. I don't mind the late hours, really, but there's only so much I can do. Even someone part-time to run the copiers and wait on the counter would help." She didn't need telepathy to know she'd lost his interest. "Drop the Grady's stuff in my box," she finally said.

Piver leafed through a stack of invoices. "No one was in?" he asked again.

"No customers." She added, "Oh, wait! You did get a phone call. Your lady friend, I think. No message, sorry."

Piver held up Smith's business card. "Who's this?"

"Some guy. About the Abernathy trial. I told him to take a walk...." Her voice trailed off. She wanted to dismiss Smith as a creep, but he hadn't looked like a creep or acted like a creep or talked like a creep. Why did he have to show up in connection with such a creepy subject?

Piver gave her an odd look. She tried a bright smile. "But we have Grady's now. Good job, sir. I knew you could sell them."

He unlocked his office door. Kerry scowled at his back. On days like this, she thought he didn't care about the business at all. If he hated it so much, why didn't he sell out and find some other pie in the sky to chase? He disappeared into his office and shut the door. Wheeler-dealers, she thought sourly. They chased anything that looked like a quick profit, then gave up when it turned out to be plain hard work.

"I'm nothing but a flunky. Slaving away like it matters," she muttered. Maybe it was time to find another job. Her friend and sometime business rival, Richie, had dropped several hints that she'd make a great manager in one of his copy-shop franchises. There was excellent money in that, too. Maybe she could buy her own franchise. The banks wouldn't touch her for an operation like Copy Copy, but they might be willing to listen to a proposal about an established franchise. She looked around the shop. By comparison, Richie's franchise outlets were big and impersonal. As much as Piver frustrated her, she still loved Copy Copy. She knew almost all of her customers by their first names, and they knew they could rely on her for quality service. "Face it, Byfield, you're small potatoes at heart," she told herself as she went back to work.

By six o'clock, Kerry felt caught up enough to leave. She slipped her work in progress into a folder and backed up her day's computer work onto floppy disks.

The doorbell sounded. Kerry turned around, ready to say, "I'm sorry, we're closed."

A harassed looking young woman waved a piece of paper, and cried, "Oh! I'm so glad I caught you. I know it's late, but I just have to make a slide out of this. I have a presentation in the morning and our office copier is broken."

Unfortunately, Piver didn't pay overtime. Kerry told herself, *Inconvenience today, valuable customer tomorrow.* She smiled and murmured, "Sure."

Making a simple slide turned out to be difficult. The woman had smudged her typewritten paper. She groaned, finding a few typos. Kerry patiently cleaned the smudges with a gum eraser, then whited out the typos. In a practiced hand, she made printed corrections that the woman swore looked better than the typed letters.

Then Kerry pointed out that the woman had made her margins too narrow. When she framed the slide, some of the copy wouldn't fit. That set the woman into a semihysterical panic attack. Kerry tried reducing the document. It was still readable, and the margins were wide enough. She made the slide on a transparency sheet. It was perfect.

"You are so helpful!" the woman gushed as she paid her bill.

"That's what everyone tells me," Kerry said, resisting a glance at her watch. "Good luck with your presentation."

Kerry saw the woman out, then flipped the Closed sign on the door. She closed out the cash register, then shut down the three copiers: the big high-speed, the color copier and the little self-service Xerox machine. She locked the back door and cleaned out the coffeepot. Finally, she knocked, then poked her head into Piver's office. He was on the phone, his feet on the desk. He stopped talking and glared at her.

"Excuse me," she said. "I'm going home. Want me to lock the front door?"

He waved at her to go.

She took that to mean he wanted the door left open. She took out her car keys before she left the shop. Humming, she plotted the quickest way to finish the Grady's order as she walked to her car. Menus first, she decided. They would take the longest and need the greatest amount of proofing and customer approval— A movement startled her from her thoughts. She gasped to find a man leaning against her Nova.

Chapter Three

Recognizing Tarkington Smith's tall, lean form, Kerry relaxed a little.

He patted the Nova's hood and said, "Nice car. A classic. I haven't seen one of these in a long time. Sixty-eight?"

"I told you I don't want to talk to you."

She glanced back at the row of storefronts. Plano Place shopping center formed a giant, lopsided X. On the nearest side of the center were dental offices, a beauty shop, a lawyer's office, a video-game arcade and Copy Copy. All of them, except for the arcade, closed at six. The parking lot was deserted.

Kerry took a few steps backward. She said, "I'm very sorry. I'm not a mean person. It's just that I'm tired of being called a liar. Please get away from my car." Her leg muscles tensed. She was ready to run at the first sign of a threat.

"Twenty minutes. I promise, if I upset you, then I won't bother you anymore. Okay?" He pointed at the other side of the shopping center. "We'll go over to the frozen-yogurt place. Well lighted, lots of people. You can leave anytime. I really need to talk to you. I need your help."

He sounded sincere. Kerry felt herself wavering.

"Or I could buy you dinner. Hungry? We can get a pizza or whatever you want. Name the place."

Kerry suspected that talking to Mr. Smith was a lot like a visit to the dentist. It was better to just get it over and done with. She said, "A cup of coffee. Twenty minutes."

"Good enough." He fell in beside her and they went to the frozen-yogurt shop.

He put a large coffee in front of her before sliding into the pink vinyl booth. Kerry scalloped the rim of the disposable cup with her fingernails, watching Smith dump four sugars and two nondairy creamers into his coffee. She tensed again, ready to walk out the moment this man insinuated she was a liar.

He smiled at her. She tried to figure out if he was handsome or not. His nose was broad and oddly flattened; his jaw flared, bony and strong. His eyes were so deep seated and thick lashed, she couldn't tell their color. His age was indeterminable. Crow's feet at the corners of his eyes and the deep smile lines in his cheeks said he'd been around awhile. But his thick shock of chestnut hair, haphazardly cut and hanging around his shoulders, and the glint of gold on his left earlobe made him seem younger.

The way his gaze fixed on her—intense, sharp and quirkily merry—made him strangely attractive. Her rational mind rebelled at his attractiveness. Some of Quintas's legal assistants had been attractive, too. Until Quintas himself had her on the witness stand. This was not the time to have her head turned, not when it meant dredging up the very unpleasant recent past.

She steadied herself. "What do you want, Mr. Smith?"

"Facts."

She laughed, but the sound was hollow. "Robert Marsh warned me about you. He said you're a trouble-maker."

Smith lifted an eyebrow. "I am."

The admission took her aback. "He told me not to talk to you."

"It's a free country. I want facts, but no law says you have to give them."

"I found out the hard way that the American justice system isn't interested in facts," she said, hating the bitterness of her tone. "At least, lawyers aren't. I told the truth, Mr. Smith. I'm not going to change my mind."

"I believe you," he said.

"You do?"

"Sure."

She felt surprised, but she believed him.

"But I need more than the truth. I need facts." He held up a hand, as if holding something between his finger and thumb. "If I show you a coin that's black on one side and white on the other, and you say it's black, then that's the truth. If I say it's white, that's the truth, too. What I need is the fact that the coin is black *and* white." He spoke with a Texas drawl as warm and comfortable as a pair of old shoes. It didn't match the burning intensity of his eyes, but the intelligence behind the words did. "The prosecution based its case around your eyewitness account. I think the truth was told, but not all the facts."

"Facts," she repeated, and blew on her coffee. "I saw him running out of his house with a shotgun. I picked him out of three different lineups. His legal team set up two of those lineups. Each time I picked him out, they tried to make me think I was guessing. I wasn't.''

"Do you know how hard it is to get a conviction based on a single eye witness?''

"I didn't convict him. The jury did.''

"You didn't see him murder his wife.''

"But I did see him leave the house with a shotgun. Mr. Smith, this is painful for me. I'm a very private person and I was ripped apart. Quintas even accused me of accepting a bribe to say I saw Abernathy. I feel like I've been through a war. Why can't you forget it? They convicted him.''

"Maybe Quintas and his crew went after you so hard because they're right. Bill didn't do it.''

"The jury thought he did.''

Smith leaned forward and folded his fingers, looking very earnest. His eyes gleamed darkly. "Bill Abernathy was tried because the spouse is always the first suspect and because you claim you saw him. Everything else was purely circumstantial. There was no murder weapon and no motive. No witnesses said Bill threatened his wife.'' He cocked his head. "In fact, Quintas subpoenaed forty-eight character witnesses to tell why Bill couldn't have and wouldn't have murdered Louise.''

He looked at Kerry sympathetically. "Discrediting witnesses is sometimes the best tactic a trial lawyer can use. It's nothing personal. Unfortunately for Bill, you were better than his lawyers. I happen to think tearing up witnesses ought to be outlawed, but that's neither here nor there.''

"I did see him.''

"You saw something. I think you were supposed to think you saw him coming out of that house. I think somebody used you.''

Kerry blinked in confusion.

"Two hundred thousand dollars," he said.

"What?"

"Exactly." He drummed a swift tattoo on the table-top. "I heard my old buddy was convicted. The first thing I thought was that he went nuts and blew her away." Smith sipped his coffee, grimaced and added another sugar. He held up a finger. "First thought, and it lasted about one second. I know Bill. He's honest. Always has been, always will be. When he tells me he didn't murder Louise, I believe him."

A troubled line appeared between his eyebrows and he looked away, his gaze distant. He stirred the coffee with a hot pink stirrer. "The whole thing's been one big mess. His attorneys couldn't get him to cooperate. When the press got a whiff of that, they blew it up to make him look like a deranged lunatic. It wasn't guilt— it was grief. He loved Louise, loved her the way most folks can only dream about. Then she was murdered. He was arrested and to top things off, by the time he'd made bail, there'd been a mix-up at the mortuary—did you hear about that? Bill was planning a funeral worthy of her and then a paperwork error caused the mortuary to cremate Louise. He never even had a chance to say goodbye. I don't think he believes or understands she's really dead."

Kerry blinked slowly. Smith's intensity was genuine. Right or wrong, he believed every word he said. She murmured, "Oh, that poor man."

Smith lifted his shoulders in a rueful shrug. "I was vacationing all summer down in the Gulf. If I had known what was going on up here in Dallas, I could have done something earlier. Quintas did a good job, but he just doesn't know Bill the way I do."

"What's that got to do with the money?" Kerry asked. She took a sip of the plastic-tasting coffee.

"I've been in town three weeks and done more reading than in the past three years. What I find interesting is that Louise recently withdrew $200,000.00. Bill doesn't deny Louise took it. She handled all their financial affairs. What he denies is that she gambled with it or used it to pay off a boyfriend."

Kerry had not followed the particulars of the case, but she recalled the stories about some love letters the police had found. "The theft of that much money sounds like a pretty good motive."

Smith dismissed the idea with a toss of his head. "Bill didn't care," he said emphatically. "You have to understand that Bill comes from old, old money. You might say that touching the stuff was beneath him. That was his attitude. Before he got married, accountants handled his affairs. Afterward, it was Louise. Until the trial, he didn't even know how much he was worth. I can't say I admire that, but it's just the way Bill is. And Louise wasn't a gambler. The investigation turned up gambling slips and a bunch of other hoorah, but I don't believe they were hers."

"Why not?"

"Because she wasn't the type to play the odds. She went for a sure thing, always."

"How can you know that?"

"I met her at the wedding. Call it a hunch. I can't explain those gambling slips yet, but I will. That money is out there somewhere."

As nutty as his theory sounded, integrity surrounded Smith like an aura. Reservations aside, Kerry was interested. "I don't get it. What do you want from me?"

He gestured with his folded hands. "Tell me why you were at the Abernathy house."

"A delivery."

"I read the transcripts. Do you know what I picked up that Quintas didn't? Nobody asked you why."

"Copy Copy makes deliveries. There's nothing unusual about it. I make deliveries all the time."

"What are you, twenty-one, twenty-two?"

She frowned at him. "I'm twenty-five."

"Pretty young. Attractive, female. So you run a delivery to a stranger's house at 9:00 p.m. That sounds pretty dangerous to me. It's sort of above and beyond the call of duty. You strike me as reasonably cautious. So why?"

"He wasn't a stranger. He'd been in the shop before."

"Once." Smith laughed at her surprise. His laugh was deep, throaty and nonthreatening. "I came prepared, Kerry. May I call you Kerry? Pretty name. Anyway, do you know why he went to Copy Copy?"

She shrugged.

"The owner called him. Nolan Piver asked him to look over some sort of stock distribution."

"So? I don't understand what all this has to do with me."

"I'll get to it." Smith tapped his index finger. "Fact—Bill was asked to go to Copy Copy. He talks to you, just long enough so he isn't a stranger. Fact—he says he never ordered the legal forms you were delivering."

"Yes, he did. Piver took the order."

"In person?"

"Over the phone. And they're standard forms. I had them on disk and only needed to make some minor

changes before I printed them. Quintas asked me about
that at the trial, too. He tried to make it sound like I'd
made up the whole bit about the forms. I didn't. Piver
talked to him.''

"He talked to someone. It wasn't Bill."

"The jury believed me."

"I believe you, too. Black coin or white coin? Okay,
next fact. You deliver said legal forms to the house at
nine o'clock at night. You start to ring the doorbell and
a man carrying a shotgun runs out of the house—"

"Knocking me down."

"Knocking you down. He gets in a car and takes off.
The shotgun scares you, so you get back in your car
and go down the street to a convenience store. You call
the cops. Curious, you cruise by the house, find it surrounded by cops, see the ambulance and then get out
and tell your story."

"That's right. I never saw the body. I never went
into the house. But I saw him. There was a light on in
the foyer. When he opened the door, I saw his face."

"And you've seen him before. He's pretty good-
looking. Blond hair, blue eyes, stays in shape. Girls always looked at Bill. Girls remember him."

Kerry thanked the heavens this man hadn't gotten
ahold of her in court. Quintas only succeeded in making
her more stubbornly certain; this man made her think.
"If it wasn't him, then who was it?"

"That's what I have to find out. Why were you at
that house at nine o'clock at night? Your shop closes
at six. Four on Saturdays."

"Those are customer hours. I work late a lot of times.
In this business there are always deadlines. They have
to be met." She tore little half moons out of the coffee
cup's rim. "I think I was putting together a brochure. I

can check my records. I'm telling you, it isn't unusual for me to work late.''

"You the only employee?"

"Now I am. Jack quit in July." She made a face. "And if Piver doesn't hire somebody to replace him, I'm quitting, too. He's got me doing everything. In fact, tonight is the first night in weeks that I've left before seven o'clock.''

"There was a man working in the shop at the time of the murder?"

"Yes. Jack Retter."

"But you were sent to make a delivery late at night, to a man's house. Why you and not Jack? Would you have sent a young woman out on that delivery?"

Kerry ripped at the cup. "I don't know how to answer that."

"I'm upsetting you," Smith said gently. "I'm sorry."

"I'm the one who's sorry, Mr. Smith. I don't think I can help. I know what I saw. I didn't want to get involved, but I had no choice. *I saw him.* I don't know what else I can tell you.''

Smith tapped his fingers rapidly on the tabletop again. "I'm under a lot of pressure here. Bill goes up for sentencing in one week. After that, nobody is going to give a damn about this case.''

Kerry wondered at the power of those dark eyes. She'd heard about burning eyes, but this was the first time she'd ever seen them. He looked at her as if she was the only thing in the world to see. Waves of pleasant discomfort washed over her. She tugged her skirt and shifted on the vinyl seat.

"If I don't find enough to make a case real quick, then nobody is going to care enough to look into it. I don't want to upset you, but this is a fact. The prosecutor's case was built around you. The motive the prosecution came up with looks damning on the surface, but it's shaky. Bill swears Louise didn't have a boyfriend or a gambling habit. I believe him.''

Smith glanced at his watch. ''Let me take you to dinner. Let me tell you what I know so far. Maybe you know something, anything, that can help. Maybe you forgot something.''

The sensible part of her told Kerry to stand up and walk out, but those intense eyes held compelling power. His smile formed boyish dimples in his craggy cheeks.

''Help me,'' he said.

''This is crazy. I don't know why I'm doing this,'' Kerry muttered. ''I'll buy my own dinner. And I drive my own car,'' she finished, her voice stronger.

He jumped to his feet. ''Fair enough.''

The parking lot was dark. Her blue Nova sat under a pinkish arc light. She fished in her purse for her keys. Unfortunately, the lock decided to stick. She jiggled the key until it turned, then tugged the door handle. Muttering, she gave Smith a sheepish look and went around to the passenger side.

''Do that a lot?'' he asked. ''The door sticking like that?''

''It's a classic,'' she said, and opened the passenger door. She crawled in, then rolled down the window. ''Do you know Lucky's over on Coit? Go up the road and turn left. It sits on the right in the shopping center.''

''I can find it.''

''They have great cannelloni, and it's quiet.''

A dark gray Mercedes 250SL purred into the parking lot. It stopped in front of Copy Copy. Nolan Piver came out and locked the door. He hurried to the Mercedes as if he'd been waiting for it.

"The owner?" Smith asked.

"Yes." Kerry squinted at the Mercedes, hoping to finally get a look at the woman who had Piver looped around her no doubt expensively manicured finger, but tinted glass and darkness kept Kerry from seeing her. Kerry waved as Piver looked across the parking lot at her; but he ducked into the car and its engine roared to life.

"Nice car," Smith said.

"I thought you liked classics." Kerry started her car's engine as she watched the Mercedes leave.

"He married?"

"You ask a lot of questions."

"It's my job."

"Piver is divorced. Which is your car?" Smith pointed at a white Ford pickup parked in front of a dentist's office and Kerry said, "I'll meet you at Lucky's."

"WHY ARE YOU STOPPING?" Nolan Piver demanded.

"Because of that man," the woman beside him said, her eyes glittering with feral light. Her voice remained sweet and even. "Smith."

"He doesn't look like a private investigator." Piver turned his head, guilt stricken. "He was in earlier today. Kerry told him to take a walk. She said she wasn't going to talk to him."

"I see."

His chest tightened and his heart felt too big for it. "There's nothing to connect us! Kerry doesn't know who you are. Nobody does. Please, baby, just forget it.

Kerry can talk all she wants. She doesn't know anything.''

"Smith is dangerous.'' The woman's gaze locked onto the white Ford pickup truck. She licked her lips, and her smile twitched. "Anybody he talks to is dangerous.'' She put the transmission in reverse. "There are holes. I don't want Smith sewing them shut.''

"We lay low. That's the plan. Business as usual and that's all. You're scaring me.''

"Don't be a wimp, darling. We've come this far. Why stop now?''

"You aren't going to hurt Kerry! Damn it, I forbid it.''

The woman's honeyed laughter filled the Mercedes as she backed out of the parking space, then turned to follow the pickup truck. "As long as Kerry keeps her big mouth shut, she has nothing at all to worry about.''

Piver hunched on the seat, watching the white truck. It turned left on Coit, then into a parking lot. His heart fluttered when the driver parked next to Kerry's Nova. "There's no way Kerry can connect us. Nobody can ever connect us.''

"No way,'' came the soft, deadly reply.

How did I get into this? Piver thought. It had seemed so simple at first to move some cash into legitimate business accounts. Money laundering was illegal, but relatively safe. After all, who looked twice at a copy shop? He didn't even know about the murder until afterward! "Let's take a small vacation. You and me, baby,'' he said.

"No PI is going to make me run,'' the woman snapped.

He couldn't see her face in the darkness and he was glad. He didn't want to see it. Piver pulled out his roll of antacids and popped one into his mouth. He wondered if she knew about him dipping into her till. Could she know? It scared him to contemplate what might happen if she found out. The rich interior of the Mercedes felt like a cage. He cracked the window so he could breathe.

His companion reached past him and opened the glove box. Piver jerked as she pressed a heavy weight into his hand.

"What's this for?" he whispered as he felt the icy contours of the automatic pistol.

"Insurance." She settled back on the driver's seat and rested her hands over the steering wheel. Street lamps reflected off her rings and the pearly polish on her nails. As if musing aloud, she said, "If Kerry recants her testimony, then the case reopens. You don't want that, darling. I don't want that." She drew a deep breath. Her exhalation moved the expensive scent of her perfume.

Piver swallowed hard, gripped by the urge to fling open the car door and run.

The woman continued. "Smith loves to talk. Unfortunately, he loves to listen, too. He has a way of making others talk." She chuckled, soft and low. "He fancies himself quite the ladies' man. It would be a terrible shame for Kerry to start thinking, really thinking, about what she saw that night."

"There isn't anything for her to think. You took care of the details. You said so."

"Of course, I did." The edge was back in her voice.

Nolan waved the pistol. "What am I supposed to do with this?"

"When the time comes, I'll tell you, darling. Don't I always know just what to do?"

IT WAS WEDNESDAY, and only two tables were occupied in the little Italian restaurant. Kerry took a booth near the back and sat facing the door. The dining room was dim. Light bulbs were hidden by red glass wall fixtures. Candles and carnations in fat vases made the cloth-covered tables look festive. She relaxed. The service was nice here, and forgiving of the lingering diner.

Smith arrived within minutes. Watching him walk made Kerry decide he was an exceptionally handsome man. He had a loose-limbed, graceful walk that showed off the tight leanness of his body. Still, there was something off kilter about him that she couldn't put her finger on. He had a reckless, possibly even dangerous, air. The way the two women sitting at the table near the door watched him told Kerry she wasn't the only one affected by his presence.

She sat straighter, unconsciously eager to hear his resonant voice and anticipating those dark eyes locked on hers. Then she caught herself and sat back. Confusion gnawed at her. She'd listened with tolerant amusement to girlfriends talking about the zap of finding the perfect man, of having everything click—his looks, his values, his way of talking—of just plain knowing all the stars were aligned and everything meshed. Kerry had never believed a word of it until now. Something was happening between them. She couldn't explain it or rationalize it or logically pick it apart. It was just there, and to have it happen in connection with one of the worst experiences of her life seemed unjust.

He slid into the booth. "That Nova have air conditioning?" he asked as he picked up the menu.

"No."

"So you had the window down that night. Did the door stick?"

Completely lost, she asked, "What are you getting at?" The waitress distracted her. Kerry ordered cannelloni, a salad and ice tea. Smith asked for the same, along with a basket of garlic and Parmesan bread sticks. Kerry made a point of asking for separate checks. Then as soon as the waitress left, Kerry asked, "What does my car have to do with anything?"

"I'm trying to picture this. The driveway is in the front of the house. You drive up with the window down. It's a nice neighborhood, so you don't roll the window up. The door sticks. You shove on it. You say to heck with it, grab what you're delivering and scoot over to the passenger side. You take a minute to straighten your clothes, then walk up to the house. Am I right?"

"I don't know. I suppose. They didn't ask any of this at the trial."

"You start to ring the doorbell. But this guy—"

"Abernathy."

"Comes barreling out, knocking you down."

"Right. No...he opened the door. He jerked it open. While he was standing there, I recognized him. Then he ran. He hit my shoulder and knocked me down."

Smith's gaze fixed on her again. "Ever hear a shotgun? It sounds like a cannon. Under the right conditions, you can hear it for miles."

"The neighbors didn't hear it."

"No one heard the shotgun. I can sort of understand the neighbors. The house is surrounded by trees and bushes, and most of the neighbors were out that night. Across the street is the golf course. But you were in front of the house. Why didn't you hear it?"

"He shot her before I arrived."

"Then why was he running *before* you rang the bell?" Smith suddenly clamped a hand over hers. Startled, she stared at his hand. His fingers were long, his nails blunt, his skin warm and covering hers possessively. Her insides shifted a few degrees off balance.

''Tell me again—why were you, a young woman, sent to a stranger's house at night?''

His touch and tone shocked her into the past. Images crystallized like a video. She had been working on the *Tiger's Tidbits* newsletter. Jack ran the copies, cussing the whole time because the high humidity made the paper wrinkle. He finally finished, and she was stuck with the folding. Piver took Abernathy's phone call and told her to deliver the forms. He wrote the address on the back of one of Copy Copy's cards. The car door did stick when she tried to get out. She beat her shoulder against it, trying to spring the stuck catch. It finally opened. The front yard of the Abernathy house was well lighted. There were even lights set into the concrete steps that led up to the front door. Kerry blinked, shivering with the memory.

''Tell me,'' Smith urged.

She did, her talk interrupted only once when the waitress brought their tea, salads and bread sticks. When Kerry finished, she felt exhausted, as if she'd run up a long, steep hill.

Smith dumped four packets of sugar into his tea and stirred it idly, his spoon clinking. ''Tell me about Piver.''

She smiled in confusion. ''He doesn't have anything to do with this.''

''He's the one who sent you to Abernathy's. Tell me. It's probably nothing.''

Kerry bristled. ''He certainly didn't murder Mrs. Abernathy.''

''Tell me about him.''

"I don't know what to say." She thought about it while she picked the olives out of her salad, savoring each one. Smith offered her a bread stick. She couldn't resist the crunchy, garlicky deliciousness. "He's my boss," she finally said with a shrug.

The waitress brought the cannelloni. The cheese crust bubbled, smelling of heavenly oregano. Kerry warned Smith about the hot dishes while avoiding his expectant gaze. He had her off balance; he was too easy to talk to. Every instinct told her to trust him, but she wasn't used to following instincts or hunches or intuition. She liked everything tidy, in order and explained clearly. Impulsive behavior was a sure path to trouble. Didn't everybody know that?

"Mr. Piver's a wheeler-dealer. He got into this business because desktop publishing is the wave of the future." She dabbled at her salad, seeking chunks of feta cheese. "I really don't know much about him. He's divorced. I don't think he has kids. He likes to take long lunches. He has a girlfriend, but I've never met her. He's my boss. He signs my paychecks. What do you want?"

"How long has he been seeing his girlfriend?"

Kerry shrugged. "A few months, I guess. That was her Mercedes. She calls but never leaves her name. And she never gets out of her car." Kerry held out her hands in a helpless gesture. "It's none of my business anyway."

"You've worked for him a long time."

"Look, Nolan Piver is a deal maker. This part of Texas is full of guys just like him. He's a type, a caricature of a Texas tycoon, but he isn't a murderer. He didn't even *know* Louise Abernathy."

"Maybe not, but that's something to find out." He crunched a bread stick.

"It must seem strange that I know so little about him, but what is there to know? He's superficial. If the talk isn't about money, he has nothing to say." She took another bread stick and studied the bumpy, lavalike crust of melted cheese. "It isn't so strange he sent me out that night. He takes me for granted. He says hop, and I might grumble, but I hop."

"Maybe so."

"What makes you so sure Abernathy is innocent? Okay, you don't like the murder motive the prosecution came up with, but so what? I read in the paper every day about people who've been murdered for a lot less."

Smith made an okay-okay gesture. "I knew Bill in law school—"

"You went to law school?" Surprise made her giggle. Of the professions Kerry might have matched with this rugged, drawling Texan, law would have been her last choice.

"Harvard," he said, using a Boston accent so that he sounded just like Ted Kennedy.

Kerry laughed.

"It's true. Bill and I were roommates. Just a pair of country boys at war with all them Yankees. I went to work in the D.A.'s office down in Houston. Bill went to work for a big firm here in Dallas. We kept in touch, got together sometimes and did some fishing. After I quit the D.A.'s office, Bill's firm hired me a few times. The buddy system, you know." He cocked his head, looking thoughtful. "One thing Bill has never been able to do is lie. It's a handicap for a lawyer. He isn't lying to me now."

"I saw him."

"You saw somebody. And know what I think, Kerry? The more I look around, the more I think Bill was set up. I think somebody used you to do it."

"How can you say that?"

"You're a perfect witness, honest and intelligent. From what I saw in the transcripts, you have nothing to hide. You were used."

"You make this sound like a conspiracy. Why?"

"That's the kicker. If I can't figure out why, I can't build a case anybody is going to look at."

"This is pretty farfetched, Mr. Smith."

"I told you I'm desperate. I don't have any hard facts for you. But I believe, deep down where it counts, that you were more than an innocent bystander. I think you were deliberately picked because you *are* innocent."

She met his gaze. It was a mistake. His eyes distracted her. Was he married? Where did he live? Her questions were stupid and beside the point.

He made a rueful gesture. "I'm probably beating my head against a wall. I know for certain I'm asking too much of you. But I need too much. I need corroboration. I need evidence." He rapped the tabletop with his knuckles. "Motive. I have a hunch this all boils down to motive. Who really wanted Louise Abernathy dead? Or who wanted Bill Abernathy blamed for her murder?"

"What about Louise, then?" Kerry asked.

Smith held his hands palms up. "She's a puzzle. The lady came out of nowhere. Bill can't give me much there."

"How can that be? He was married to her."

"Hell, love does funny things to a man. She was good-looking and kept a beautiful house. She did all the things a lawyer's wife is supposed to do. I've been digging around like a madman, but I can't find out where she came from or who her people were. I've got a lot more digging to do.'' He closed one eye slowly. ''And you're all I have. Will you help me?''

''I don't know how I can.''

''Then help yourself. If I'm right, then you're as much a victim as the Abernathys. Somebody went to a lot of trouble to set you up as a sucker.''

Smith's words slowly sunk in. Was she a sucker? No, that was too ridiculous. She was just in the wrong place at the wrong time. Still, Smith seemed too sincere and too intelligent to feel so passionately about a lost cause.

''I don't know about you, but knowing somebody used a nice young woman's sense of honesty and justice turns my gut. Rates right up there with kicking puppies,'' he said.

The words distressed and annoyed her. Maybe she was a little too helpful sometimes, a little too quick to say yes when she wanted to say no, but she was certainly not a victim. ''Even if I believed you, what could I do?''

''Come with me to Abernathy's house.''

Chapter Four

"I can't believe I'm doing this," Kerry said to herself. She waited until Smith parked his truck and got out before she left her Nova. For once the door didn't stick.

She eyed Smith warily. He had invited her to call an assistant district attorney named Bob Ward. She did, from the pay phone in Lucky's. Mr. Ward assured her Tarkington Smith was who he said he was. He'd added, "Take care now, miss. He's a little eager out of the chute." Uncertain what that meant, but satisfied Smith wasn't an ax murderer and that someone knew she was visiting the Abernathy house, she'd followed him to the Oak Fair Country Club community in Plano. She didn't feel so safe now. It was dark, the October air was chilly and traffic was light.

A faint fishy smell wafted on the breeze, along with a whiff of horses. Across the street, the golf course looked empty and black. Despite the beautiful neighborhood, with its air of gentility, the place gave Kerry the creeps.

"This is where you parked your car that night?" Smith asked, walking down the long, curved driveway. He kept a measured pace, as if judging distance.

"Isn't this illegal or something?"

"Nope. The case is closed. I have Bill's permission. I even have keys." He rattled a set. He returned to Kerry's side. She told herself it was just a house and that there were no such things as ghosts. She edged closer to him.

"I'm not going in that house." Cold seeped through Kerry's blouse and she hugged her elbows.

Smith reached into the back seat of her car and picked up her suit jacket. He draped it over her shoulders.

"Didn't the police go over the house? I mean, that's their job, isn't it?" she asked.

"I'm looking for what they didn't look for," he said, walking up the steps. "What shoes were you wearing that night?"

She looked down at her low-heeled pumps. "Probably some like these. Why do you ask?" She looked nervously at the houses on either side. One was dark, but the other showed lights both upstairs and downstairs.

Smith opened the front door of the Abernathy house. "Are you *sure* this is all right?"

He nodded. "After I close the door, walk up the steps." He turned on the outside lights.

She did, wincing as each click of her heels echoed. She jumped when he opened the door. She said, "Can I go now? I need to feed my cats."

He thumped the doorjamb. "Pay half a million, and you should get better construction. I guess the neighborhood means a lot. I heard you plain as day."

"There. He heard me coming and panicked. Can we go now?"

Smith walked through the foyer. A luxury car cruised past the house. A sports car drove past in the opposite direction, then the street grew quiet again. Kerry imagined neighbors asking each other, ''What kind of ghouls are at the Abernathy house?'' She sidled inside and shut the door.

''SHE DOESN'T KNOW anything?'' the woman asked.

Piver felt tension fill the Mercedes. He pictured her as catlike, with tense shoulders, black eyes and ears laid flat as she concentrated on her prey. Tail swishing. He hated cats. ''There's nothing for her to know,'' he whispered. He scrubbed his sweaty palm on his trouser leg. The pistol felt like a million pounds crushing his lap.

''Do you want to go to prison, darling? I don't.''

''I haven't done anything!''

Her laugh was full and throaty; it iced his blood. ''No, dear, of course you haven't done anything. You acquired that money entirely by accident. Silly me.''

''Stop it.'' He grabbed her hand. ''Let's go to Vegas tonight. We can hop a plane. We'll get married, honeymoon. It'll be terrific. When we get back, we start over. I have it all figured out. I sell the shop, liquidate, then everything goes into your boutique—''

''Spa, darling. It'll be a spa.'' She lifted his hand to her mouth. She kissed his fingers, one by one. She whispered, ''Get rid of Kerry. She doesn't realize how much she knows. It would be terrible for you to go to prison because of her.''

''What am I supposed to do?''

''Shoot her. You do know how to shoot that thing, don't you?''

He shoved the pistol at her. ''You shoot her, damn it.''

She patted his cheek. ''Don't disappoint me too deeply, darling.''

Piver clutched the gun and stared past a pyracantha hedge toward the Abernathy house. He felt sick. The hold she had on him consisted of a thousand tiny barbs. They tore and festered, burying themselves deeper every day.

"This is her fault, really. She's so damned innocent. A victim." The woman snorted her derision. "Victims deserve what they get. She's asking for it. The world is too tough and ugly for her. It moves too fast. She's in our way. She's a problem. And how does my big, strong man take care of problems?"

He forced a scowl. Maybe it *was* Kerry's fault. She wasn't supposed to talk to Smith. She shouldn't have come to the Abernathy house. If only she wasn't so stupid.

THE THOUGHT THAT SOMEONE had actually died in this house chilled Kerry. Still, it piqued her curiosity, morbid as it was. What kind of man murdered his wife?

The foyer was tiled with terrazzo, and it was icy cold. Cut flowers rotted in a dusty vase atop a reproduction of an antique secretary. The lid was down, and the cubby type drawers were open.

Smith turned on lights. Kerry slipped her arms into the sleeves of her jacket, wondering if he might turn on the heat, too. She wrinkled her nose at the dead crickets and dust balls along the base boards.

"Kerry?"

"What?"

"Go back out. Close the door. Walk up and down the steps."

Rolling her eyes, feeling like an idiot, she did what he wanted. She hoped nobody saw her. "Why do I do this to myself?" she muttered. "Stray cats, and now stray detectives. Piver walks all over me, Mom walks all over me, and now this crazy man walks all over me...."

"Kerry?" Smith beckoned from the doorway. She entered the house. "I can't hear you unless I'm in the foyer. He couldn't have heard you unless he was standing in here."

"Maybe he heard the car."

"Maybe." Smith stalked away again.

His tone was so skeptical, Kerry followed to argue. "Nobody else was worried about this."

"Yeah, I asked about that. I spoke to Shanlin, and he doesn't like it, either. But the D.A. said there was no need to upset you. Your memory was good enough."

Kerry remembered Detective Shanlin, the man in charge of the investigation. She'd spoken with him once. "My memory is good. Robert Marsh interviewed me I don't know how many times. What possible difference—" She came to a sudden stop and clapped both hands to her mouth. "Oh, gross," she whispered through her fingers.

The tape outline of Louise Abernathy's body was still affixed to the silvery blue carpet of the formal dining room. A dark stain spread from the place where her head once lay. Rusty black spots and splatters marred the silky wallpaper and ceiling. Dead ferns and philodendrons wilted in ceramic pots. A coffee cup sat on the long, cherrywood table. Kerry remembered all the pictures Quintas had shoved in her face when he tried to make her recant her testimony.

The one of Louise Abernathy's hand loomed horribly vivid. Despite the blood and butchery, it had once been a beautiful hand. Slender fingered and elegant. A hand to arrange flowers or hold a piece of Baccarat crystal.

Smith's eyebrows raised in alarm. "You all right?"

The cannelloni she'd eaten was doing flip-flops in her stomach. She shook her head and backed out of the room.

"Sorry," he said. He touched her arm lightly, reassuringly. She gave him a wan smile and wished she was brave. He walked past her, then up a flight of stairs. Too spooked to stay downstairs alone, she followed.

She focused on the decor. Every wall surface was papered, trimmed and hung with pictures, mostly oil landscapes of the type Kerry recognized as investment art. Upstairs, the place looked like a layout from *Better Homes and Gardens.*

They entered the master bedroom. Kerry whistled. It was like a French palace, with white-enameled furniture, swagged drapes and glittering crystal. She ran her finger over the satin bedspread and found dust.

"Some place, eh?" Smith asked.

"It's something, all right." Curious in a macabre way, she looked around for a hint of Louise Abernathy's personality. Everything seemed too perfect, too impersonal. The room seemed better suited to a store display than a home.

Smith searched an armoire. He moved quickly, scanning, barely moving what he touched. He hummed a country-sounding tune. At the same time, Kerry peeked inside a bedside cabinet. She found a few copies of *Barron's,* an issue of the *Wall Street Journal,* and a trade-paperback copy of *In Search of Excellence.* She imagined what people would find if she died. Cat toys under and behind the furniture, paperback novels scattered wherever she finished reading them, a pink box of Mr. Bubble in the bathroom, old envelopes and paper-clipped stacks of coupons. Bits and pieces of her life were everywhere. There were no bits and pieces here. It was creepy.

"What are you looking for?" Kerry asked.

"Anything the police or Bill's lawyers might have missed. They found the gambling paraphernalia in here and the love letters, too. It was a good investigation. Very thorough. Perfect procedure." He looked around, his gaze thoughtful. "Too perfect. With all that good stuff on the surface, there was no need to dig deeper. That's my job."

He leaned his back against the armoire and studied the bed. "Quintas pushed for a quick trial. He believed in Bill's innocence, and a quick trial is the best way to weaken the prosecution's case. The more I look into it, though, the shakier everything seems." He cocked his head. "Quintas screwed up when he didn't talk to you. He did a good job investigating you, but he was too busy digging for dirt to consider something as simple as talking. Eyewitnesses make lousy evidence. People see what they expect to see, then interpret it. But I have a feeling the D.A. okayed a quick trial because he wasn't interested in uncovering more evidence."

"What?" Kerry threw up her hands in incredulous dismay. "Do you read all those awful books about the Kennedy assassination? And believe those cockamamie conspiracy theories?"

"That isn't what I meant. Okay, maybe it's what I meant. It just seems strange to put so much faith in you, unless somebody knew something they didn't want falling into the hands of the defense."

"I'm lost. And I think you're paranoid."

"Rules of discovery. The way it works is that whatever the defense uncovers they hold on to, but whatever the prosecution finds, the defense can demand and use. What didn't the prosecution want the defense to find?''

''This is ridiculous.''

''This case was sloppy. It makes me wonder why.''

''You're paranoid,'' she said.

''Since the guy who wrote the love letters never stepped forward, it makes me think he's involved. A boyfriend makes a better suspect than a husband. But he's a phantom. Quintas went crazy trying to find him. He even got himself in trouble by accusing the D.A. of making the boyfriend up. I tend to think that Louise liked a certain type of man. It would have been somebody who looked enough like Bill for you to mistake the two.''

''I was positive it was Mr. Abernathy. I still am. I have a good memory for faces.''

Smith returned to his search and invited her to look behind a door. Kerry opened it, revealing a closet the size of her living room. She fingered the silk blouses and cashmere skirts, awed by the variety. She recognized top-designer quality. The neatness awed her, too. Everything was arranged by color. The skirts and slacks were hung on special hangers. She chuckled to find the hangers were like the kind in motels, attached permanently to the rods. Each suit wore a dust cover over the shoulders. Shoes were mounted on trees. The air held a faint sachet of potpourri and cedar.

She frowned. ''Hey, Smith, come here.''

He popped into the closet. ''Find something? Wow, the lady did like to dress.''

''Or at least liked to shop. My mother would love this. But look.''

He walked inside, his quick gaze flickering high and low. Then he shrugged.

"Men," she muttered. She pointed out gaps between the clothes. There were two empty hangers in a row of red blouses, three among the green and six empty spaces in a line of dress suits. There were empty spaces on the shoe trees, too. The gaps stood out in the compulsive neatness like missing teeth.

His expressive face revealed the idea hitting him. He said, "Almost like she packed for a trip."

"She was running away with her boyfriend and Mr. Abernathy stopped her the only way he could?" Kerry offered. She opened a pink wicker hamper. It held a few hand towels, underwear and other washables. She pulled out a summery cotton blouse. "That's odd." She also found a denim skirt.

Smith peered into the hamper and said, "What's the matter?"

"Well, she had all those beautiful clothes." She held out the skirt and blouse. "And wore these. These are okay, but they're cheap."

"Maybe they aren't hers?"

Kerry checked the label, then a dress on a hanger. "Everything is size five." She tossed the clothes back into the hamper. "She was probably cleaning or something."

Smith fingered a gap in the row of blouses. "Where's her suitcase?"

"You're the detective."

"Private investigator," he corrected with a grin.

They left the closet. Smith left the bedroom, and Kerry peeked into the dressing room, amused by the ring of light bulbs around the wall mirror. It was just like a movie star's dressing room. Plastic boxes held cosmetics; makeup brushes perched in a ceramic holder. Kerry lightly touched bottles of expensive perfumes. A quart-sized bottle of Chanel No 5 made her shake her head. Louise must have bathed in the stuff.

The neatness still bothered Kerry. Items on the vanity were regimental. It was as if everything had been laid out for a white-glove inspection. Bottles were lined up according to height, and everything was encased. Except for a layer of dust, everything was perfect. Louise Abernathy must have been a terror to her housekeeper.

Unable to resist, Kerry opened a jewelry box. The costume baubles disappointed her. There were rhinestones, faux pearls and trendy ethnic junk, but nothing of particular interest. Everything was of good quality, but junk jewelry nonetheless. She opened a narrow closet door. Towels and sheets were folded neatly and stacked by size and color. A spot of color under the door caught her eye. A crumpled cigarette pack was stuck among the dustballs, as if someone had tossed it at the waste basket and missed.

She picked up the pack, walked out and bumped into Smith. He caught her, holding her for a lingering moment. It was long enough for her to catch the scent of garlic and spicy after-shave; long enough for her to note that his height was perfect, tall enough to make her feel delicate, but not so tall she had to strain to look into his face. She felt his reluctance to turn her loose.

"No suitcase," Smith said, releasing her.

Kerry held up the cigarette pack. "A clue, Mr. Smith. I haven't seen any ashtrays. Does Mr. Abernathy smoke? Did she?" Smith's frown told her she'd found something he wasn't expecting. "I bet her boyfriend smokes. Maybe her suitcase is stashed at a hotel. Maybe she'd already left Mr. Abernathy and came back for something." Kerry tapped the jewelry box. "I know how you can find out for sure. Check her safe deposit boxes. She must have had real jewels, and she didn't keep them here. She wouldn't walk out on him without taking her jewelry.''

He took the cigarette pack, but looked stubborn. ''Maybe.''

''It makes sense. If he loved her that much and she was walking out, then it makes sense. Tragic sense.''

He flipped open a maroon, leather-bound book. It was an organizer, a combination address book, calendar, business-card holder and appointment keeper. ''She had a dinner party planned for the weekend after the murder, a hair appointment for that Friday and another appointment for a body wrap, whatever that is. Here's a club meeting, a riding lesson and a reminder to buy flowers. A reminder to pick up a suit from the tailor. A note about Bill's birthday. She was booked through August according to this.''

''No clues about her boyfriend?''

Smith looked disgusted. ''All the letters were signed 'D.' There were no fingerprints on the letters and no return address, just a lot of smut and I-love-yous.'' He jerked a thumb at the dainty secretary in the far corner. ''What bugs me is that the letters were found in there, in plain sight. Bill says he was always going through the secretary for a pencil or piece of paper. He would have seen the letters. He says he never saw them, and I believe him.''

Back downstairs, Smith stopped in the foyer and scowled at the door. ''This doesn't make sense. If he shot her and ran immediately, you would have heard the shotgun. If he heard you, then why was he still standing in the foyer? Why not bolt out the back door? Or into the garage? Why open the door at all?''

''Ask Mr. Abernathy. He's the one who ran.''

"Somebody called Bill at the office on the night of the murder. A man who identified himself as one of the firm's partners asked Bill to drive to Arlington as a special favor. Some briefs had to be filed first thing in the morning, and all the clerks and secretaries had gone home. So Bill went to Arlington. He said he called from his car phone and told Louise he'd be late. That was at 8:07 p.m. He had to fight evening traffic, then couldn't find the address. He tried calling the partner back, but couldn't reach him. By the time he got home, it was after ten. The coroner and police were here."

"It sounds like a pretty shaky alibi."

"Or a way to put Bill in a position in which he couldn't establish an alibi." Smith cocked an eyebrow. "Here's a discrepancy no one can explain. You claimed he called Copy Copy around eight-forty-five. Now, the calls Bill made to his house and his office are in the phone company's records, but there's no trace of the call to you."

"Did he call from a pay phone? Or from here?"

"You're suggesting he killed Louise then called you to deliver legal forms?"

"I don't know, but you're turning a crime of passion into a major conspiracy," Kerry said. "I say she was leaving him and he loved her too much to lose her."

"Maybe."

Kerry breathed easier when Smith shut and locked the front door and they walked to her car. She tugged on the driver's door. "Sorry I couldn't help you or your friend." She gave the handle a hard jerk and its sudden release made her stumble backward.

A sharp crack like an engine backfire broke the night air. Kerry jumped, wondering where the noisy car was. Smith caught her waist, slinging her around the car door. Another crack sounded; metal pinged. Smith pushed Kerry around the front of the car, toward the side nearest to the house. Kerry scrambled and stumbled. She scraped her knees on the concrete drive. Metal pinged again.

Shoving her head down, Smith urged her to run. Her heels sank into the frosty grass in the side yard. She stumbled, losing a shoe. Another crack sounded, and something hit the ground, throwing sod. Smith threw Kerry to the side and she rolled. She ended up clutched to his belly, his body shielding hers from the street. Kerry panted, her eyelids squeezed shut. An engine gunned, dogs barked, a man shouted and car tires squealed. Then the engine sounds faded in the distance. Kerry gasped for air. Her heartbeat thudded against her eardrums. It was pitch dark. Dried grass pricked like spears of ice through her clothes. Smith held her tightly, his arms locking her arms across her breast, his face pressed against her neck.

Smith strained to listen, dreading the crunch of feet on the frozen grass, but there was nothing except the sound of dogs barking. He relaxed. "Mmm," he breathed in Kerry's ear. "A big girl. Just the way I like them." He doubted she heard or cared about his observation. She trembled, her legs churning as she forced herself into a tight ball. She was scared witless, and he didn't blame her. He wasn't feeling so hot at the moment, either. He nuzzled her silky hair and murmured soothing sounds. "It's okay. It's over."

Kerry whispered, "Was that a gun?"

"I hate handguns." He snorted. "I really hate people shooting at me with handguns. You all right?"

"I don't know. I tore my stockings." She pressed even tighter against his belly. "Did he hit my car?"

Her voice rose in a panicky whisper. "I think he hit my car. *I can't believe he hit my car!*"

Smith forced down anger, saving it for later when he found the low-down egg sucker who had taken potshots at them. Right now Kerry concerned him. She made little huffing noises as if she were building up for a real good scream, and she was trembling so hard that her teeth chattered. He helped her upright, but she sagged in his arms. It was definitely the wrong time to think about how nice she felt. Her fragility was an illusion; her body was solidly fine. Her hair smelled of flowers. He couldn't help being distracted. Since the moment he had laid eyes on Kerry Byfield, thinking about her had vied with Bill's case for top priority.

"Ah, don't worry about it, sugar," he whispered. "That sounded like a little gun."

Her head snapped up and he felt the force of her angry astonishment in the darkness. She shoved against his chest. Good, better that she was mad at him rather than scared. She grumbled something about insensitive smart alecks, but he didn't catch the exact words. He held her hands and worked his thumbs against her palms until she stopped shaking and breathed easier. He found her shoe. She snatched it out of his hand. He grinned. Not only was she beautiful, but she was gutsy. He told her to wait.

She pressed against a brick garage wall as he crept toward the front of the house. He saw movement near the street and froze. A man and a woman clutched each other and looked at the Abernathy house. Neighbors probably.

"Is he gone?" Kerry whispered hoarsely.

Smith glanced back at her. The shooting proved his hunch about the murder. He was close enough to the truth to give someone a scare. His gut tightened. It was bad enough he had to involve anybody. But Kerry? There was something cockeyed about finding the woman his head, heart and instinct agreed was the girl of his dreams, then pulling her into a situation in which he could get her killed. If this wasn't so serious and promising to get worse, he might almost appreciate the irony.

A siren wailed, growing closer.

"DRIVE FASTER!" PIVER screamed. He shoved the pistol into the glove box and buried it under papers.

"Hey, watch the mess." The woman turned on the turn signal, seemingly oblivious to the police car. It squealed around the corner, siren wailing and lights flashing. "I can't believe I missed." She stopped at the intersection and stared at the red light. Her fingers tapped the steering wheel. When she smiled, her teeth looked like fangs. "Poor baby. You're just Mamma's little softy, aren't you?"

Piver licked his lips, concentrating on controlling his shaking. He'd never realized a gun was so loud. His ears were still ringing. He cut a wary glance at her. Was she angry he couldn't shoot the gun? "You don't think anybody saw us do you?"

"In that neighborhood? They don't even see each other." The traffic light turned green. "This sort of thing is beneath us anyway. I'll handle this little problem."

"What—what are you going to do?"

She guided the Mercedes effortlessly through frequent lane changes. "Don't go to work tomorrow, darling," she said, giving him that evil, cat smile. "You really don't look well at all. You can trust Kerry with watching the store for a day, can't you?''

"Don't hurt her.''

The woman glanced at the rearview mirror. "She won't feel a thing.''

Chapter Five

Kerry spent the next hour and a half freezing while four very unhappy Plano police officers argued with Tarkington Smith.

The police had taken her statement. She couldn't recall seeing or hearing a car before the shooting. She hadn't seen it drive away. The police, though polite, treated her as if she were an imbecile. Her explanation as to why she was at the Abernathy house in the first place elicited only sour sounding *uh-huh*s.

Kerry kept her face averted from the street as several people walked dogs past the Abernathy house—it was a convenient excuse for gawking. She was uncertain which was worse, being scared half to death or being a public spectacle.

She fingered the bullet holes in her car. Her beautiful little 1968 Nova, with its perfect engine and a weekly wash and wax, had never had so much as a scratch in the original paint job. It had been a birthday gift from her father, the last gift he'd given her before he died. She began shaking again. The sensation started in her knees and worked its way upward, detouring a moment to her belly to jerk the knots tighter. Her teeth chattered. "My car, my car," she mouthed, and tears burned her eyes. She blinked rapidly. She and her father had shared a love of craftsmanship and solid dependability in everything from architecture and automobiles to music and art. He had taught her to appreciate what was good and to always do her best, and that substance is always better than style. Now Tarkington Smith and his idiot theories had put holes in her car!

She wrenched away from the Nova and jammed her hands under her armpits. Her only consolation was that the police treated Tarkington Smith as if he'd opened a drug dealership in the Oak Fair Country Club. An out-of-town private investigator causing a shoot-'em-up in one of the most exclusive neighborhoods in the Dallas–Fort Worth metroplex won no prizes for popularity. Kerry took twisted pleasure from the open hostility of the police.

When the police finally left, Smith raked back his hair with both hands. He loosed a long breath as he watched the lights of the last patrol car recede. His investigation had already antagonized the Collin County D.A. Few appreciated his efforts to bust open what had been for them a very neat open-and-shut case. He couldn't afford to lose police cooperation, too. He was close to something and if the police department cut off his access to investigative reports and other case particulars, then Bill was going to rot in prison while Smith bent his nose against a hostile wall.

He turned to Kerry. She hugged herself, her head held up like a horse smelling smoke. Regret and sympathy squeezed his heart. She was scared, but doing her best to fight it. "I'll drive you home."

"No need," she said in a voice that was an octave higher than normal. She pulled her keys from her purse and dropped them. When she bent to retrieve them, she dropped her purse. Her hands trembled as she gathered her lipstick, wallet and comb. He crouched to help her. He handed her a package of tissues and repeated his offer. She sat on the passenger side of the Nova and buckled her seat belt.

On the drive home, he tried to draw her out with neutral conversation about the Dallas Cowboys and the weather. Except for mumbled directions, she rode in silence. She stared straight ahead, her hands clenched on her lap. He parked in front of her apartment building, leaned his forearms on the steering wheel and studied the nondescript, two-story row complex. It was just like a hundred other apartment complexes all over north Dallas, with cute names like Charter Arms and Seven Trees. Hers was called Parkway Manor.

Doors faced the parking lot. The first-floor apartments had fake stoops to match the fake brownstone design. A balcony walkway offered access to the upper apartments. Street lights made gray-yellow puddles in the parking lot. The bass rhythm of somebody's stereo pulsed. Traffic hummed in the distance. It didn't look safe to him.

"Think they'll catch the guy who shot at us?" she asked hopefully. Her voice sounded stronger.

He looked at her. With her rounded forehead and chin and small nose, she looked a lot younger than twenty-five. Put her in a miniskirt and too much eye makeup, and she could pass for a teenager. Still, there was nothing young or flaky about her inner fortitude. Her wide eyes glistened like dark pools, but she showed no sign of breaking down.

He gave her question consideration. The neighbors hadn't seen anything, and the police hadn't seen anything suspicious on the scene. "Not a chance. I don't think you ought to be alone. Whoever's gunning for you—''

"Gunning for me?" Her jaw dropped. "Gunning for me? No way! I'm a nice person, Mr. Smith. I don't make enemies, and people don't go gunning for me." She jabbed an accusing finger in his direction. "You, on the other hand, strike me as a crazy person. If I'm in any danger, it is caused by association with the likes of you!"

"Now you're mad at me." Those were the wrong words.

Her voice rose. "You drag me through a death house. I get shot at. That cop lectured me as if I were a teenager caught riding a skateboard in a shopping mall. I— I ruined my only pair of black panty hose. There are holes in my car. *Holes in my car!* Go away!" She pushed open the car door and almost fell in her haste to escape. She snatched her purse then stomped up the sidewalk.

Smith raked back his hair and told himself that anger was better than panic, even if it didn't make things any easier for him. One thing was certain, he wasn't leaving her alone. He locked the Nova before following her to a first-floor apartment. He jingled her keys.

She groaned and rested an arm against the door. "Please go away and leave me alone."

"I need to call a cab. Can I use your phone?" He held out the keys.

Kerry drew deep breaths and counted to ten, slowly. She took the ring of keys and fumbled through them for the house key. The cats met her inside the door, chittering and complaining about each other in their squeaky, Hello-hi-how-are-you meows. Kerry pointed at the phone on the kitchen counter. Smith sat on a barstool, and Keystone jumped onto his lap. Smith picked up the handset while he absently stroked the big tabby's ears.

"The phone book is under the counter," Kerry said, and kicked off her shoes. Her knees ached. Still, inside her home, surrounded by normalcy, she felt much, much better.

"Now isn't it funny. I'm in town three weeks and can't find anything. Everywhere I go I have to make appointments. No one wants to talk to me. I talk, and they watch their watches. I hook up with you, and all of a sudden somebody's interested. Why is that?"

She didn't know and didn't want to know. She excused herself and went into the bathroom. She examined the damage to her knees, stripped off the ruined stockings, then washed the scrapes. Wincing at the sting, she dabbed on Mercurochrome. At least her hands had stopped shaking.

"Somebody doesn't want me talking to you," he called out.

"I don't want to talk to you," she muttered, and jammed the stockings in the waste basket—$4.95 down the drain. That plus however much it would cost to patch her car. Tarkington Smith was an expensive date. She giggled, then clapped a hand over her mouth. If she laughed now, she'd never quit. She hugged her knees. *Get a grip, Byfield. It's over. No harm done. It's over.*

"Are you all right in there?"

"Fine," she replied. "I need to change. I'll be out in a minute."

In her bedroom, she slipped out of her skirt and jacket. Both were stained with reddish mud. She folded them and made a mental note to drop them off at Toby's Cleaners. She pulled on jeans and a pink sweatshirt with

Minnie Mouse smiling on the front. She ran a brush through her shoulder-length hair, then stopped in the bathroom to take two aspirin and brush the garlic off her teeth.

She found Smith on the couch with all four cats vying for his attention. Dash curled around his boots. Midnight made a vain attempt to tame Smith's unruly shock of hair. Keystone lay on his lap. Even Lucy, whose temperament was aloof at best, perched on the arm of the couch, as if considering whether to allow him to pet her. A little surprised to find she felt normal, Kerry decided it was too much effort to stay angry at a man who liked cats.

"Did you call a cab?"

"We need to talk." His long fingers found the sensitive spot behind Midnight's ears. The black kitten's purr rumbled in the quiet room. "I know you're upset, but this is important. Talk to me. You know by now there's something wrong."

Kerry sat on the other end of the couch, her knees together, her hands folded on her lap. "Mr. Smith, I am going to share something with you. I would appreciate it very much if you will listen. My father was in the military. I spent most of my life moving. I promised myself that when I was an adult, I would find a place to root and stay there. I like routine. I like knowing exactly what I'll be doing tomorrow. I don't bother people, and I don't like being bothered. My mother calls me a very dull person. She thinks it's a criticism, but I take it as a compliment. Do you understand what I am saying? Being your partner in some sort of adventure holds absolutely no appeal— Please stop looking at me like that."

One eyebrow quirked. His gaze was attentive and warm enough to melt glass. "Like what?"

"Like—" *Like I'm beautiful and you can't get enough of me.* She stood abruptly and went to the counter that separated her kitchen from the living room. She sat on a stool and rested her chin in her hand.

His cowboy boots clicked on the linoleum as he stepped off the carpet. "Got anything to drink, sugar?"

"There's Coke in the fridge."

He poured two sodas. "Where was the car?"

"I don't know. I never saw anything. I just heard—"

"Not tonight. Last June."

She thought for a minute, then lifted a shoulder. "I don't know. It wasn't in the driveway. I heard him leave, but I don't remember seeing the car."

"Can you remember what kind of car it sounded like?"

"Even if I heard it right now, I couldn't tell you anything about it."

"Bill has a three-car garage and all that driveway, but his car was nowhere in sight. Make sense?"

She sipped her Coke. It tasted funny mingled with toothpaste. She smacked her lips.

"Triple garage. Two cars. Enough room in the driveway for ten cars. People don't park on the street in that neighborhood. Nobody parks a Jaguar on the street in any neighborhood."

"You aren't going to quit, are you, Mr. Smith?"

"Can't, sugar."

"Stop calling me sugar."

"Stop calling me Mr. Smith."

Throwing up her hands, she cried, "Enough! You are turning something simple into a complicated mess! I admit that I don't know much about the case, but com-

mon sense tells me that if twelve people on a jury were
convinced that Mr. Abernathy killed his wife, then it's
a pretty sure thing he did.''

"Well, now—"

"Stop. Look, I want to believe you. You seem like
a very trustworthy man. I also believe you believe every
word you are saying. Except for one thing. You keep
talking about hunches and funny feelings, but you don't
have any evidence. I'm the one who saw Mr. Abernathy
with the shotgun.''

Smith started to say something else, but she shut her
ears and refused to look at him. An unwanted image of
William Abernathy formed in her mind. The man
wasn't feeling guilt, just grief Smith had said. That rang
true. He'd looked like a pitiful man in shock, shaking
his head in mute denial as her accusing words had filled
the courtroom. What-ifs gnawed at her conscience.
What if she had to prove her innocence? What if all the
evidence was stacked against her and she couldn't deny
it? What if every face held accusation and every ear
was closed against her cries?

Her gaze fell on her desk and the computer on top
of it. Facts and figures—she could understand them. She
also admitted she wanted to help Tarkington Smith, if
only to rid him of the delusion that William Abernathy
was innocent. "I have an idea, a practical idea, if it
works," she said. "Can you find out Louise Abernathy's Social Security number?''

"Why?"

"Because Mrs. Abernathy was wealthy and wealthy
people don't deal in cash. They use credit cards and
checks.''

"True." Openly interested, Smith leaned his forearms on the countertop.

"I think there's a way to prove that she was leaving him." Kerry met Smith's gaze with challenge and caught the slight narrowing of his eyes, but bulled ahead anyway. "I know what you believe, but I also know what I saw. Only one of us is right. So let's make a deal. If I can prove she was leaving him, you admit that's cause enough for him to kill her. Then you get out of my life and leave me alone."

THE TELEPHONE STARTLED Robert Marsh. Holding a finger on his place in the law text, he picked up the handset and balanced it under his jaw. "Marsh," he said absently.

"It's me."

The sound of her voice grabbed his full attention. He sat straighter. "Why are you calling me at home?" he demanded.

"Remember that phone number you mentioned? The one I might need if I ran into certain problems?"

He grinned in admiration. She was good. She never named names. Her words were full of insinuation, but never specifics. The grin faded as it occurred to him what she wanted. A chill ran up and down his spine and his feet felt cold. He remembered a documentary about African Cape hunting dogs. They were weird, long-legged dogs. They looked as harmless as collies, but once a pack set its sight on a zebra or wildebeest, nothing distracted or stopped them until they had a kill. He blinked slowly. He'd given her a little technical advice, tampered a little with the evidence and guided the police investigation. It had been lucrative and the risk factor had been acceptable. Now, however, she was talking about raising the body count. It was too risky.

"Are you there?" she asked.

"I'm here. Listen, let me give you a piece of advice. Lay low. There's no need to panic."

"I never panic," she said icily. "Give me the phone number."

He curled his lips inward. How could he have been so stupid as to boast to her about a man like Rex? He was a psychopath who'd torture his own mother for fifty dollars. Marsh considered telling her Rex was out of circulation, but doubted she'd believe him. "That's a very valuable piece of information."

"Really? Hmm, I wonder if it's as valuable as the information I'm looking at right at this moment."

Cape hunting dogs patiently sought out weaknesses and knew their prey better than the prey knew themselves. "You're bluffing."

"That's right. I'm bluffing."

He closed his eyes and slumped. She wasn't bluffing. God only knew what she had. With elections coming up and the press busily scurrying about in search of a whiff of scandal, it needn't be much. Just a few juicy names and figures planted in the ears of the right people and his political career was over before it began.

Tarkington Smith, he thought bitterly. Everything had been perfect until that cowboy roared into town, charming file clerks and secretaries into handing over official records and making a pest of himself at police headquarters. He deserved to get himself killed. Marsh gave her the phone number.

She hung up without saying goodbye.

He slammed down the handset then jumped up and paced, his slippers scuffing the Persian rug on the den floor. He suddenly stopped. Kerry Byfield? Had she been talking to Smith? Was her name going on Rex's shopping list? He shook his head to clear the thought.

Kerry Byfield was a genuinely honest woman who believed implicitly in her testimony. Nothing Smith might say could shake that belief.

Still, it might be best to find out for certain.

Chapter Six

Smith asked, "How?"

Kerry jerked a thumb at her personal computer. "That. With Mrs. Abernathy's Social Security number, I might be able to find the hotel where she stashed her suitcase."

His cockiness disappeared. His lips tightened into a stubborn line. Kerry said gently, "I've been more than willing to listen to your side. Turnabout's only fair."

With a grudging nod, he murmured, "You're right."

"Then is it a deal? I find the evidence, and you get out of my life." She leaned forward and added sternly, "And you fix the holes in my car."

"You have the prettiest green eyes I've ever seen." He arched his eyebrows devilishly.

She slapped the countertop. "That's it! I'm trying to be serious and helpful, and all you—"

He rattled off a string of numbers. Kerry stiffened in surprise. "Louise Abernathy's Social Security number," he said.

She gawked, incredulous, but knew it was too outrageous a lie for anyone to tell. "How did you know it?"

He tapped his temple with his index finger. "Perfect

recall. I'm cursed. Of course, I save money on notebooks.'' He took a pencil from the jar she kept by the phone and scribbled the number on the edge of an advertising circular.

Kerry blinked at the number, then pulled the phone near. ''Uh—actually, I've never done this before. I have to call someone first.''

He was giving her that look again. Unable to look at his face, she stared at the phone. She grew warm under his gaze and questioned her own motives. Searching for information with the computer seemed a way of keeping him around, not of getting rid of him.

She dialed a number, then let it ring. Her friend Blackie picked it up after the fifteenth ring. ''Don't hang up, it's me, Kerry.''

Blackie grunted.

She explained what she needed quickly. Blackie laughed at her. She grinned, abashed. How many times had she lectured him about the evils of computer hacking? Or about the sanctity of personal records?

''This is important,'' she said. ''Can you help me?''

''Got a pencil? You're in luck. I had to run a credit check on that guy who wants my motorcycle. I've got some new passwords for the NCB.''

She wrote quickly, taking down a list of codes and passwords to get into the National Credit Bureau's computer. Blackie offered numbers for a travel agency and a major banking network. She said it was unnecessary. He told her it was better to have too much than too little and gave them to her anyway.

After she hung up, Smith eyed the list of numbers and codes. ''Who'd you call, the FBI?''

''Better. A friend of mine from my users' group at my computer club. He's a genius. A little odd, but I like him. His hobby is computer hacking.'' She made a face of apology. "He spends all his time locked up with his computers. He's probably broken into every system in America. I don't think he's a crook, but God help us all if he ever decides to turn into one.'' She eyed the list glumly. "This is illegal. I'm not used to doing illegal things. I've never even had a parking ticket.''

"Truth isn't always pretty. Sometimes finding it is downright ugly. I just keep telling myself that what I'm doing is right.''

Kerry caught a funny quality in Smith's voice. Was he apologizing? Was he sorry to involve her in this mess? She liked to think so and liked him better because of it.

She turned on the overhead light and then the computer. After hooking the telephone into the modem, she typed in the command to activate the communications program. The PowerComm logo appeared. She pressed return and the menu appeared. She selected autodial then typed in the phone number for the National Credit Bureau.

"That's all there is to it?'' Smith asked, watching over her shoulder. "I don't fiddle with my computer much. I just write some reports and do my bookkeeping.''

"I'm surprised,'' Kerry said. "If you need information, this is the only way to go. These things aren't necessarily better, but they're faster than searching file cabinets or libraries.''

The NCB computer answered the phone. A bright blue-and-yellow logo appeared across the top of the screen. Under it were requests for company and authorization codes.

Kerry took a deep breath. "Here's felony number

one. Computer larceny. NCB is a paid-subscriber system. Somebody somewhere is paying for this.'' She typed in the company code, then a seven-digit authorization code. A request for a password appeared. ''Felony number two. Electronic invasion of privacy.'' She typed 987NNU150; it showed on the screen as asterisks.

''Welcome to the National Credit Bureau.'' The greeting flashed on the screen. Then a menu listed the options available.

She said, ''This is a data base. You've used them before?''

Smith pulled a bar stool close so he could watch over her shoulder. He said, ''A little.''

She pressed a key for the help menu. She typed another key to bring up the search menu. She explained. ''This is a network data base that compiles complete credit histories. What's good and bad about it is that it's so complete. It's updated continually with new information, but they're pretty slow about deleting entries. That's good for us, I hope. From what I hear, it takes a long time to convince the powers that be that someone is dead.''

She typed the find command. ''Social Security numbers are unique. Names and addresses change, but not the numbers.'' She laughed softly. ''I went with a friend of mine when she bought a waterbed. It wowed her when the clerk ran a full credit check through NCB in less than four minutes. I clocked it.''

''That's scary to contemplate.''

''You got it, cowboy.'' She turned on the printer. ''Want to hide in America? It can't be done. Not as long as computers are around.''

She typed in Louise Abernathy's Social Security

number. "I can't believe I'm doing this. Blackie will never let me live it down."

She looked over her shoulder. Smith had put on a pair of horn-rimmed glasses. The contrast between the glasses and his long hair and country clothing made him look curiously vulnerable. Gone was the tough, raffish air. He looked bookish, even sweet. He met her gaze and her skin tingled. Her mind rebelled again with the unfairness of lousy timing. How could she get to know him better when all he cared about was this terrible murder?

Information filled the screen with a flash of color. Kerry pressed the command for a printout. The rasping hum of the dot-matrix printer began.

"That's it?"

"Uh-huh." She stared at the jumble of credit transactions on the computer screen, wondering which one was going to cause Smith to finish his business and walk out of her life. "It'll take a few minutes. My old printer is slow." She cast him a sideways glance. "It's a classic."

"What else do you do with this thing?"

"A little of everything. I customize data bases, and do some free-lance bookkeeping and typing. I've tried my hand at writing game programs. I can't seem to come up with anything original." The way Smith absorbed every word unnerved her. She wasn't used to that much attention. "There it is."

She exited the NCB network and felt relieved that the FBI wasn't pounding on her door to arrest her for electronic trespassing. She tore off the sixteen-page printout, and handed it over.

Smith took the page and his Coke to the couch. The cats swarmed him, Midnight batting the trailing paper.

Smith read quickly, then scanned the list of codes Blackie provided and asked if Kerry could break into the banking network.

She was on the computer until midnight. She tried not to think about her phone bill; at least half the computer calls were long distance. The more she found, the more Smith wanted. A few times, she had to call Blackie for more information. The printouts made trails, which the cats thought heavenly, all over the living room floor. By midnight, they had a woman's life in dot-matrix print.

Kerry yawned as she helped Smith gather the papers into orderly stacks. She'd had two Cokes and a cup of instant coffee, but she was exhausted.

"This is strange," he murmured, removing his glasses and rubbing his eyes.

"I have to go to work in the morning," she said. She'd begun to get a headache. "I need to go to bed."

"I don't want to leave you alone. That jerk with the gun is still out there."

Her belly knotted in remembered fear. She glanced at the door. It was fitted with a dead bolt and chain, but the door itself looked as flimsy as cardboard. Without a word, she went into her bedroom and fetched a blanket and pillow. She dropped them onto the couch next to Smith.

"Don't get any funny ideas, okay? I'm only letting you stay because I'm too tired to argue with you anymore. Good night, Mr. Smith."

With a chuckle in his voice, he called to her back, "Night, sugar."

KERRY SMILED AS SHE LOOKED down at Smith. He was stretched out on the couch with his head on one arm and his feet hanging over the other, outside the blanket. He wore white socks. Keystone and Dash were curled on his belly. Midnight had wrapped herself under his chin, her nose tucked under his hair. Lucy made a trim, gray ball on a stack of paper on the back of the couch.

In repose, without the distraction of those dark, dancing eyes, Smith's face was especially handsome. He was definitely not pretty. At some time his nose had apparently been broken, then had healed crookedly, and his skin was coarse from too much time in the sun, but he was a looker. No doubt he'd had more than his share of success with women. That's what made him so cocky. She chuckled softly. Had he actually said all those outrageous things to her yesterday?

Kerry made coffee. The cats wandered into the kitchen. She fed them. It startled her to find that Smith was sitting up and watching her. She felt stupid in her ratty flannel robe, with her wet hair wrapped in a towel. "I've enough time to take you to your truck, Mr. Smith," she said.

"Good enough. Call me T.K." He yawned and raked his fingers through his hair. He went to the bathroom. When he came out, Kerry wondered about the basic unfairness of life. Men looked great in the morning and women looked lousy. Even tousled and needing a shave, he looked ruggedly alert. She wondered if he liked camping and hiking. What might it be like to wake up in the woods on a chilly morning and look across the embers of a fragrant fire at his smiling face?

"Am I right about Mrs. Abernathy?"

"Do you cook?"

"Yes."

"Good, because when I'm right, you're making me

dinner. Can you fry chicken? It's hard to find a woman who fries chicken right these days.''

She gaped for the few seconds it took for his teasing tone and wink to register. She laughed. ''Did you or did you not find something?''

''Possibly. I need to do some checking around.'' He leaned an elbow on the counter. ''Every time I look at you, you get prettier and prettier.''

She stammered, ''Umm—if you're h-hungry, help yourself.'' She hurried to her bedroom and shut the door.

As she dried her hair, she studied her face. Except for her green eyes, which were her best feature, she thought she had a common appearance. Oval face, nondescript nose, okay mouth, hair that was neither blond nor brown and a so-so figure. She preened, looking at herself from different angles. Not exactly a so-so figure. A little lush in the curves by fashionable standards, but proportioned.

She caught herself and laughed. Prettier and prettier, indeed. The man was a shameless flirt. He probably picked up loose women in bars. For all she knew, he was married. She pitied his possible wife. The poor woman was probably stuck in the house with four kids while sexy hubby gallivanted around in his pickup truck looking for pick ups.

She dressed in a dark red skirt and a cotton sweater with a red design that brought out the lights in her fawn-colored hair. She applied a dab of mascara, some blush and lipstick, and put on a pair of red button earrings. She slipped on her shoes. Calm and in control again, she left the bedroom.

Smith was eating a bowl of cereal. The sugar bowl sat open beside him.

"How do you stand so much sugar?" she asked. "It makes my teeth ache just to watch you."

He made a face at his Crispy Bran. "How do you eat this stuff? It tastes like wood chips."

"Actually, I don't eat it. It just makes me feel virtuous to buy it." She poured a cup of coffee. "Is there a Mrs. Smith?" She hoped the question sounded casual.

"Just Mom."

That still didn't rule out girlfriends, mistresses or a fiancée, but a little tingle shook her insides anyway. She nodded at the tall stack of printouts. "What did you find in all that stuff?"

"Questions. Lots and lots of questions. For instance, it looks like she's been married at least three times before, or she's changed her name. I can't tell. And she filed for bankruptcy twice. Once a personal, the other time when a beauty shop she owned went under. The lady had expensive tastes."

Considering that picture-perfect Oak Fair house, Kerry agreed. "Then she married Mr. Abernathy for money?"

"A possibility. Here's another goody. Last April, she bought a shotgun from Sears and Roebuck and used her charge card to pay for it."

Kerry nearly dropped her coffee.

"Why a shotgun?" Smith chewed cereal slowly, frowning. "There's golf, tennis courts, stables, but no trap or skeet at Oak Fair."

"A gift?" Kerry offered.

"Not for Bill. He didn't hunt. He fished a lot, but wouldn't hunt. I know that for a fact because I've been trying to get him to go hunting with me for years."

"Could *he* have used her charge card to buy the shotgun?"

"Maybe. Here's another thing. Who is Randi Mae Firkins? There's a life-insurance policy to the tune of $150,000, payable to Randi Mae. Louise bought the policy last April. The insurance company has already paid off. There's a notation on here that might mean they paid double indemnity. The only address is a post-office box in Richardson."

"Her mother?"

"I'm going to find out. Louise was a busy lady, and the police investigation barely skimmed the surface. Again, I couldn't find anything out about safe-deposit boxes, but these reports verify her withdrawal of $432,900—in cash."

"And you still say she wasn't gambling?"

"Bet good money on it."

"So what now?"

"I have to talk to Bill. There's some other checking I need to do. I've still got more to read." He patted the stack of paper. He made a rueful gesture. "There's so little time."

Kerry touched his hand with her fingertips. "When you show Mr. Abernathy the facts, you might not like what he tells you."

"Sugar, that boy was sick with love for Louise. If she wanted money, all she had to do was hold out her hand. Bill's no Rockefeller, but he was pulling in six figures annually. And he inherited a goodly sum from his family. If all she wanted was money, why leave him?"

"Her boyfriend. She loved another man."

"If she was bankrolling a boyfriend, why would *he* want her to leave Bill? I'm thinking that this paper trail leads straight to our mystery man. I'm thinking he grew too expensive and Louise threatened to cut him off."

"Wait a minute. If the other guy killed her, then he has to be Mr. Abernathy's double. Plus, he had to set this up by calling Copy Copy so I would be there to see him. Even you have to admit it's too farfetched."

"Maybe."

Smith was quiet on the way over to the Oak Fair Country Club. Kerry concentrated on the hectic rush-hour traffic. As she drove through Oak Fair, she passed Lincolns, Cadillacs, Jaguars and other expensive cars, their drivers intent on another day of wheeling and dealing.

The Abernathy house looked shabby in the daylight. The windows were dirty and the shrubbery unkempt. The shaggy lawn, untended all summer, was brown and weedy. A few old newspapers moldered on the grass. Kerry wondered if the house would stay empty forever. That struck her as very sad.

She pulled into the driveway next to Smith's truck. He unbuckled his seat belt, then turned those dark, sparkling eyes on her. Before she had time to react, he pressed a kiss to her lips. Stunned, her mind blanked while her mouth greedily absorbed the feel of his lips. A heady scent of spice and maleness filled her head, and her hands went slack on the steering wheel. It was a sweet kiss and over far too soon.

He grinned and winked. "First time I ever spent the night with a lady and didn't get so much as a kiss. Can't ruin my reputation."

She imagined herself sternly ordering him out of her car and giving her head a haughty shake to let him know that his impudence wasn't appreciated. Instead, the corners of her mouth twitched. She watched him fetch the printouts from the back seat.

"See you later, sugar." It sounded like a promise.

He strolled jauntily to his pickup. With a sigh, Kerry put the Nova into reverse. Her mouth still tingled by the time she reached the Plano Place shopping center and parked her car. She checked her lipstick in the rear-view mirror. "Get a grip, Byfield," she told her reflection. "Even if he is sexy, he's definitely too good to be true." Sobered, knowing something this good could not possibly happen this fast, she went to work.

Piver wasn't in. Kerry went through the routine of turning on the copiers and powering up the computers and printers. She checked the fax machine, but nothing had come in during the night. By nine o'clock, she had coffee made, had opened the cash register and was seated before her computer, working on the Grady's pizza parlor menu.

A man came in to pick up an order of business cards. Another called to see if his cards were ready. A college student brought in a huge stack of papers to copy on the self-service copier. The machine befuddled the student, so Kerry took the time to walk the customer through the operation. A salesman called wanting to know if they were satisfied with their fax machine. A businessman called in changes for a report.

Then a woman came in to copy a lease. Despite her elegant designer clothes, she managed some foul curses at the results. The college student's papers had shed dried correction fluid on the self-service copier's bed. They showed up as black spots on the woman's photocopy. Kerry soothed the woman's temper while she cleaned the glass plate. She didn't charge the woman for the ruined copies.

Feeling harassed, Kerry glanced at her watch. It was nearly eleven and there was still no sign of the boss. Back at the computer, she squinted at the screen, wondering if a Bodoni font or a novelty font like Circus suited Grady's. The phone rang. "Copy Copy," she said. "May I help you?"

"Piver here."

"It's about time. I'm going crazy."

"I'm sick, Kerry. I won't be in today."

"Oh, gosh, I'm sorry. Can I do anything for you, sir?" She thought he did sound awful. "Is there anything you need?"

"Uh—no—just take care of things. If Henry Oldenfeather calls, he'll want the figures— No, tell him the papers are with my lawyer. I'll get back to him as soon as I can."

"Oldenfeather, papers with the lawyer. Got it. Well, you take care then. I sure hope you feel better soon."

Kerry hung up the phone, sighing. She poured herself another coffee and braced herself for a long, long day. The doorbell tinkled and she turned. The sight of Robert Marsh took her aback.

"Hello, Kerry. Long time no see," he said cheerily. He wore a pin-striped suit. The gray at his temples was more pronounced than she remembered.

"What are you doing here?" She winced, knowing her tone was rude. She smiled to make up for it.

"I was in the neighborhood, and it's lunchtime, and I thought that maybe a certain young lady had forgiven me by now."

"Oh." She relaxed and took a second to save her work to disk. She rose and smoothed her skirt. "No need for forgiveness, Mr. Marsh."

"Robert."

"No need, Robert."

"Would you care to do lunch with me?"

She shook her head. "The boss is out sick and I'm

minding the store. But thanks anyway.'' She giggled. "I thought you'd come because of Tarkington Smith."

Marsh placed a hand on the countertop. His skin had the golden glow of a tanning parlor tan. He had very white, manicured fingernails. "Oh, yes, Mr. Smith. Has he been bothering you?" The tone was smooth, but something hard behind it rubbed Kerry the wrong way. "I reiterate my warning about that cowboy. He was fired from the D.A.'s office in Houston for a scandal involving ethics. He's a troublemaker. What did he say to you?"

"He thinks William Abernathy is innocent." She shrugged, trying to seem light despite her anger. Who did he think he was to come in here speaking poorly of T.K. Smith? "He and Mr. Abernathy are friends."

"Abernathy is paying a lot of money for that friendship."

Kerry bristled. "He seems sincere to me. Excuse me, I have work to do."

Smith wore the kind of smile used car salesman plaster on their faces before telling a buyer about the extra costs of dealer prep. "Practiced sincerity. From what I've seen, he likes to practice it on lovely young women."

Her jaw dropped. Robert Marsh had come all this way just to express his dislike for Tarkington Smith?

"You seem too intelligent to fall for his line of crap. Tell me what he's up to and I'll put a stop—"

"I think you better go, Mr. Marsh." Being rude left a bad taste in her mouth, but Kerry stood her ground.

His shoulders stiffened and his fingers tensed on the countertop. The same look of angry disgust she remembered from the trial came over his face. The same look he'd had when Quintas surprised both of them by bringing up Mike. It was a look that said she'd lied to him and betrayed him. She didn't like it any better now than she had then.

A man laden with ungainly rolls of blueprints entered the shop. Pointedly ignoring Marsh, Kerry lavished attention on the customer. Marsh finally left.

The afternoon trade proved light and Kerry finished typesetting the menu. She took the copy into the back room to attach the Grady's logo and make a mock-up.

At five minutes before six, she heard the doorbell. Wiping her ink-stained hands on a rag, she went to the front. "May I help—" Her words and smile faded.

A skinny, almost emaciated man shifted jerkily in front of the counter. A woman's stocking mashed his nose and lips. He grasped a gun with both hands. "Cash register!" he barked.

As if from far, far away, she heard herself say, "This is a copy shop. There isn't much cash—"

"Open it!" He waved the gun wildly at her face.

A calm inner voice coached, *Cooperate. Give him what he wants. He's more nervous than you are. Mall security will be by any minute, or someone will look in and call the police. Get a grip, Byfield. Stay calm and pay attention to details.*

The gun held her complete attention. The black bore swelled hypnotically. Kerry punched at the register keys. A tinny beep sounded. She slowly looked down at the cash register. There were thousands of dollars worth of expensive copiers and computers, but Piver had gone cheap on the cash register. It was an older model and unforgiving. Until she corrected her error, it would remain stubbornly locked and beeping. *I'm going to die because Nolan Piver is a cheapskate.* Her throat closed.

"What's that?" the robber cried. The gun dipped and rose and dipped again. Kerry followed the sickening rise and fall. He leaned forward and the gun touched her arm, scraping her skin with reptilian iciness. Her flesh shriveled.

I'm going to die. She stammered, "I—I can fix it. Just a minute." She pushed the Clear key. The beeping wailed like a siren.

The robber glanced at the tall, wide windows. It was dark outside, and except for the lights of passing cars and starburst patterns of the parking-lot lights, the windows looked black. Waiting, hoping for a security guard or a passerby to walk in and demand to know what was going on, Kerry punched buttons; the beep pierced her ears like white-hot needles.

The robber jerked his head toward the door. "C'mon, c'mon!" he ordered.

The bright blue glass cleaner beckoned. Without thinking, Kerry grabbed the spray bottle and when the robber faced her, she squeezed the spray trigger with both hands. A cloud of ammonia vapor surrounded his head and the spray filled his eyes. He screeched and grabbed his face. Kerry dropped the bottle and ran.

SMITH SAW THE blue flashers as he turned into the parking lot. Scalp prickling, he sat taller. As he drew closer to Copy Copy and saw the patrol car parked in front, his chest tightened. He jerked the wheel hard, then slammed on his brakes. He threw the pickup into Park and grabbed his keys. Why the hell had he let Kerry go to work?

He rushed inside the shop. When he saw Kerry standing in front of the counter, he had to stop and catch his breath. Her face was pasty pale and she had her arms wrapped so tightly around herself it was a wonder she could breathe, but she looked unhurt, even calm. She spoke in a normal tone of voice to a female police officer.

Another officer tried to stop Smith. Kerry looked at him. "Oh, T.K. It's okay, officer, he's a friend," she said, not even realizing she had used T.K.'s nickname. Then in a breathy rush, she babbled about robbers, guns, a faulty cash register and glass cleaner. The words trailed away and she cast the police officer an apologetic smile. "What were you saying?"

Smith put his arm around her shoulder. She clutched his wrist with an icy hand. The police officer asked her about the make and model of the gun. She didn't know. Was it an automatic or a revolver? Smith explained the difference and she said she thought it was a revolver. The police asked her to approximate the size of the bore. She drew a dark circle on a scrap of paper, frowned at it, then added to it until it was the size of a fifty cent piece.

The officer shook her head, saying, "Sorry, miss, there ain't no such thing."

"That's how big it looked to me," Kerry muttered.

After the police left, Smith asked, "What happened?" Admiration burned inside him. Except for her white face, she was calm and cool.

She told him about the attempted robbery. She had run out the back way and called the police from a dry cleaner's. When they arrived the robber was gone.

"Glass cleaner?" he asked, chuckling at the thought of the creep's unpleasant surprise.

"I have to clean the glass on the copiers two or three times a day—I need to sit down."

He reached for a chair, but as he pulled it around,

Kerry sank slowly to the floor. With odd grace, she fell to her knees, then to her haunches. Alarmed, he dropped to one knee beside her. "Hey, you're okay. It's all right."

"I have to call Mr. Piver." She looked up at Smith with stricken eyes that shimmered, then overflowed.

Smith gathered her against his chest. Her tears soaked through the front of his flannel shirt. It was a delayed reaction, he knew, and he made no attempt to stop her crying. He stroked her soft hair and without quite realizing it, kissed her forehead. He murmured nonsense against her smooth skin, drinking in the smell of her flowery shampoo. Her sobbing subsided. She snuffled and sniffed. He cupped her chin and lifted her face. Her eyes were red and puffy, but her color was good.

"You all right, sugar?"

Her embarrassment touched him. Releasing her was one of the hardest things he'd done in a long time. He eyed the door with longing. He wanted to take her somewhere safe, let her eat a nice meal and maybe drink a glass of wine and forget all this nastiness. She found a roll of paper towels, then turned her back on him and blew her nose.

"I've gone my whole life never even looking at a gun, and now in two days…" She wiped her eyes with a towel. One long shudder racked her body, then she lifted her chin. "What are you doing here?"

"I needed to talk to Piver."

"He's out sick." She blew her nose again.

Anger flared inside Smith hot and tight. Kerry was loyal to Piver, and if his suspicions were correct, Piver didn't deserve the honor. What he deserved was a busted nose and about fifty years in prison. The police had spoken to Piver during the initial investigation. A cryptic note in the files had said, "Nolan Piver can't remember his own breakfast." Piver had denied that he had ever spoken to Abernathy. "Damned convenient."

Kerry gave Smith a wary look. "Why did you want to talk to Mr. Piver?"

"Louise Abernathy wasn't a stranger. She used her MasterCard in Copy Copy on February 9 of this year. Another thing, you don't advertise deliveries. Not in your phone book ad or in here." He looked at the white lettering on the windows that advertised copies, fax service and desktop publishing.

Kerry wiped her nose again with an absent swipe of the towel. "Go back. Louise Abernathy was in here?" She beckoned for Smith to follow her. In the back room she opened the cabinet. She pulled out a paid invoice. She handed it to Smith. "That's Mr. Piver's handwriting."

"And he spoke to her more than once. She ordered invitations on the fourth and paid for them on the ninth."

"So what does it mean?"

"I don't know."

Kerry said, irritably, "Louise probably thought we did a nice job, so she did us a favor by sending her husband here for his business."

Still loyal. Smith said, "About those deliveries. Other printing places advertise deliveries. You don't."

Kerry hunched her shoulders and crossed her arms. "It's a loss leader. We do it for regulars and big orders. It's worth the hassle when they think we care about their schedules. Repeat business is very important to us." She went back to the invoices again. "Heck. That invoice for Abernathy was used as evidence in the trial."

"$32.49," Smith said. "That's how much the order

was for. So he wasn't a regular customer, and that's not a big order. So why did Piver send you out at night to make that delivery? I have a feeling he'll have an interesting answer for me.''

Chapter Seven

Smith held the door for Kerry, admiring her spunk. She'd given him no arguments about driving her home, but on the way she'd managed to laugh about the cash register freezing up and her spraying the robber with glass cleaner. She was growing battle hardened and bouncing back from shock with a survivor's aplomb. He just hoped nothing else happened for which she'd need that resilience.

The cats met them inside the door. He scooped up the black kitten, tickled by the way she went limp in his hand, her purr rumbling like an outboard motor. "By the way," he said, "Bill gave me another tidbit today. It takes another chunk out of the theory that Louise was leaving him. She sold her car because she wanted a Jag to match his. They applied for vanity plates. Sweet1 and Sweet2."

Either Kerry had ignored him or hadn't heard. He guessed she had ignored him. He shrugged it off, thinking philosophically that if he could ever convince Kerry Byfield, he could convince any judge in the county. Kerry had gone to change her clothes. He called that he'd fix them something to eat.

He poured two glasses of Coke. While he rummaged

for something to eat, he decided he liked her apartment. It was neat, but the clutter said she wasn't fanatical about cleanliness. He liked the cozy, permanent feel, too. She owned good stoneware dishes, quality cookware and utensils and nice furniture. None of it matched, but all was of good quality. Too many singles lived like Gypsies, waiting for marriage before investing in household goods.

He knew a lot about her from reading the court transcripts. She was college educated and had been born in Colorado. Her father had been in the army. She had been engaged once but never married. Surface stuff. Her apartment revealed details. Pinks and yellows predominated, telling him she was basically a cheerful person. Cartoons stuck on the refrigerator indicated a sense of humor. Her house plants were in bad shape, but the cats had a lot to do with that. She liked to read romance novels and science fiction. She saved old magazines and coupons. Art work dotted the walls, all of it original, much of it having an amateurish cast. He guessed the pictures were gifts from artistic friends.

Except for a refrigerator filled with yogurt, skimmed milk and vegetables—no goodies in sight—he liked everything about her. As he piled salad fixings on the counter, he chuckled. He'd dated many women, good-looking women, interesting women, and none of them had really meant anything. Now, for the first time in his life, love had snatched him by the ear and said, "Pay attention, boy!" It was a screwy situation, but he liked it.

He was slicing tomatoes and cucumbers when she came into the kitchen. Lettuce drained in the sink. Eggs boiled on the stove. He said, "I figure you like salad since your fridge is full of veggies." He admired the neat fit of her rounded hips and long legs in her blue jeans.

Her mouth pursed primly. She scooted around the counter and sat on a bar stool. Scraping chopped vegetables into a bowl, he grinned. He even liked her prissiness.

"I had a strange visitor today," she said. "Robert Marsh. He doesn't like you."

Smith snorted. Robert Marsh was the kind of man he hated to see in a courtroom. Cases were games: winning was everything. Marsh didn't give a damn about people or justice as long as he kept his conviction rate high and his name in the papers. Smith waggled a knife at Kerry. "He's told me as much to my face. He figures I want to shake his easy conviction. He's right. What did you tell him?"

"Nothing. He called you a troublemaker."

"I already confessed to that."

"He said you were fired from the Houston D.A.'s office because of ethics." Challenge tinged the words.

Smith's grin faded. "I quit. But he's half-right, it was a matter of ethics." To her questioning look, Smith said, "It's a cruddy story." A hunch said she was checking him out and that whatever Marsh had said bothered her. Yet, something stubborn tightened inside him. His days as an assistant D.A. were past, but old shame gnawed at him. It was the only time in his life he had ever quit anything, the only time he had ever felt like a loser.

"What happened?"

Good question. He was still trying to figure it out. He began tearing lettuce into a bowl. Finally he said, "A boy was shot. Nine years old. The bullet entered just under his rib cage, ricocheted off his spine and tore off the bottom of his right lung. He lost three quarters of his blood and his heart stopped twice, but he lived. He was paralyzed, and brain damaged, but alive.''

Smith caught the horror in Kerry's eyes, but kept going. ''It was a domestic case. The mother's boyfriend threatened her, and the kid jumped to the rescue. I went after the boyfriend with child abuse, endangerment, assault with a deadly weapon and attempted murder. The boyfriend said it was an accident. He was cleaning the gun. The mother didn't want to testify, but I knew I could get her story on the stand.'' Memories plagued him. He could still smell the antiseptic stink and hear the soft whispery nurse's shoes and the whirrs, beeps and *chunk-chunk*s of life-support machinery. He remembered friends telling him to back off, that he was too involved and that he had lost his objectivity.

''I really admired that kid. He was tough, a real fighter. I'd finish work and go over to the hospital and sit with him. He was so damned alone. His mother proved her loyalty to the boyfriend by staying away from the hospital. She said all the tubes and machines made her nervous.

''Anyway, the D.A. told me to expedite the case and arrange for a plea bargain down to simple assault. We were in the middle of a financial crunch and it made perfect sense. Except to me. I told the old man to fill a hole, and he assigned the case to another prosecutor. So I quit. It was more a conflict of interest than a case of ethics.''

Silence crowded the apartment. Kerry's eyes had become soft and thoughtful. Smith saw pity. He said brusquely, ''Yeah, well, mostly I quit because I hate being told what to do.'' He turned his back on her and busied himself at the sink. *The past is past,* he told himself sternly, *forget it.*

Kerry stared at his back, sorry for encouraging him to talk. There had been pain in those dark eyes. Even his voice had changed, turning blunt, cold and clipped. There was a lot more to Tarkington Smith than easygoing cockiness and smart-aleck comments.

Flustered, wishing she knew the right words to say, Kerry noticed the light blinking on her answering machine. Disturbed by the thick silence, she pressed the playback button.

Her mother's voice said, "Call me, sweetie. It's urgent. I just have to talk to you right away."

She dialed her mother's number.

Angela Byfield chirped, "Hello," in that sing-song voice she used on the telephone. Kerry identified herself, and her mother cried, "Darling! Where have you been? I haven't heard from you in ages."

"I saw you on Sunday, Mom," Kerry said, grinning sheepishly. *Urgent, right,* she thought. Everything concerning Angela was urgent.

"I know this is late notice, but you simply must come to the house on Saturday, about sevenish. I insist. Don't dare put me off. I'm throwing a party for Eve. It will hurt her deeply if you don't come."

"She's *your* friend, Mom. Saturday is sort of—"

"I insist. Eve's son is coming. Darling, he's divine. Thirtiesh, drives a BMW…"

Kerry's head ached as her mother went on and on about the merits of Eve's son, Randall Westworth. Since Kerry's father had died, Angela Byfield's one continuing interest was seeing Kerry married. Preferably to a rich man who owned a big house and drove a nice car.

Kerry interrupted, "Mom, I'm seeing someone."

A long pause. "You are?"

Those words held buckets of interest. Kerry closed

her eyes, wondering why she did this to herself. Now Angela would want all the details. Why not grow up and tell her the truth? *Because Mom uses information the way a ninja uses knives,* she thought, answering herself.

"This isn't one of your computer geeks, is it?"

"I wish you wouldn't call them that." Kerry glanced at Smith. He was tossing the salad. Trapped, she said, "Uh—no—actually, he's a lawyer."

"A lawyer! Oh, my God, tell all, dearie, tell all. Is he good-looking?"

Kerry studied Smith. He was the kind of man who set a woman into auto-primp mode. The casual rebelliousness of his earring and long hair gave him a raffish, dangerous air. The way the fabric of his shirt strained over his shoulders when he moved promised a superb body. Maybe she wasn't lying that much about seeing someone. She just wished this conversation were taking place a few weeks or months from now. Time enough to get to know T.K. better and know for certain if anything real was happening between them.

"I can't talk right now, Mom. He's fixing me dinner."

"Fixing you dinner? Why isn't he buying you dinner? Really, you are much too casual about these things. How long have you been seeing him? Why haven't you said anything? You never tell me anything. I feel so shut out of your life. You're my only child, and I only want to know because I care." Angela sighed, dramatically.

"Look, Mom, I have to go. I've had a really bad day. I'm starving. I didn't have time for lunch—"

"Well you could stand to lose a few pounds, you know. I have this marvelous new diet. You fast two days a week, then eat whatever you want the rest of the week. Lawyers' wives are always thin. You'd be surprised at what a difference only ten pounds can make.''

Kerry gave her thighs a glance, then frowned. ''Mom, I have to go.''

''Bring him to the party. I want to meet him.''

''I don't think that's a good idea—''

''I insist. You don't know how it breaks my heart to know the only people you meet are those computer geeks with their thick glasses—''

''Mom! Uh—T.K. has plans for Saturday. He can't make the party. Hold on a minute.'' Kerry covered the mouthpiece with her hand and whispered, ''Now I've done it. I do this to myself every time. It's my mother. She insists I bring you to a party.''

He looked serious and beckoned for the phone. ''I'll take care of it.'' Embarrassed, she handed over the receiver. Smith introduced himself, then listened. He nodded and said, ''Uh-huh,'' and ''Yes, ma'am.'' Just as Kerry was congratulating herself on slithering out of yet another predicament, he said, ''I'd love to attend, Mrs. Byfield. See you there.'' He handed over the phone.

Aghast, Kerry put the phone to her ear again in time to hear Angela say, ''...charming man. I'll see you about sevenish. Dinner at nine, darling. Want me to make you a hair appointment with Jocelyn?''

''No.''

''Black tie, dear.''

''That'll go great with his blue jeans. Bye, Mom.'' She hung up, then snapped out, ''Why did you do that?''

Smith grinned roguishly. ''I figure it's about time I met your family. You can't hide me forever. Secretive relationships never work out. Things need to be out front, above board.''

''Smart aleck. It's black tie.''

''No problem.'' He dumped the boiled eggs into the sink and ran cold water over them.

Keystone jumped onto the counter. Kerry took him off and held the big tabby, running her fingers through his fur. One of these days she was going to get even with T.K. Smith. She grinned, thinking an evening with Angela might be payback enough.

The phone rang. Kerry put the cat on the floor. Hoping it was Angela calling to cancel, she mouthed, ''Keep your mouth shut,'' to Smith, then answered the call. It was Piver.

''Well, hi. Are you feeling better?''

''I tried to call you at the shop.'' He sounded brittle. She hoped he didn't have the flu that was going around.

''I was there past seven-thirty.'' She quickly explained what had happened. She emphasized that nothing was stolen and no damage was done.

''Did you get a good look at the guy?'' he demanded.

His strange tone caught her off guard.

''Kerry?''

''Uh—no. He had a stocking on his head. I couldn't even tell what color his hair was, but nothing was taken. Mall security said they'll keep a good eye on the place. The police said they'll cruise the parking lot tonight. I gave them a report.''

''But you're all right.''

''Yes—well, no. It's been terrible, actually, Mr. Piver. Just yesterday some guy took potshots at me over in the Oak Fair Country Club. A hit-and-run sniper. It was awful.''

''Did you see him?''

"No."

"Is it the same guy?"

She grimaced in exasperation. She had expected sympathy, not grilling. "I don't think so. The police said the robber was probably a kid. The kind who robs convenience stores. Why he tried to rob us is beyond me. There was only about seventy-five dollars in the register."

Smith beckoned with his fingertips. Kerry shook her head.

"So you didn't see the guy who shot at you?"

"No. Are you going to be in tomorrow? There's a man who wants to talk to you. He's a private investigator. It's about the Abernathy case. You know, that murder trial."

Piver made a strangled sound. Kerry debated offering to lend him a humidifier to clear his congestion. He demanded, "Why does he want to talk to me?" Now he sounded angry.

"You don't sound too good, sir. Have you been to a doctor?"

"I don't have anything to do with the Abernathy thing."

"He's just doing some background check—"

Smith pulled the phone out of her hand. "Piver? Tarkington Smith here. I'm working for William Abernathy. I'd like to ask you a few questions, if you don't mind—" He frowned at the phone. "He hung up on me."

"I don't blame him. He has the flu. Give the man a break." She slammed the handset onto the cradle.

"Does he make a habit of calling you at home?"

She didn't want to admit that tonight was the first time. She shook her head.

Smith grunted and shook a bottle of poppy-seed salad dressing. "Piver told the police he didn't call Bill and didn't remember him at all. He's lying. He's the one who asked Bill to come in the first place, on legal business."

"Piver's a salesman. He talks to hundreds of people every week."

"He lied."

"The police didn't think so."

Smith put salad into bowls. "Look, every police department in America is understaffed and overworked. They must of been jumping for joy to get an easy case like this one. I'm not saying they botched the investigation, but from the moment you fingered Bill, they just went through the motions. I say Piver lied and that he might have had a reason for doing so."

"He's a salesman, not a murderer!"

"Maybe."

Kerry realized when Smith said "maybe" it meant "no way." She said, "Fine, so what happened? Piver dropped seventy pounds, dyed his hair blond, had Louise buy a shotgun, used it to murder her, then let Bill take the blame. How can I have been so stupid? It makes perfect sense."

"We know for a fact he knew Louise and Bill. So that means he lied to the police." Smith tapped a fork against the countertop. "Have you ever caught him doing anything illegal?"

His doggedness brought out Kerry's stubborn streak. Even though reason said he might be on to something, she spoke defensively. "He's just another yuppie whose goal in life is to own a new foreign-made luxury car every year."

Smith gently reminded her that they were on the same side. It wasn't exactly true, but she calmed down.

"Illegal? He's substituted cheap stock for good stuff. He's lied to the Xerox rep about how many copies we've run so he can stay within the service contract. Penny ante. He calls it 'good business.'"

"Can you get me his Social Security number?"

She groaned and dropped her head against the counter. "Why are you doing this to me?"

"You're a trooper." Smith pushed a bowl of salad toward her and gave her a fork and knife. He rummaged through her bread box. "We should have stopped by the supermarket for rolls. Hmm, whole-wheat muffins. Looks good."

"Why Piver? I'm telling you, he isn't a murderer. He couldn't have murdered Louise."

"Call it a hunch."

"I'm getting sick of your hunches."

Smith made a dismissive gesture. "These are facts. He knew Louise Abernathy. He arranged for Bill to come into Copy Copy that first time. He sent you to make the delivery."

"If you're sure, why not turn the information over to the police? Or the defense attorney? Quintas could make him confess even if he didn't do it." She took a bite of salad. Smith had mixed a little of everything and added just the right amount of dressing. It was delicious. Her appetite roared to life.

"It isn't enough." He touched her arm. "I don't want to scare you, sugar, but if Piver is involved, he's also involved in trying to hurt you. Scared men do stupid things."

"Don't be ridiculous. He might mess up my paycheck, but hurt me?"

"It isn't ridiculous. You convicted Abernathy. You could also hold the key to clearing him. If Piver thinks you're getting close then he's going to do stupid things. Take potshots at you or send some punk to shoot you during a robbery."

"Shoot me? Now you're being totally outrageous. He was a robber! If you want the truth, I think he was more frightened than me."

"Maybe." He studied the door, then the windows. "I don't think you ought to stay here."

Kerry grabbed a paper napkin out of a seashell-shaped holder. She wiped her mouth, then swung off the stool. "I can get you Piver's Social Security number." She took the phone to the computer and plugged it in. While the computer booted, she studied the lists of numbers and passwords Blackie had given her. She used a red pen to underline the number for Plano City Hall.

Piver nagged her more than she cared to admit. He had seen her and Smith together in the parking lot. He wasn't at work today, and had called her at home, which he'd never done before. Now she realized he'd never said why he'd called. Was it to see if she was dead or alive? It was like hearing a strange noise in the night. Either you got up to see that it was nothing or stayed in bed wide awake and scared until dawn. The only way to get over being scared was to prove Smith wrong.

He laid a hand on her shoulder. "I'm not trying to frighten you for the fun of it, sugar."

"I'm scared anyway. Happy?" She looked up and found him solemn. "I thought this was finished, and you're starting it all over again. And the worst thing is, you make so much sense."

Smith leaned over, close to her face. Too close. His

eyes were blue, a very dark midnight blue, fringed by thick, black lashes. He searched her face, questioning. She knew he was going to kiss her. Either weariness or curiosity—she couldn't determine which—held her still. He made a tentative motion and her chin lifted. He pressed his mouth to hers.

Nothing in her life had ever felt so right. He tasted of tangy-sweet salad dressing and smelled of spicy after-shave. His mouth was warm and ever so gentle. He ran his hand under her hair and lightly traced the rim of her ear. Kerry closed her eyes as long-dormant feelings struggled to the fore. She parted her lips, yielding, and touched her tongue tentatively to his.

Kerry sighed deeply when he drew away. His fingers trailed her cheeks and she leaned into his caress. "Despite what my mother thinks, you aren't my boyfriend." The words felt stupid and smart alecky as soon as they emerged. She wanted to take them back, but didn't know how.

"Maybe," he said, and turned his attention to the screen.

Kerry broke into the City Hall computer network and searched the data base for business licenses and incorporations. She concentrated ferociously, trying to take her mind off Smith, but failed miserably.

"Voilà," she said when she found the file for Copy Copy, Incorporated. Included in the information was Nolan Piver's Social Security number. She pressed the print command.

"Go back. Let's find out about his property holdings and such."

Kerry typed commands. "This will only tell you about Plano. He lives in Richardson. I don't know how to get into Richardson City Hall or the Dallas County courthouse.''

She started a general search using Piver's Social Security number, then typed a command to print whatever the computer found. She went back to her salad.

Smith put his glasses on to read the first printout. Kerry squinted, trying to imagine him wearing a business suit and surrounded by law books. And she licked her lips, imagining his taste and craving it again. She looked away. It wasn't right to feel so strongly about a man she'd just met! ''How long did you work in the D.A.'s office?''

''Oh, I reckon about eight years. I've always had this thing about bad guys. I figured a job as a prosecutor might suit me. It's a great job if you're looking to climb the ladder of success. It's a crappy job if you care about what you're doing. I quit two years ago and haven't missed it a lick.''

''You don't look old enough to have spent eight years in the D.A.'s office.''

He raked his fingers through his long, dark brown hair. ''Thanks. But I'm thirty-two, plenty old enough.''

She frowned and shook her head. ''I can count, Mr. Smith. Are you trying to tell me you graduated from Harvard Law when you were only twenty-two?''

He laughed, obviously enjoying this conversation. He said, ''Twenty-one. Child prodigy. I started college when I was fifteen and passed the Texas Bar two months before my twenty-second birthday.''

''Some sort of genius?''

''That's right.''

Irked to have him confirm what she already suspected, she retorted, ''If you're so smart, why aren't you rich?''

It was a dumb rhetorical question, but as he tore off the finished printout, he said, "I am. I think the term 'filthy rich' describes me pretty well. Impressed?" He winked.

Kerry sagged on the bar stool. He had to be teasing. She picked up a piece of lettuce with her fingers. "I have the most awful feeling my mother is going to like you."

"Mothers always do." His whistle was low and appreciative. "Well looky here. Your boss is getting married. He applied for the license last Friday." Smith slid the paper through his fingers. "No record that he's been hitched yet. The plot does thicken."

"What do you mean?" Kerry asked, miffed that Piver never told her he was getting married. It disappointed her, a little, that the mystery woman wasn't scandalously married. Kerry wondered if she should surprise Piver with a gift. What was hot on the market this week for yuppie weddings?

"Take a gander at who he's marrying." Smith pointed to the printout.

Kerry read, "Randi Mae Firkins."

Chapter Eight

"Oh, jeez, T.K., you were right." Kerry jammed a forkful of salad into her mouth. Randi Mae Firkins, Nolan Piver and insurance money. Everything made awful sense now. "You have to go to the police. What's his name, that detective. Oh—Shanlin—"

"With what?" He tossed the printout onto the coffee table.

"Randi Mae Firkins. Piver murdered Louise so Randi Mae could collect the insurance."

"Maybe."

"Don't do this to me!" Kerry shouted. He drew back in surprise. "You wanted the real murderer and there he or she is. Go to the police."

He patted the computer. "Let's do with Piver what we did with Louise."

Kerry jumped off the stool and paced. "No. It's not my business. This is illegal. You've got enough to prove—"

"I can't prove anything with this."

"Why not?"

"Like you said, what did Piver do? Lose seventy pounds and dye his hair blond? Randi Mae is a connection. She isn't proof. I still haven't the faintest idea who killed Louise.'' He held his hands palms up. ''I need hard evidence. I checked out Randi Mae. The D.A. investigated her as a matter of routine. She's listed in the reports as a distant relation. If I go to the D.A. now, he'll take one look and say it's all a coincidence. We need more. Now, sugar, can you break into the police computer?''

She was aghast. Would the FBI name her as the perpetrator or merely an accomplice? ''I don't think so...maybe. Why?''

''Find out if Piver owns a handgun.''

Kerry hugged her elbows. She went to the window and, glaring at Smith, pulled the drapes shut. ''This is a police matter. Not mine. I've already done the right thing. I've done more than my share.''

''What worries me is that he's scared. If he's behind this, then Abernathy's conviction put him in the clear. Having me stir things up must make him pretty nervous.''

''Then you're in danger, too. It was probably you being shot at over at the Abernathy house.''

''Yeah, well, I'm pretty good at taking care of myself. I survived all them Yankees at Harvard.'' He pulled out her office chair expectantly. ''Come on, sugar, we have work to do.''

She sat. ''Shouldn't we at least inform the police of our suspicions? Detective Shanlin seemed like a really nice man.''

''I've been talking to Bob Ward at the D.A. He isn't exactly interested but he's cooperative. If we find anything else, I intend to be in his office first thing in the morning.''

Kerry sighed and checked the list Blackie had given

her. She instructed the computer to dial a number. "Will you fix me a Coke—no, make that coffee."

While she waited for the connection, she leaned back on the chair and watched him start the coffee. She fingered the collar of her sweatshirt, her thoughts drifting away from Piver and back to Smith. She mused about not having made love to a man since Mike. She hadn't wanted to in God only knew how long. And Smith reminded her too much that she was young and healthy, and that she worked too many long hours and took herself far too seriously. Still, where was this lust at first sight coming from? Good grief, she and Mike had dated a year before sleeping together. They'd dated three years before talking about marriage. Relationships took months—no, years—to develop. You didn't meet a person one day, then start wondering the next day how your lives were going to mesh.

The connection for the NCB came up and she typed in the company code, then the password. She started a search using Piver's Social Security number and instructed the computer to print everything it found.

She went back to her salad. Smith began rummaging in the freezer. His taking over the kitchen amused her. "What are you looking for?" she asked.

"Ice cream," he said. "Cookies. Frozen Snickers bars. Don't you have anything good around here?"

"A junk-food junkie. Amazing. You look so healthy."

The printer started its whirring buzz-saw imitation; the print head whipped back and forth across the paper.

"My sweet tooth—ah-ha. You're not so pure after all." He pulled a small box of Godiva chocolates out of the back of the freezer. He looked to her questioningly and she gave him a go ahead. She grinned as he tore off the cellophane covering. "Those are a million years old. Mike gave them to me."

Smith unwrapped a piece of candy, then crumpled the foil and flicked it for Midnight to chase.

"You have pets?" she asked.

"I keep a few horses and too many dogs and a few cats. They wander in and end up staying. Who's Mike?"

She knew he'd read the court transcripts, but he apparently wanted her to elaborate. She pretended to not hear the question. "Who's watching them while you're up here?"

"A housekeeper. Her son feeds the horses for me and runs the dogs." He chuckled. "Maria used to threaten at least once a day to quit because of all the animal hair. She only threatens once a month or so now. I think she's starting to like them. So who's Mike?" Smith gnawed on the chocolate. "Don't you believe in modern conveniences? There's no TV, no microwave." He looked frustrated as he examined the rock-solid candy.

"I have a clock radio," she offered helpfully. She suddenly decided to oblige Smith. "Mike's an old boyfriend. We were going to get married, but we broke our engagement.

"What was wrong with him?"

"Nothing." She shrugged. "He took a job with NASA in Alabama, and I didn't want to go to Alabama, so we broke up." She added tartly, "I'm not carrying any torches."

"Nice to hear," he said with warm undertones her entire body responded to.

The printer stopped, distracting her. Smith collected the printout while Kerry went to the next number on her list. Tapping the keys, she laughed to herself, beginning to understand why Blackie got such a kick out of snooping in other people's private lives. The feeling of power was heady. The screen went blank. Kerry's first thought was that there had been a power outage. Her belly chilled when she saw the prompt glowing in the upper left corner of the screen.

"What happened?"

"I think I just got caught."

"What do you mean?"

"I think somebody realized I was hooked in. Oh, jeez, they put people in jail for this."

"Give Blackie a call and ask him what to do."

"He'll tell me to run to Mexico. Caught is caught. I may as well get what I can before they put me in the slammer, though." She reactivated the communications system. The computer replied with an error message.

"What's that mean?" Smith asked.

She laughed wanly. "Equipment failure. Thank heavens. No G-men breaking down my door." She reached around back and made sure all the lines were secure. They were. "That's strange." She went back to the disk-operating system and called up her utilities program. It showed everything in working order. There were no problems in any programs. She pulled a manual off the bookshelf and turned to the page on the communications system. She followed the instructions exactly for booting the system. Again, the computer replied with an error message. She picked up the handset.

"Kerry?"

She turned to him with worried eyes. She whispered, "The phone's dead."

Smith checked his watch. It was almost eleven. "Sugar, do me a favor." He checked the door lock.

"Shut down the lights and go to your bedroom. Wait, are your curtains closed in there?"

She nodded. With shaky hands, she shut down the computer and turned off the printer.

"Just make like you're going to bed." He sat on a bar stool.

She listened intently for anything suspicious. She checked the phone again and tried plugging it into another jack. Dead. "Do you have a gun?" she whispered.

"There's a .30-30 in my pickup. Don't worry about it. Just do what you usually do."

She stared in disbelief. What kind of PI was he? "In your truck? What good is that going to do?"

"Sugar, I don't believe in using handguns. Go on."

Kerry turned on the hall light, then turned off the living room lights. Smith was an alert shadow. The cats scampered toward the bedroom. Holding her breath and straining to hear only spooked Kerry further. She began to undress, then stopped. Wear a nightie while waiting for an intruder? She watched the cats play hide-and-seek around the bed. That eased her a little.

She reached under the bed and pulled out an industrial flashlight she'd picked up at a garage sale. This part of Texas was subject to severe storms, and power outages were common. The flashlight had come in handy more than once. She checked the batteries, wincing at how bright the light was. Comforted by the flashlight's weight, she lay down on the covers and turned off the lamp.

Her eyes adjusted to the dark. Midnight bounced across the bed in that funny sideways hop kittens used, then tumbled off and meowed as she tussled with one of the bigger cats. Kerry listened to traffic sounds. Somebody played a television loudly and the sound filtered into the apartment as a staticky murmur. The flashlight on her chest made her aware of her own heartbeat. Keystone jumped onto the bed, making Kerry start. She riffled his fur as he marched across the pillows then hopped with a thump to the floor. *Get a grip, Byfield, phones go dead all the time.* She began to feel ridiculous. Imagining Smith crouched in the darkness gave her the giggles. They were acting like a couple of kids giving each other the heebie-jeebies. She sat up.

She heard a metallic scratching. Her giggles died. It sounded again, rattling softly. She stared at the window. Dash jumped onto the bed and hissed, then streaked from the room. Clutching the flashlight in both hands, Kerry scrambled after the cat.

"T.K.!" she whispered. "The bedroom window."

He touched her arm and placed a finger against her lips. Cat footed, he went down the hall. Kerry followed.

She watched from the doorway as he crept along the wall until he was directly under the window. The rattling grew louder, then the pane clicked in the sliding tracks. A louder click sounded, then a gritty schussing. Kerry wanted to run, but couldn't move. The curtains ruffled, then parted. She heard a soft, masculine grunt and rustling. She turned on the overhead light.

A ski-mask-enclosed face shot up. Kerry screamed. Smith caught the intruder's shoulders and heaved. The man popped from the window like an ice cube out of a squeezed hand. Flailing wildly, he thumped the wall. Smith stumbled backward and fell over a clothes hamper. The intruder twisted, hitting the floor with a thud, but he bounced, pausing only long enough to kick at Smith before he launched himself at Kerry.

Yelping, she swung the flashlight. With her eyes squeezed shut, she didn't know what she hit, but she heard a sickening noise. It was like punching a wet bag of cement; a jolt rattled her shoulders.

"Nice shot, sugar," Smith said.

She peeked and dropped the flashlight. The intruder was stretched out on the floor, still as a stone.

"Oh, my God! I killed him!" she said in a choked whisper.

Smith jammed his fingers under the man's jaw. "Nope," he said. "You have something to tie his hands with? Hand me that scarf over there."

She gave him the scarf. For the first time in a long time, she wanted her mother.

Smith pulled the mask off the intruder's head. He was a kid, dirty, skinny and unshaven. Blood trickled off his chin where the flashlight had cut him.

Kerry gasped. "I think that's him."

"Who?"

"The guy who tried to rob the store. I don't recognize his face, but I've seen his clothes. I mean, I'm not certain, but those patches on top of patches on his jeans— the robber was ratty, just like this guy."

Smith felt under the intruder's jacket and pulled out a small, black revolver. "Saturday night special," he said, sounding disgusted.

"Excuse me," Kerry said, wearing a tight, forced smile. "I'm going to go vomit now." She hurried to the bathroom.

She wasn't as sick as she'd thought. She sat on the cool tile floor, breathing deeply and staring at the baseboards, thinking she needed to give the walls and baseboards a good scrubbing. Sunday, she thought. She'd clean the entire apartment, top to bottom. Maybe she'd balance her checkbook, too, and throw out old tax records. She'd do nice, normal busy work, with no thinking involved.

Smith knocked on the door. She pulled it open and eyed him glumly. "I went next door and called the police. They're on the way." He grinned devilishly. "You never said you had such sweet neighbors."

"Police? Can't we just dump him somewhere?"

"Chin up, Kerry. Between glass cleaner and flashlights, you do a fine job of taking care of yourself."

She slumped against the wall and began to giggle. Hearing the hysterical rise, she clapped a hand over her mouth. *Kerry Byfield, champion chicken.* Mustering control, she asked, "Is it possible to die from adrenaline overdose?"

"Don't think so. You okay?"

Kerry nodded. She busied herself by gathering the cats and imprisoning them in the bathroom before the police arrived. The cats shot her hateful looks. She knew just how they felt.

The intruder came around when the police arrived. His chin had swollen to an alarming size. His eyes were black and rolling, glassy and unnaturally bright. The scarf was exchanged for handcuffs. Demanding a lawyer in a cracked, squeaky voice, he was led away. Kerry only had to give her name to the policemen. Smith did the rest of the talking.

"You ought to have proper locks put on those windows, miss," a policeman said.

"I'll do that," Kerry said, thinking she'd get a large, mean dog while she was at it.

Her neighbors, Sharon Courtland and Becky Sind, peered into the living room. They looked scared. Kerry assured them as best she could that the intruder wouldn't be around again.

Sharon said, "You're lucky your boyfriend was spending the night."

"He isn't my boyfriend."

Sharon and Becky brightened, peering at Smith, who was speaking earnestly to a police officer. Sharon raked back her mane of blond hair.

"He's cute," Becky said. She was nineteen and cute herself as she tugged at the hem of her flimsy excuse of a bathrobe. "Who is he? I never see guys over here."

Kerry said, "A business associate." Her eyes narrowed. "Don't waste your time. He's gay."

"Bummer," Sharon said.

"All the best-looking guys are," Becky said with a snort.

"I know," Kerry said, managing a straight face. She urged the girls back to their apartment and made them promise to make sure their door and windows were secured.

After the police had finished their reports and left, Smith said, "Pack a bag. You're getting out of here."

"What?"

"Somebody wants you out of the way. You aren't staying here."

"My cats," she protested, even though it was the best idea she'd heard in two days.

"I'll take care of them. Until we get this straightened out, you need to lay low."

She nodded, knowing she wouldn't be able to sleep here anyway. Even with all the lights on and Smith here, she was scared. She packed quickly, taking the barest necessities. Smith put the window back in its track. Kerry made certain the cats had plenty of food and water, then Smith hustled her to her car.

"My mother lives over in Carrollton—"

"You aren't going to your mother's. Whoever wants you out of the way knows where you work and where you live. Do you want him following you to your mother's house?"

He drove her to downtown Dallas. She stared at an art deco building, her eyes fixed blankly on what looked like a giant jukebox. Memories played over and over in her mind, like a video loop: waving to Piver across the parking lot as he ducked into the Mercedes; the robber screaming; Piver's call to her house; Piver locking his door, his secretiveness and the strange looks he gave her. He'd sent her out on a night delivery to a man's house....

"I believe you," Kerry said. At Smith's questioning look, she continued, "Mr. Abernathy. I believe he's innocent. I believe I was used, and I believe somebody wants me out of the way." She shook her head. "I don't believe it's Piver. He's involved somehow, but I think he was used, too."

Smith parked the Nova in the Sheraton Hotel parking lot and they went to his hotel room. It was an executive suite, with a separate bedroom, a full bar, and fresh flowers on the table. There were real oil paintings, and the television wasn't chained to the wall. Perhaps he wasn't kidding about being rich, Kerry thought.

Smith dropped her bag on a damask-covered chair, then went to the phone. "Take the bed. You look beat." He dialed.

"Who are you calling at this time of night?"

"Bob Ward. I want to be present when they question that kid. Ward's the only string I have to pull in this town. Go on, I'll fill you in later."

Too exhausted to argue, she went to bed. The last thing she heard was Smith's coaxing drawl. She felt sorry for Bob Ward. No one stood a chance of winning an argument against Tarkington Smith.

WHEN KERRY WOKE, she yawned and stretched. The bed was comfortable, and the sheets were silky. She glanced at the bedside clock—8:55 a.m. She gasped, startled wide awake. She tore out of bed and jerked open the door. Smith was gone. She slammed a fist against the doorjamb. She hated being late. She searched for her keys. They were gone.

She called Copy Copy, hoping Piver had come in early to open the shop at nine. To her relief, he answered the phone. "Mr. Piver," she said quickly, "I'm terribly sorry. I overslept. I don't have my car. I'll be in as soon as I can. I'll take a taxi. I'm really sorry. I had an awful—"

"Don't bother coming in, Miss Byfield," Piver said coldly.

Short hairs lifted on the nape of her neck. Was he a murderer?

"You're fired."

She drew away from the phone. "Fired?"

"That little stunt you pulled last night is the oldest trick in the book. I'm deeply disappointed in you." His voice held the warmth of a cold snap in Alaska.

Kerry squeaked. "What stunt?"

"Reporting a theft to cover your robbing the till. You're damned lucky I like you or I'd call the cops. As it is, I just want to forget your betrayal of my trust. I hope there's nothing else missing when I go over the books. You better hope there's nothing missing."

"Mr. Piver, I am not a thief! Mr. Piver?" She was speaking to a dial tone. "Fired? You can't fire me." She set the handset gently on the cradle.

She sank to a chair and sat with her hands dangling between her knees. Anger burned deep inside her, flaring and shooting sparks. She'd given him two years of hard work, of building a clientele, of mastering a complicated computer system and dozens of programs, of running all of his gofer errands. Fired? She thought of all the dirty words she knew and couldn't find one foul enough to express her feelings.

Kerry glared at the phone. "What are you hiding, Piver? Just what's behind that locked office door you don't want me to find? And you owe me two weeks' pay. Call me a thief? I'll show you thief." She dialed Blackie's number.

He answered after the twentieth ring. She said, "Don't hang up, it's me, Kerry."

"Baby, do you know what time it is?" he groaned.

"Time for a vampire like you to crawl out of your coffin and save my life."

"Whoa, you sound upset."

"I'm more than upset, Blackie. Three times in two days I've had someone try to kill me. Now I just got fired. I can't go to my apartment." Blackie was chewing noisily on something. She gave him a quick synopsis of what had happened since Smith had walked into her life.

"Heavy," Blackie said. "What do you want?"

"I want everything you can find out about Randi Mae Firkins." She spelled the name out for him. "A name is all I have."

"A challenge. Okay, where can I reach you?"

She had to check the room number, then told him, adding, "Call as soon as you get anything. I owe you, buddy."

"Does this mean you'll go to bed with me?" he asked.

"I don't owe you that much. How about a lifetime supply of Twinkies—delivered."

"You got it. I'll get back to you."

Kerry called room service and ordered breakfast. Staring into space didn't make her feel better while she waited, nor did staring out the window. She called her mother.

"Hello, darling."

The normalcy soothed Kerry. She managed a wan smile as she settled back in preparation for some tidbits of gossip or a recounting of a shopping trip or even some minor harassment about her life. "I cut you off last night. Sorry. So I just—"

"Isn't this funny? Someone called for you. I told him you didn't live here anymore. I told—"

Ice filled Kerry's belly. She clutched the phone with both hands. "Who?"

"He didn't leave his name. In fact, he was rather rude. Probably one of those computer geeks. I think—"

"I have to go, Mom. There's someone at the door."

"Oh—well—but you didn't tell me—"

"Bye." Kerry put the phone down. "Who is it?" she called.

"Room service."

She let a young man in. He set a large tray on the table. He eyed her scruffy flannel robe as she signed the tab. She fished in her purse, came up with $2.70 in change, all her cash, and tipped him. The waiter rolled his eyes as he walked out.

She poured a cup of coffee, knowing she should shower and dress. What for? She now had no job, no life and no apartment. People were calling her mother's house when she hadn't lived there in years. She sipped the coffee and tried to feel more angry than scared.

BLACKIE CALLED KERRY a few minutes after eleven. "You picked a weird lady."

"Explain."

"No credit history. Zilch. Not even a gas-station charge card. She's held one job. Get this, she's been a waitress in the same truck stop for sixteen years."

"Got an address?" He did, and Kerry wrote it down quickly. "Waxahatchie, huh? Anything else?"

"Yeah, waitressing must pay pretty good. She drives a Mercedes. Late-model 250SL. Nice chunk of car. What's weird is I can't find out how she paid for it. The feds are getting sticky about paying cash for that sort of stuff."

Kerry almost heard the light bulb clicking on inside her head. "What about the previous owner?"

"Hold on a second."

Kerry listened to shuffling paper.

"Here you go. Louise Abernathy. Isn't that the broad who got herself whacked?"

"Uh-huh. And somehow this doesn't surprise me. What about banking records? Has she been making large deposits?"

"Nada."

"Is this all on hard copy?"

"Yes."

"Can I come by later to pick it up?"

"Sure. Knock three times so I know it's you. I'm working on the Macrotech program."

Kerry hung up and grimaced at the Waxahatchie address. She muttered, "As Alice said, 'curiouser and curiouser.'" Coincidence? Connections? She went over the past two days, especially yesterday. Nolan Piver had been acting strangely for a long time. He'd been locking his office, shutting the door and dating a mysterious woman who never gave her name or came inside the shop. He wasn't the only weird one. Kerry thought about Robert Marsh and his dislike for Smith. The more she thought about it, the odder it seemed. Was he involved in this, too?

When Smith finally returned, Kerry was draped over a chair, eating room-service chicken salad and watching soap operas. "I think I've been missing out on things. This is really interesting," she said. "See that blond woman? She's pregnant, but I think she has to choose between three possible fathers. And none of them is her husband." Kerry aimed the remote and clicked off the TV. She turned Smith a baleful eye and said, "You took my car and left me stranded."

"Sorry," he said and drank out of her ice-tea glass. He made a face, and she took the glass away before he dumped sugar in it. "Did you call Piver?"

She smiled coldly. "He fired me."

"Good."

"He accused me of stealing money from the cash register— What do you mean 'good?' I have bills to pay. I have four dependent cats who'll starve on the streets."

"You're too good for that job, sugar. You're hired."

She bristled. "It was a great job. I loved that job— What?"

"A hundred bucks a day, plus expenses. I need your magic on the keyboard." He hid a yawn behind his hand.

"I'm not taking charity from you."

"Okay, one fifty a day, but that's my top offer. And

I get to drive.'' He headed for the bedroom. ''You should have been there last night. Once that jerk started talking, nothing could shut him up. And Bob Ward is on our side. Nothing official, but he's willing to look at everything we can dig up. I think we have a chance, sugar. I really do.''

She trotted after him. ''What did he say? The jerk, that is, not Mr. Ward.''

''You were right. He's the same one who tried to rob Copy Copy.'' Smith tossed his shirt onto the bed.

Kerry did a double take. His tanned upper body was lean and chiseled, whippy with muscle. A body that beautiful ought to be against the law, she thought. Her nerves began jumping, screaming, ''Me! No, touch *me* first!''

Smith sat down and began to tug off his boots. ''I don't want to scare you, but that guy was supposed to…make certain you don't plug into any more data bases.''

Lost in musing about how his skin might feel or if that muscle-ridged belly was as rock solid as it appeared, she said, ''Huh?''

''He says he never heard of Piver. The jerk's a coke freak. He swears his dealer, some guy named Rex, gave him the gun and the addresses. The gun's an orphan. There's no tracing it.'' Smith made a disgusted noise. ''Drug freak—had less than thirty bucks on him. Murder is cheap these days.''

Kerry focused on the doorframe. It was white enamel, very smooth and cool under her fingertips. ''So who is Rex?'' Smith stood to unbuckle his belt. Kerry did an about-face. ''Do you want something to eat?''

''Order me a steak sandwich, fries and ice tea. Let

me grab a shower, and then I'll tell you everything else.''

Twenty minutes later he came out, toweling his hair, barefoot and wearing blue jeans. His skin glowed from the hot water. Room service arrived. Kerry grinned at the way the waiter fawned over Smith. He must know a soft touch for a good tip, she thought. She studied the way Smith's jeans fit and the neat taper of his waist from his broad chest. After he closed the door, they exchanged a look charged with *I want*. It caused a tender imbalance deep inside Kerry.

Her sensibility rebelled. It was the dangerous situation charging her senses, not his sun-browned skin and muscular body. Fiddling with the notes from Blackie's phone call, she said, ''I have news for you.'' Her voice sounded funny. She cleared her throat. Staying in this room with him was dangerous—relationships that happened too fast burned bright and hot—then out. She needed distance to consider him rationally.

He dumped sugar into his tea, then yawned, stretching like a big, sleek cat.

She handed him the Waxahatchie address. ''Randi Mae Firkins.''

Smith brightened visibly. ''Good day's work all around. How'd you get this?''

She told him about Blackie and about the Mercedes. He ate the steak sandwich in big, hasty bites as if he were starving. Like her, he showed no surprise that Randi Mae was the woman in the Mercedes. He flopped back in a chair, holding the plate of French fries in one hand. The line between his eyebrows deepened.

''Can I ask a stupid question?'' Kerry said. ''It's been bugging me. What about Robert Marsh?'' She sat on a chair and leaned forward. ''It's been bugging me since he showed up yesterday. I mean, first he called me before you showed up, then out of the blue, he showed up where I work. Your conspiracy theory keeps sounding more and more sensible. So why not Marsh?''

Smith chuckled but shook his head. ''As much as I want to agree, sugar, I'm afraid he's not a suspect. His involvement is worse, it's politics. Bradford Lowell is coming up for reelection, and Ward tells me Marsh is gearing up to run against him.'' He yawned, then rubbed his face with both hands.

Kerry mulled that information over, disappointed. The more she considered Marsh, the more he seemed like the perfect villain. ''I told you it was a dumb question. So what about the other guy, the robber's boss…?''

''Rex. He's a mystery man. Ward said he'll check around. He didn't laugh me out of his office when I told him what I thought about Piver.'' Smith regarded another French fry. ''The drug freak was supposed to kill you as soon as you opened the cash register. He said Rex was adamant about it looking like a robbery.''

Kerry closed her eyes, thanking God that Piver was so cheap when he'd bought that balky register. She didn't need Smith to tell her what the guy was supposed to do in her apartment.

Smith picked up the Waxahatchie address, studying it while he ate the last of his fries. Then he said, ''Let's go to the morgue.''

Chapter Nine

"The morgue? No way. Forget it. I absolutely refuse to look at any dead bodies."

Smith's eyes sparkled as he hid another yawn behind his hand. "The newspaper, sugar. The morgue is where they keep all the back editions and files at the newspaper." He laughed softly, then sipped his tea.

"Oh. Why?" She tapped the Waxahatchie address. "Let's go visit Randi Mae."

"I'm too tired to drive all the way to Waxahatchie right now. Besides, I've got a theory and I need some facts to back it up. I think Piver, Randi Mae or both of them were blackmailing Louise. That would explain the money Louise withdrew." He slumped back on the chair and stretched out his long legs. "Maybe she threatened to expose them."

"Blackmail? I can't see Piver as a blackmailer." Kerry winced at the memory of him firing her. How could he accuse her of theft? "Okay, maybe so. It seems pretty stupid for Louise to take out an insurance policy payable to a blackmailer, though. I think we ought to go to Waxahatchie. If Piver is getting scared, then Randi Mae is, too. She might decide to run."

Smith yawned again. His eyelids drooped.

"Did you get any sleep last night?"

He shook his head. "I'm good for a few more hours."

"You look ready to drop." She touched his arm, but drew away from the appeal of his shower-warm skin. *Keep your mind on business,* she warned herself. "I have a better idea. You get some sleep. I'm going over to Blackie's. He has the printout on Randi Mae. I think I can get him to run a check on Piver for me."

"Nope. You aren't going anywhere without me."

"Piver doesn't know about Blackie. Besides, he's at the shop, and he can't leave since there's nobody to watch the place. Murderer, blackmailer or whatever, he still has a business to run. Get some sleep. I have to do something to earn my one fifty a day." She tapped her chin. "Can I count getting the bullet holes patched in my car as an expense?"

"Get estimates first." He picked up the phone.

"Who are you calling now?"

"Car rental. Your Nova stands out. I don't want you followed."

It didn't take long. Kerry wondered at how easily he managed to have the car-rental people deliver a Mustang to the hotel. The little car handled well. She took 75 north toward Richardson, where Blackie lived.

She made one stop at a supermarket, to pick up a couple of boxes of Twinkies and a box of Ding Dongs. She paid by check and while the clerk studied her driver's license, she hoped Smith wasn't kidding when he'd said he'd hired her. Her checking account balance was an embarrassment.

At Blackie's apartment, she knocked three times, waited a minute, then knocked three times again. Blackie answered the door. He weighed at least three hundred pounds. His IQ matched his heft. His stained clothing clung to his corpulent contours as if growing there like mold. His apartment was dark, and foil covered the windows. It smelled like a locker room. She suspected Blackie only left the apartment to attend the monthly users' group meetings. She handed him the grocery bag.

"Thanks," he said. "Now I don't have to go shopping."

Kerry had been to the apartment before. Still, the strangeness took her aback. The living room was crammed floor to ceiling with computer equipment. Most of it was strung together from bits and pieces he'd picked up from previous jobs at places like Xerox and Texas Instruments. The air glowed with green and yellow light. Stacks of paper and electronic equipment boxes formed a labyrinth through the one-room apartment.

"What are you working on, Blackie?"

"A debug utility for Macrotech. It's a pain, but it pays the rent."

"Why don't you get some lights? You're going to ruin your eyes."

He blinked in amusement behind his thick, black-rimmed glasses. "I'm a vampire, remember?" He handed her a slim stack of paper. "Your system crash?"

"My phone line was cut. Now I'm scared to go back to my apartment." She drew a deep breath. "Can I ask you another favor? Will you run a check on Piver for me?"

She should have known better than to think Blackie needed coaxing. He seemed pleased to do the electronic snooping; it gave him a recreational break.

While Blackie went to work, Kerry took the printout

on Randi Mae to the kitchen area and read it by the overhead stove light. She tried not to look at the overflowing sink and greasy stove.

Blackie was faster than she was. He had two phone lines. He could dig up information as fast as his printers could spit it out. While two printers ran at full draft speed, he wheeled his chair over to a different terminal.

"See my new third-world turbo charger?" he asked proudly.

Kerry was impressed at how quickly he brought a utilities program on line. He said, "Got bugs galore in this system, but the speed makes it worth it. A 486 processor and twenty megs of RAM. I can own the world with this baby."

"Who makes it?"

"Taganachi. They're new. Too bad all their research and development is in Japan. I'd love to break into their programming mainframe." He grinned ruefully. "Lou is letting me try this system on spec. Love at first byte. He's suckered me in again."

"What else have you got to spend your money on?"

Blackie thought for a moment, then lifted a beefy shoulder. He laughed. "So that creep fired you, huh? Want me to clean out his hard disks?"

"No thanks, Blackie." She eyed him, hard, suspecting he might do it anyway just for the fun of it. "If T.K.'s right, Piver's got enough trouble. T.K. thinks he might have been involved in blackmail along with murder."

"Heavy." Blackie raked his black hair away from his face. "So what are all your yuppies going to do without you cleaning up their grammar and making their newsletters look pretty?"

The last thing she wanted was guilt over what her

customers were going to do. She said, "That's Piver's problem."

"Go free lance. It's a great life. You can take all of Piver's business."

"I haven't got the money for a decent laser printer. And I need a copier. No money for that, either."

"Hit up your old lady. She's loaded."

Kerry groaned mentally. Her mother would love the chance to play Mommy Warbucks, if for no other reason than to prove that Kerry couldn't make it on her own.

Blackie added, "And I can get you the latest version of Ventura Publisher or Aldus Pagemaker if you want. Free. I made a new buddy on the bulletin board. He can get anything."

"Jeez. Piver accuses me of being a thief. Now you want to make me one. If I ever go free lance, I'll buy my own programs. Play with your new toy and don't worry about me." Kerry focused on Randi Mae.

Blackie finished the search and handed her a loose stack of printouts two inches thick. A phone rang. Blackie had his computers programmed to answer only authorized callers. If it was someone on his list, his computer would answer. The phone stopped after seven rings.

"Why don't you get an answering machine?" Kerry asked as she shifted her purse strap on her shoulder.

"Nobody I want to talk to," Blackie answered.

"How much do I owe you?"

"Don't worry about it. I'll just tack this onto Macrotech's bill. Their accounting department will never know the difference."

"You're going to get caught some day, Blackie."

He threw back his head and laughed. "Figure the

odds.'' He nodded sagely. ''The trick to it is brass. Chumps who lose their nerve are the ones who get caught. They waste their time trying to cover every track and hang themselves. Too many details are dangerous. Remember that.''

Kerry saw herself out. She stood in the parking lot, confused for a few moments until she remembered she was driving a white Mustang. As she buckled the seat belt, she was half tempted to stop by Copy Copy, to remind Piver he owed her a paycheck—and to give him a piece of her mind. He'd hurt her feelings with that blatant lie about the cash-register theft. Smith was right about Piver getting nervous and doing stupid things. Firing her was stupid. Until Piver did that, she'd wanted to believe in his innocence. Now she wanted him guilty. She eased the Mustang into the 75 south traffic toward Dallas. ''Oh, Tarkington Smith, what have you done to me?'' she muttered, glancing at the stack of paper on the seat beside her. ''I had a swell life before you showed up.''

He had upset her thinking about men and life in general. Ever since college graduation and calling off the engagement with Mike, she had concentrated on her job and had absorbed herself in routine. She'd had no distractions. The men she met, customers and the men her mother ferreted out as son-in-law hopefuls bored her. Earnest businessmen in uniform dark suits, trendy ties and carefully styled hair who spouted fashionably obscure buzzwords just weren't her style. Their fascination with expensive cars and the stock market didn't interest her. Turning down the occasional few who asked her out was easy. She just said no.

Tarkington Smith was different. He made her think about the way she looked and the way he looked. She told herself it was just his way, that he hit on every woman he met and was a natural-born charmer. But then, how did he make her feel so special? She pulled into the Sheraton lot and parked the Mustang next to her Nova. She stared up at the hotel, wondering if he was still asleep.

She muttered, "You and your darned hunches, Smith! No way. I'm not some animal who's going to go trotting off wherever instinct leads me." In the back reaches of her mind, she heard his amused, *Maybe*.

Kerry read on the elevator ride to the seventeenth floor. The information on Piver was terse and broken down into numbers. It began to make a little sense in bits and pieces. The elevator pinged softly and the doors schussed open. She stepped into the hallway. When she turned a corner, she stopped short.

A man stood in front of T.K.'s door. He wore a cheap, brown suit. The jacket hung clumsily off his rounded shoulders. He stood too close to the door, his face almost against the wood. He held his right hand inside the jacket.

Clutching the stack of papers, Kerry took hesitant steps. She squinted at the man, trying to place him. He had a furtive air that made her scalp prickle.

The man knocked hard and called, "Room service, Mr. Smith!"

Her sneaker-clad feet silent, Kerry broke into a run. She screamed, "No!" as the door opened a crack.

The man spun around. He pulled a gun from his jacket.

"Don't open the door, T.K.!"

The fan-fold continuous-feed computer paper flew like giant streamers of confetti when she threw it. Running backward, the man batted wildly at the paper.

Smith shot out of the room low and quick, grabbing for the man's legs. He got armfuls of paper instead. Kerry slammed herself flat against the wall, gaping as the man disappeared around the corner. Smith grabbed her arm and jerked her inside the room. He slammed the door and locked it.

"I'm the target?" she whispered harshly. "Me, huh? Did that guy say, 'Room service, Miss Byfield?' No!"

Smith clamped a hand over her mouth. She glared at him. He grinned. His eyes were sleepy slits and his hair stood in wild spikes. He said, "You're gorgeous when you're angry. Something to do with your big green eyes, I think."

She wrenched her face away from his hand and cried, "Call security!"

"Why? That jerk is long gone. Calling them means another hour wasted with the police."

He kissed her. She resisted—for a moment. His mouth was sleepy sweet and male musky. His hands gripped her shoulders. She wrapped her arms around his lean waist, shocked by the sudden demands of her body. His slow, probing tongue was provocative. Everything from the iron strength of his hands to the supple skin of his hard back held an allure that weakened her knees. Her pounding heart changed tempo from a jackhammer to a flutter, as if taking wing. When he broke the kiss, she blinked slowly. As if savoring the taste, he licked his lips. He rubbed his nose very slowly, very lightly against hers and caressed her shoulders.

"Why did you do that?" He was giving her that look again, and it worked. She felt beautiful and desirable, drowning in his eyes.

His eyes seemed black, the pupils rimmed by the deep glint of midnight blue. "I'm trying to take advantage of you, sugar. Do you mind?'' He had the sexiest voice she'd ever heard and the most deliciously wicked grin.

"I certainly do," she said weakly. The feel of satiny skin over taut muscle drew her fingertips. She traced the ridges of his shoulder blades. She swallowed the thickness in her throat. "I am definitely not the type of woman who indulges in casual affairs."

"Just checking." He released her and reached for the doorknob.

Kerry blinked dreamily, musing whether or not being taken advantage of was such a terrible thing. Then she realized he meant to open the door. "Wait! He might still be—" She pressed against the wall. "T.K.!"

"He's gone. What do you want to bet that was Rex? Did you get a good look at him?" Smith scooped up the printout and her purse. "I wonder how he figured out I was here?"

She huffed in exasperation. "You have to call the police. This is too much to handle."

He tried to put the papers in order. "Fine, we go to the police. They take another report and ask why I don't get my butt back down to Houston where I belong. Then Lowell asks Bob Ward why he's bothering with me. And Bob is spooked because, right or wrong, he has to work in that office. Then that's it." Smith shoved the mess of papers at her. "Fix that. I'm going to pack."

"T.K.—"

"I heard the Embassy has an indoor swimming pool. Know if that's true?"

"How can you be so calm? Doesn't anything bother you?"

Again, he gave her that wicked grin. "Lighten up. I won't let anything happen to you."

It surprised Kerry to realize she believed him.

TWO HOURS LATER, they were ensconced in a suite at the downtown Embassy Hotel, eating a Domino's pizza, drinking Coke and trying to make sense of Piver's life.

The Embassy Hotel was smaller than the Sheraton, but in some ways nicer. Reproduction antique furniture in Victorian style, wool carpets in muted colors and a profusion of philodendrons and asparagus ferns gave the sitting room a homey air.

Kerry and Smith sat on a rug, the pizza box between them. Both of them were encircled by fans of computer paper.

Kerry used a red pencil to circle items of interest on a banking statement. "He's been making a lot of deposits into his business account in the last year. Look, $7,640.00 here, another for $6,821.00. There's a whole string of them. Copy Copy isn't bringing in that kind of cash. I know that for a fact."

"He's not so stupid after all," Smith said. "Any cash deposits over ten grand have to be reported to the feds. And those odd amounts are probably backed up by a lot of phony bookkeeping... Bingo."

"What?" She leaned over to see what had him interested.

"It's been bothering me that he hasn't cut and run. I mean, okay, he gets away with murder and gathers a very tidy sum of cash. He's got Randi Mae and a Mercedes. Why not head for Mexico?"

"He has a business."

"That's been steadily losing money." Smith flipped back a few pages. "His profit last year was on paper, created by some shuffling and a credit extension. He's in the hole. Here's the reason he's sticking around." He handed her a page.

Kerry's eyes widened. Piver was paying, via check, $4,800.00 a month to a private nursing institution called Lambeck Quality Care. She grabbed the stack of paper that concerned his banking statements and found his personal account. Piver had been making that monthly payment for at least a year.

"Oh, T.K., this is so sad."

"That's so expensive. Whoever is in that nursing home is costing him a pretty penny. Any ideas?"

"He's never said."

"It explains why he's hanging around. And why he's desperate that this case doesn't reopen. Maybe it's his mother in there. And what we see may only be the tip of this particular iceberg. There might be other costs— doctors, prescriptions, special nursing. The man is deeply in debt."

Kerry groaned, lying back on the floor and staring at the spray-flocked ceiling. "Why couldn't he have been a gambler or a drug addict? Or a Mafia hit man? Why'd he have to murder Louise to get money for the care of his mother?" She turned her head to look sadly at Smith. "Maybe we have this all wrong. How can he be evil if he loves his mother? Maybe it's just circumstantial. Maybe there's another killer. One we haven't thought of yet."

"Maybe." He enclosed her hand in both of his. "If Piver is innocent, he has nothing to fear from us. If he isn't, then loving his mother isn't enough excuse to murder a woman. Keep that in mind." His voice dropped. "Louise Abernathy was looking at the man who stuck a shotgun in her face and pulled the trigger."

Kerry felt sick, remembering the horrible photograph

of the hand. It was as if Louise had thrown up her hand in a desperate attempt to protect her face. "You have a way with words, Tarkington Smith." She sat up and grabbed a pile of papers. "We keep looking, right?"

"Right."

Kerry used a legal pad to make notes, ignoring his smirk. She didn't have his photographic memory. She added up the deposits Piver had been making into personal and business accounts. It was a lot, but nowhere close to $432,900.00. She tried to imagine what it felt like to sit on a huge bundle of cash, unable to spend it because of a guilty secret.

Smith muttered, "That Randi Mae must be pretty stupid."

"What's that?"

"Randi Mae. Why hasn't she opened any bank accounts? That insurance money is legal. Is she toting around a purse full of twenties?"

"Do you think she gave it to Piver? They are getting married."

"You've never had a good look at her?"

Kerry thought hard, but had to shake her head. "I couldn't point to her if she was standing in front of me." She watched Smith pull the phone near. "Who are you calling now?"

"Bob Ward. We need more help than your computer can give. Mother aside, Piver is going to get spooked and hightail it if we don't act fast."

He punched numbers quickly on the phone. He pointed at the two-liter bottle of Coke. Kerry refilled his glass.

"Ward? Tarkington Smith here. Yeah, real glad to hear your voice again, too." He winked at Kerry. "Listen here, buddy, this mess is getting deeper and deeper.

I need to convince you of the wisdom of getting some warrants and maybe a state auditor or two. Uh-huh. Oh, yeah? You don't say?''

He put his hand over the mouthpiece, then whispered, ''That kid we caught yesterday keeps confessing. He's pretty shaken by cocaine withdrawal and is willing to cut any deal in order to get a fix. Yeah, Bob, I'm here. Go ahead.... You say he ID'd Rex's car. It's a late-model Buick. Rex wouldn't by any chance be about, oh, say five ten, about one eighty with sandy-colored hair?...I thought so. We've met. He's packing a piece, too. I'll tell you later...Now?...The Embassy, downtown Dallas, room 2811...Sure enough, out here.'' He hung up.

''Oh darn,'' Kerry said. ''You should have asked him to find out if Piver owns a handgun. I forgot to ask Blackie.''

''I'll ask him later.''

''Why can't we just turn this over to Mr. Ward and be done with it? He has all the resources, doesn't he?''

Smith patted a stack of paper. ''Ward can't do anything with this. It's information gained in direct violation of Piver's rights. And wouldn't the D.A. just love that?''

''Then what good is it? Why am I going crazy trying to read this stuff?'' She looked at her watch and groaned.

''Because I'm not a law officer, I'm not bound by rules of evidence. I can use this to nudge Ward into finding something he can use. Maybe he'll get a warrant to look at Piver's books. I wish we'd caught Rex. I bet he can sing a pretty tune about Piver.''

Kerry took another slice of pizza, then caught a glance at the fit of her jeans. She was a size ten, but a very curvy size ten. She put the slice back into the box. Then she retrieved it, determined that no man was going to make her crazy about her figure.

She watched Smith nudge his reading glasses higher on his nose. She imagined him in college at the age of fifteen. Had the older students intimidated him? Had he been bookish? Or had he always owned this irrepressible cockiness? She pictured him as a teacher's pet. No, she amended, with his quick mind and ready wit, he had probably been a teacher's nightmare. "Are you really filthy rich?"

"Don't I look it?" He took the last slice of pizza.

"No."

"My granddaddy was in oil, and my daddy was smart enough to get out of oil before the big bust. Ever hear of Westdynamics?"

"Who hasn't? Software development, electronics... space research."

"That's Dad."

She arched her eyebrows. "What does your father think of what you do?"

Smith made an odd face. "He thinks I'm a jerk."

She related to that. She suspected her mother thought she was a jerk, too. "Why?"

"He's a Harvard man too, and he'd hoped I would follow in his footsteps. When I worked in the D.A.'s office, I heard how I was wasting my education. Now I hear how I'm wasting my life." He made that odd face again. "What father doesn't think his son is a jerk? But I'm still rich. So tell me, sweet thing, like me better knowing I can keep you in chinchilla?" His words were teasing, but his entire posture was serious, even slightly challenging.

She responded, "Money isn't a real high priority with me."

He lifted his shoulders in a lazy shrug. "Oh, well. I'll come up with something." That held a promise. Kerry found herself extremely interested in seeing if he could keep it.

BOB WARD ARRIVED within the hour. He was a tall, gaunt man with a cadaverous face and intelligent eyes underscored by purplish, baggy circles. He wore a dark suit, a string tie and cowboy boots with a lustrous shine. He had a gravelly Texas drawl and a firm grasp when he shook Kerry's hand.

Kerry at once liked and pitied him. He looked dragged out and to-the-bone tired. He sat and lit a cigarette.

"Here's the facts I've found." Smith explained how Nolan Piver knew Louise Abernathy, and how it was strange for Piver to send Kerry on a night delivery. He emphasized that Louise had purchased a shotgun. When he reached the part about the insurance policy payable to Randi Mae and the fact that Piver and Randi Mae Firkins had taken out a marriage license, Bob Ward puffed more rapidly on his cigarette. The ash grew long, threatening to spill onto the carpet. Smith continued to spout hard facts about the $432,900 withdrawal, and Piver's deposits to his business account that were larger than Copy Copy's revenues. Ward looked very interested.

"Here's my theory," Smith said. "Randi Mae and Piver were blackmailing Louise. But Louise decided that whatever they had against her wasn't bad enough to keep shelling out the cash. Or maybe she'd dipped into the piggy bank as far as she could go. I think she not only told Piver no, but threatened to call the police. Piver and Randi Mae then arranged for her murder. As for the gambling slips and love letters, I think those were planted. Consider the corroborating evidence. Witnesses testified seeing Louise in bars and hotel lobbies with a man, but no one identified the mystery lover. No one overheard any conversations or saw any public displays of affection. For all we know, Louise could have been talking to accountants or interior decorators. And what about the gambling slips? They were anonymous. If they hadn't been found in Louise's bedroom, no one could have said who they belonged to.''

''What about the bank tellers who testified?'' Ward challenged.

Smith shrugged. ''They testified that Louise seemed 'nervous' about withdrawing large amounts of cash. So? It seems to me that withdrawing blackmail money would make her a lot more nervous than taking money for a horse race.''

''Interesting theory, Smith, but what the hell am I supposed to do with it?'' Ward stubbed out his cigarette, then immediately lit another. He shook his head. ''You found my soft spot when you came to me with this lost cause of yours, boy. But damn, this is stretching things.''

Trying to hide her disappointment, Kerry asked, ''Why do you say that, Mr. Ward?''

''Well, one, it ain't illegal to collect on an insurance policy. Two, just because Piver's filling his pockets with cash don't mean it's coming out of Mrs. Abernathy's purse. Three, Randi Mae and Piver getting hitched is purely coincidental. That connection is weak as a silk thread in a bull's nose.''

''But what about that awful man who tried to kill

me? What about that Rex guy?'' Kerry clenched her fists, wanting to pound them against the floor.

In a matter-of-fact voice, Smith told Ward about the man in the brown suit at the Sheraton.

Ward swung his head. "Sounds like it's possibly Rex." He waved his hand and smoke swirled around his head. "I believe every word y'all are saying. But Bradford Lowell has me on the hot seat right now. He's been stacking up my cases so's I need a shovel to get to my desk. He ain't impressed with fiddling around with a closed case. Hard evidence. That you ain't got. Lowell's real unfriendly about this sort of thing. And with elections coming up, he's getting meaner than a three-legged bear at a dog race."

Kerry looked at Smith and wondered how he managed to appear so optimistic.

Smith asked, "How about warrants? Have we got enough for you to search Piver's house or office?"

"Possible. No guarantees." Ward leafed through the stack of printouts. He chuckled. "Where'd you get this stuff, Smith? Especially these here that say 'Confidential'?"

"Found them lying around. You know how it goes."

"Yep." Ward read for a few minutes, his pale eyebrows working up and down, then set the papers aside. "You write me up a report and give me all your facts and figures. Maybe I can't get him on the murder, but looks like there's some stuff the IRS will be interested in. We can get him sideways."

"Take what we have," Kerry said.

"Can't do that, Miss. This stuff's hotter than a pimp's pinkie ring. I can't go snooping around in a person's private affairs without a good reason before the fact. Have that report on my desk Monday morning, and I'll figure out some way to get those warrants." He looked between the two of them. "You missed something there in that old theory of yours, Smith. Who shot Mrs. Abernathy?"

"I'm working on it."

"You do that."

Kerry said, "What if Piver decides to run? If he's behind trying to kill us, then he's scared. What if he runs?"

Ward made a resigned gesture. "Convicting Abernathy was a nice little feather in the hat band. Lowell and Marsh aren't about to lose that feather without a bigger one to take its place. If Piver runs, y'all are just going to have to chase him. On the other hand, if you get some hard evidence, there ain't no place that old boy can hide." He tapped the stack of paper. "I ain't going to ask how you got this. But you keep looking. There's a whole lot more than a simple murder here. Judging by the ruckus you two are causing, it's gonna get worse. If your theory is anywhere close, Smith, we're talking conspiracy, extortion, tax fraud and a whole passel of other things."

"How about a wiretap? Piver talks to Randi Mae on the phone."

Ward's laugh emerged throaty and dry. "Want to hear what Lowell thinks about wiretaps? Tell you what though, let me get the IRS boys in on this. They're a determined bunch. I'll put that bug in a few ears." He lit another cigarette, seeming not to notice the one already burning in the ashtray. He reached inside his jacket for his wallet and extracted a business card.

"Give that old boy a call. He can keep an eye on Piver for you all while you're checking. With any luck, he can give you warning if it looks like Piver is going to run. He owes me a favor or two you can collect.''

"I appreciate it, Ward. I appreciate everything.''

Ward shook hands with Smith. He made a gallant gesture at Kerry. At the door he stopped, saying, "Watch yourself, Smith. You're dealing with nasty characters. I've issued an APB on that Rex feller. You let the police handle that one.'' Smith assured the gaunt assistant D.A. that he could take care of himself. Ward left.

"What now?'' Kerry asked.

"I have a report to write. You go to bed. I'll pick up a typewriter tomorrow and you can type this thing up for me—''

"One fifty a day is pretty steep for a typist,'' she teased.

"You asking for a raise, Miss Byfield?''

"Good night, T.K.'' She headed for one of the bedrooms in the double suite. Then she stopped and slapped her forehead with her palm. "Jeez! I have to call Mom. She's going to kill me for canceling out like this.''

"Why cancel? We can make it tomorrow night. No problem.''

Kerry looked askance. "If you think buttering up my mother is the way to get on my good side, you are sadly mistaken.''

He grinned. "Maybe.''

Chapter Ten

Kerry brushed her hair, listening to Smith, who was in the shower, doing a fair imitation of Willie Nelson singing "Three Days." He stopped the water and the singing, and soon entered the sitting room with a towel around his waist. The dusting of hair on his chest curled with dampness. Her body jerked with a tingling shock and she began blindly rummaging in her purse. She had to get out of here. He was too sexy and too darned casual about his state of undress for her to think straight.

"Did you order breakfast?" he asked.

"Oh. No, not yet." She reached for the phone, trying to keep her observation of his long, muscular legs covert. Nobody had the right to look that good.

As he walked back into the bedroom, he called, "We'll pick up something on our way to Plano to get my truck."

He was thinking too fast for her again. "You aren't going in to talk to Piver, are you? What are you going to say to him?"

"Not yet." He popped his head out of his bedroom door. "Think there's some way we can get into his office?"

Thoughts flashed to her set of office keys. She said, "That's illegal entry. I was fired, remember?"

"Maybe."

She didn't like the sound of that. What would an arrest look like on her résumé? Every job application had a space for listing arrests and convictions. Maybe free lancing was the way to go. Nobody cared if a free-lancer was a felon.

On their way out, Smith asked for her car keys, then stopped at the desk. He spoke to a young man wearing a Grateful Dead sweatshirt. Kerry gaped as Smith handed over her keys, displeased even after he assured her that the man would treat the Nova like a baby when he parked it in a downtown parking lot.

He made another stop in front of an exclusive men's clothing shop. Kerry waited in the car, wondering if this sort of place rented tuxedos. It didn't seem like it. The shop had tinted windows and displayed its logo in tasteful gold script. Smith emerged within minutes, carrying two large garment bags.

"That was quick," she said.

"I had my tailor send my measurements. Suit's off the rack, but it'll do."

She hid her surprise. "You dearly love showing off to me, don't you?"

"I have to get lucky someday."

He made another stop. This time at Sears. Together they picked up a portable typewriter, a pair of wide-brimmed Stetson hats and mirrored sunglasses.

The thought of disguises set Kerry to giggling. She giggled all the way to her apartment. It was nerves; they'd been jangling since the minute T.K. Smith walked into her life. But, she had to admit there was something especially dashing about him in the gray

Stetson and dark glasses. She wished she possessed his easy-going aplomb.

When he parked the car, fresh nervousness gripped Kerry. She pulled her hat brim low on her forehead, then peered suspiciously around the parking lot and at the apartments, looking for strange men and strange cars.

She expected the worst inside her apartment, but except for the loudly complaining cats, everything looked all right. The phone even worked. Kerry changed into a pair of clean slacks and a sweater, then packed a more substantial bag. She added her one formal gown and high heels.

"I hate leaving my cats alone."

"What about taking them to your mother's?"

"Mom has Yorkies. They hate cats."

Kerry thought she had her emotions under control, but when they reached the Plano Place shopping center, her mouth went dry and her palms started to sweat. She kept hearing the robber shouting at her to open the cash register, and then the rattle of her bedroom window popping out of its frame. She tucked her hair under her hat and pushed her sunglasses higher on her nose. When Smith told her to wait in the car, she didn't give him any arguments. She crawled over the transmission console and into the driver's seat.

Instead of going to his truck, Smith sauntered to a maroon Chevrolet Impala parked in front of the dentist's office. He approached the driver's side, leaned casually on the car's roof and talked to the person inside. Then he came back to her. "Meet me at the hotel. I'll follow you."

"Who were you talking to?"

"Friend of Bob Ward's named John. He said Piver

came in about nine-thirty and opened the shop at ten. Business as usual.''

"I don't get it. Why make attempts on us, fire me, then go on with business as usual? It doesn't make sense.''

"He's done some stupid things, but he's done some smart things, too. Besides, he's got mom to worry about in that nursing home. That gives us a little time. Anyway, if Piver tries anything, John will follow through.'' He leaned through the window and planted a friendly kiss on her lips. "Drive careful now, you hear?''

That was hard to do when she spent more time looking in the rearview mirror watching for him—certain he meant to do something reckless—than watching the road ahead. She was the cause of only two near wrecks by the time she reached the Embassy Hotel. To her relief, Smith pulled in not long after her. But instead of going to the suite, he urged her into the truck for a trip to the newspaper library.

"What do you possibly hope to find?'' she asked.

"According to what we know, Louise spent her entire adult life in the Dallas metropolitan area. If there's some sort of black secret, it'll be here.''

It didn't take Smith long to find a good old boy who was willing to show them the cataloging system of the *Dallas Times-Herald* morgue. Soon, both of them were armed with stacks of microfiche and seated before viewers.

"What am I looking for?'' Kerry asked.

"Anything. Louise was a mystery. No family, no friends…no past. It might not be much. An illegitimate birth, an arrest, or an involvement with a crime figure.''

"Previous marriage maybe? Is Bill Catholic?''

"No.''

"Her bankruptcies? Maybe we already have the blackmail material. We don't know what kind of woman she was or how guilty she felt about her past. She hid that from him. Maybe it was enough."

"Maybe," Smith said and started viewing.

Kerry searched back issues of the paper until she thought her eyes would fall out. The viewing screen was larger and brighter than a computer screen; it gave her a headache. They took one break for a late lunch, but otherwise sat glued to the viewers. Kerry used all her logical skills, cross referencing, deductive reasoning, but she felt as though she were in a maze with a million dead ends.

"Well, well, well," Smith murmured.

"Find something?"

"Serendipity."

"What?"

"It means—"

"I know what it means. Finding what you're looking for when you aren't looking for it. What have you found?"

"This picture."

She looked at his screen and frowned when she found a newspaper dated three weeks after the Abernathy murder. He was supposed to be searching the past. Smith pointed to a small photograph in the lower right-hand side of the screen. "I was looking to see if a reporter mentioned something the police or the D.A. missed. But look at this picture."

It was a grainy, badly lighted photo of a man. Kerry read the caption, learning the man was a suspected cocaine dealer named Thomas Nordoff. His decomposing body had been found by some picnickers in Mountain

Creek Lake Park. He'd been murdered in what the police investigators called an execution-style killing.

Bewildered, she asked, "Friend of yours?"

Smith went to find the employee who'd been so helpful. Kerry studied the article, but couldn't see the connection between Louise Abernathy and a cocaine dealer. Smith returned after about thirty minutes. He handed her a five-by-seven-inch color photograph.

"It's Aber— No, it isn't." Eyes wide, she looked hard at Smith's viewer. Her stomach tightened, then settled lower, icy cold. She gaped. "It looks just like William Abernathy. Well, not exactly like him, but, jeez, it's close."

"Same facial features. And according to their files, same size and coloring. The Thomas Nordoff case is still open."

"Either you found something, or this is a really weird coincidence." Kerry swallowed the guilty sour taste in her throat. If she saw this cocaine dealer coming out of Abernathy's house, she'd swear it was Abernathy on a stack of Bibles, under oath. She handed Smith the photograph. "How can we find out if this is coincidence or not?"

"That's a puzzle." He disappeared again. When he returned, he looked angry. "The detective in charge of this case is out of town for the weekend. I talked to some flunky who couldn't find the file. He said to call back Monday. Dead dope dealers don't rate much priority in Dallas."

"Did you call Ward?"

"I left a message."

Kerry caught a glimpse of a clock on the back wall. She gasped and checked her watch. "T.K., it's after five. I told Mom we'd be there at seven."

He grinned, but his gaze was distant. "Okay, let's get out of here. I need to check in with John anyway."

Back at the hotel, Kerry headed for the shower. She felt strange remembering how sure, how absolutely one-hundred-percent positive she was that she'd seen William Abernathy coming out of that house. Yet that cocaine dealer had looked just like him. Even if he turned out to have nothing at all to do with the murder, it still made her realize that what she saw and stood by for three days on the stand might be totally wrong.

That was what Smith meant by eyewitnesses making interpretations. She'd seen a man who looked like Abernathy coming out of Abernathy's house, ergo, she had seen Abernathy. How was she ever going to apologize to William Abernathy?

She dried her hair, leaving it to fall in silky light brown sheets to her shoulders. She clipped one side up and back with a rhinestone barrette. She put on evening makeup, taking extra care, telling herself it was to keep her mother's criticisms at bay, but knowing she wanted to look nice for Smith. She eased into her dress, settling the low-cut bodice over her full breasts and slipping the crisscross string straps into place. She studied herself in the full-length mirror attached to the door. The red-sequined gown glittered and shimmered, showing off her full hips and small waist. It was slit to midthigh. Would Smith like it?

Smith adjusted his bow tie, then straightened the shoulders of the European-styled tux. A flash of bright red caught his eye. As he turned to Kerry, his heart squeezed and a rise of desire caught him off guard. She was stunning. Lush curves beckoned his hands; her creamy skin looked tasty enough to eat. As he forced his gaze to her face, she lifted her eyebrows, then immediately lowered her eyelids. Her smile was sweet, causing him to straighten his shoulders and lift his head like a rooster strutting in a yard full of hens.

"You look great, T.K.," she said, her soft voice going softer.

In turn, he loosed a raffish wolf whistle. "Sugar, you're gorgeous."

Her lips twisted in a smirky smile. "Mom bought me the dress. She says every lady needs one drop-dead dress."

He touched the center of his chest. "I think it's working. Oh, my aching heart."

He settled her wrap over her shoulders. His fingers lingered; her shoulders were smooth as butter. Wanting to make love to her formed an ache deep in his groin. But those little startled glances she shot him sometimes, the way she backed away from his touch and the way questions sometimes seemed poised on the tip of her tongue told him to go easy. She wanted to take things nice and slow? That was okay with him. When he was with her, he felt an odd contentment, and if it took a lifetime for them to get to know each other better, that suited him just fine.

He shrugged into a black woolen greatcoat with a red silk lining, then hung a dapper white scarf under his lapels. He cocked his arm. His chest swelled at the soft purse of her lips and the flutter of her fingertips on his forearm.

He guided her downstairs, then out front into a waiting stretch limousine. Her giggle was soft and breathy, with no hint of nervousness, just pleasure. Was he showing off? As he watched her play with the console that controlled a TV, radio and CD player, he decided he was showing off. But what better use for money than giving a beautiful woman the giggles? He tried calling Bob Ward on the car phone, but had no luck. He decided to forget business, for a few hours anyway.

He carefully filled two tulip glasses and offered one to her. When this case was finished, he determined he was going to take her down south to his beach house in Galveston. He'd fix her big, lazy breakfasts and take her out on the boat to watch the dolphins play in the Gulf. He handed her a glass. Murmuring that she didn't drink, she waved it away.

"Perrier," he said. He lifted his own glass to her. "I don't drink, either."

She accepted the glass. "What do you do on Sunday afternoons while you watch football with your buddies?" she asked. "I figured you for beer and popcorn."

"Soda pop and corn chips," he replied, and her giggles started all over again. He turned his gaze out the smoky dark windows. One more minute of her shining eyes and sweet laughter and he was going to embarrass himself. He said, "I wonder how we find out if Piver and Randi Mae are married yet?"

"There's no way to find out until Monday. Why did you ask?"

To Smith it grew unclear why he'd asked. "Just wondering." His mind churned with details about the case, but it was an insensible jumble. It was too hard to think when her flowery perfume was much more interesting. His mind's eye was busy forming a picture of Kerry on the beach at sunrise with her blue jeans rolled up over her calves, while she exclaimed over discovering seashells.

She said, "Mom's a little...on the pushy side. You

may have talked yourself into something you're going to hate.''

"Mothers are supposed to be pushy. It means they love us. What about Dad?''

Kerry looked at the passing traffic and grew solemn. "Daddy died a few years ago.''

Smith bit back the urge to say something light. Feeling thirsty for every detail of her life, he urged her to talk.

"He was in the army. I think I've lived just about everywhere,'' she said. "We were down in Fort Hood when Daddy found out he had cancer. He'd been in twenty-nine years, so he retired. Mom loved Texas, especially Dallas, so we moved here.'' Sadness washed over Kerry's face, yet there was a lot of love and fondness, too. "Daddy was a survivor. He went through I don't know how many operations, but they brought the cancer under control. He opened a defense-contract consulting firm, then he had a heart attack. Can you beat that? He survived cancer, then died of a heart attack.'' She leaned over and took Smith's hand. "Don't get me started. I get soupy about Dad.''

He entwined his fingers with hers. "You were close?''

She nodded. "A lot of people think army colonel and see a discipline freak who marches his family around. Daddy wasn't stuffy at all. He was pretty funny. He coached my softball team and gave me his medals on Halloween so I could dress up.'' She rolled her eyes. "Mom, on the other hand— Well, you'll meet her. I love my mother, but she's hard to take.''

Smith kissed the back of her hand. Nothing in his life had ever felt so certain as knowing right now that he was going to spend the rest of his life with this green-eyed beauty. He said, "She sounds like my kind of woman."

"Is there any woman who isn't your kind of woman?"

"Why, Miss Byfield," he drawled. "Are you accusing me of laxity of morals?"

"Just checking."

The limousine pulled into the large, circular driveway in front of the Byfield house. Kerry noticed the usual Jaguars, BMWs, Cadillacs and Lincolns that marked one of her mother's parties. Her mother called it "cultivating the right people." Kerry sensed that after a lifetime as an officer's wife, moving every two or three years, Angela Byfield had never learned how to make real friends.

The driver opened the door. Smith helped Kerry out of the limo with casual elegance. She eyed the house. She had never liked it. A tract mansion, she called it, pseudo-elegance for the nouveau riche. It perched on a three-quarter-acre lot, was beautifully landscaped and looked very much like all the neighboring houses.

Angela Byfield had lost what she most treasured when her husband died and now made up for the loss by collecting things. A big house, a flashy social set, jewels, bric-a-brac, clothing and cars. Kerry thought her mother had no sense of self. Now that she wasn't the colonel's wife, she didn't know who she was. Kerry pitied her mother and hated herself for pitying her. She wondered if the day would ever come when she could face her mother, adult to adult. She loved her mother and knew Angela loved her, but she always felt strangled anyway.

She said, "Don't mention to Mom that I lost my job. She'll like that too much. And whatever you do, don't mention anything about the shootings. She'll go into hysterics."

Smith offered his arm, and together they went to the front door. Kerry rang the bell.

Belinda answered. Dressed in her formal black maid's outfit, she looked pleasantly resigned. "And how are you this fine evening, Kerry?" she asked in her dry voice.

"Just fine. I see by the crowd that Mom has gone all out again. Belinda, this is Tarkington Smith. T.K., Belinda Forester, keeper of the royal nuthouse."

"Now, Kerry, you watch your mouth," Belinda chided, then carried the wrap and greatcoat away.

"Kerry! Darling," Angela called. "You're almost unfashionably late." Taking both of Kerry's hands, she made kissing motions on either side of Kerry's face.

"You look terrific, Mom," Kerry said, and meant it.

Angela's latest face-lift had finally relaxed so that her skin didn't look taut and shiny as if stretched by a too-tight hairstyle. She was slim, platinum blond and garbed in a knockout gown of snowy white silk.

Kerry introduced Smith. Angela stepped back, doing that funny little trick of shifting her weight so that she looked both flirtatious and proper at the same time. She extended a perfectly manicured hand that flashed with diamonds.

Smith kissed her hand. "I see where Kerry gets her beauty, ma'am."

"She looks like her father, but thank you." Angela tucked her hand under his arm. "I wondered when that girl of mine was going to meet a charming man. Come, darlings, I'll introduce you to everyone."

Rolling her eyes, Kerry followed them into the formal living room. She greeted people she knew as she made her way to where the caterer had set up a bar. She ordered a ginger ale and watched her mother circulate with Smith. She decided he was by far the best-looking man in the house. His tux was cut broad in the shoulders and draped slightly, emphasizing his taut leanness; his boiled shirt was startling white against his dark tan. He wore his hair slicked back, and the earring gleamed, rather devilishly. It surprised her to note he was also enjoying himself. He talked easily to Angela's friends and listened with open interest. Kerry ordered a Perrier for him and carried it across the room.

"Darling," Angela said. "This is Randall Westworth. Need I say that he is disappointed to learn you are out of circulation?"

Randall smiled stiffly. He was of medium height. His reddish hair was carefully moussed. "So, Smith, Angela tells me you're a lawyer. I'm into investments myself."

Smith murmured his thanks as he took the sparkling water. His gaze caressed Kerry, lingering and warm, before he turned to Randall. He said, "Actually, I don't practice anymore. I'm a private investigator."

"Oh." Randall looked flustered as he took in Smith's expensive clothes. "Good money in that?"

"Not much. Good hours, though."

"That's investments, there. Good hours, twenty-four hours a day. Work, work, work. It's a dog's life, but if you don't keep plugging, the other rats get ahead."

Angela said, "Randall is very successful. He just bought a new BMW. It's beautiful."

"That's right," Randall said proudly. "I picked it up on the gray market. I stole it for five grand under the dealer cost. What a deal. What do you motor around in, Smith?"

"A pickup truck." He cut an amused glance at Kerry. "Pretty handy for hauling hay."

Angela looked bemused. Kerry knew that at any minute she was going to embarrass herself by bursting into brays of laughter. Angela whispered in Kerry's ear, "He's a terrible tease, but I like him anyway." Angela insisted on leaving the boys to their talk and took Kerry aside. She demanded to know details, but Kerry fended her off with vagueness until Angela was forced to attend her other guests.

Kerry politely listened to Mrs. Newburn talk about the latest in cosmetic surgery, Claire Haven expound on the wonders of Oleg Cassini's new spring collection, and a Dr. Ridenour explain how the best art investments weren't in paintings, but in sculptures. But she kept her eyes on Smith.

He fit in, but not exactly. He listened more than he talked, sipping Perrier and nodding attentively. Kerry finally figured out what made him so attractive. Self-confidence, not an inflated ego, not bravado or machismo, not even rampant cockiness. He just plain liked himself, and he liked everyone else because of it.

Just like Daddy, she thought, smiling. He didn't need an expensive car or fancy clothes, and he didn't need to boast about his skills on the stock market or tell everyone what he did to prove who he was. She imagined Smith could talk as easily to the queen of England as he talked to a gas-station attendant. He knew who he was and he liked it. By the time they sat down to dinner, she had come to the conclusion that she had never met anyone like Tarkington Smith and that no past experience applied. Maybe trusting her instincts was not only reasonable, but right.

Randall, who was seated across the table, said, "Your mother tells me you're into computers, Kerry."

"Desktop publishing," she said.

"Good money?"

"No." She poked at her steamed broccoli with her fork. She watched Smith talk to Claire Haven. Though in her sixties, Claire giggled like a girl in response to his charming drawl.

"You aren't making the right connections," Randall said. "The real money is in corporate in-house publications."

"That's a problem. If they're in-house, they don't need me."

Randall waved a hand. "Connections. Consulting is where the money is. I know some people who can match up piece A with piece B and give you a piece of that corporate pie."

Smith swung his head around. Kerry could see he was thinking something. She asked, "What?"

He said softly, "For a couple of smart cookies, we sure are dumb. I'll tell you after dinner."

Kerry thought dinner would never end. When everyone was retiring to the living room for coffee, Smith asked to borrow the phone. Angela blandly bade Kerry to show him to the den. When Kerry shut the door, Smith tapped his temple with a finger. He said, "What do you want to bet that the gun used to murder that cocaine dealer is the one that was used to shoot up your Nova?"

She leaned her backside against the mahogany executive desk. "What makes you think so? More importantly, how can we possibly find out?"

"We spooked Piver and Randi Mae. Suppose they followed us to the Abernathy house. Piver panics, grabs the gun and starts shooting. He thinks about it, realizes he isn't the right man for the job and then he gets Rex. I bet you the farm that Piver was the triggerman on Abernathy's impersonator.''

''Farfetched, but then everything we've found is far-fetched. How can we prove it?''

He picked up the phone. ''Piece A and piece B. Bullets. Hard evidence. If ballistics show that the bullets match, then we've got enough cause for Ward to apply for a warrant. And if his boys find that gun, then bingo. We've got enough to reopen the case.'' He called Bob Ward and left a message on the answering machine, looking frustrated.

Kerry laughed suddenly, and picked up the phone.

''You're right, we are dumb, T.K. No, not dumb. It's what we call in the computer business, 'having infor-mation overload.''' She dialed Blackie's number. She listened to it ring. ''We need connections. Bullets, Rex—everything ties in. Let's find Rex.''

''How?''

''The great thing about searching data bases is cross referencing. We know his first name and we know what kind of car he drives. It'd take a million years to go through the information by hand, but I bet Blackie can do it in a few hours— Don't hang up, it's me, Kerry.'' She explained what she wanted, grinning as Blackie as-sured her it was a piece of cake. She gave Smith a thumbs-up sign. After she hung up, she said, ''It'll take him a while, but he'll find something. He always does.''

She didn't have time to protest when T.K. gathered her into his arms. ''You're not only beautiful, but smart. How did I ever get along without you?'' he asked.

''You seem to have done all right for yourself.'' She

ran her fingertips under his silky lapels. Oh, yes, maybe instincts were the right way to go.

He searched her face. "'All right' isn't good enough, sugar."

She drowned in his eyes, unable to care that he'd caught her looking at him.

"Have I told you how beautiful you look tonight?"

"You're the man with the memory." She ran her hands boldly over his shoulders. "But surely I pale in comparison to you. You have every woman in this house all but drooling." She lifted her face, meeting him halfway.

His kiss was warm, the passion restrained but there. He stroked the sensitive nape of her neck. His fingers raised delicious torment in her. She pressed her softness against his lean, strong body, and her breasts ached with deep demands.

"Really, Kerry," Angela said.

Kerry sprang away from Smith, feeling the blush creep over her cheeks. Her mother grinned wryly from the doorway. She seemed pleased.

"I assure you my intentions toward your daughter are strictly honorable, Mrs. Byfield."

Angela held up a hand. "Don't you dare be honorable, you darling devil. You will sadly disappoint me."

"You two are a match made in heaven," Kerry breathed. She turned to a wall mirror to see if she needed to make any repairs. She fluffed her hair with her fingers and wondered at the odd, soft sparkle in her eyes.

KERRY CAME OUT OF THE bedroom to find Smith reading the Sunday paper. She peered over his shoulder as she poured a cup of coffee. "Seeing if you made the gossip columns?"

"Seeing if Piver took the plunge and got himself hitched." He grinned at her. "I had a good time last night. Angela is quite a lady."

"Do you want to hear what she had to say about you?"

"Sure."

Cocky so and so. Going through life expecting to hear the best. "She said if I let you slip away, then I can consider myself disowned. It's going to be your fault when I break her heart."

He put his gaze back on the paper. "Maybe."

She veered away before giving in to the temptation to run her fingers through his hair. "Did you speak to Bob Ward?"

"He called and left a message at the desk. I called and left a message on his machine." As if in reply the phone rang. Smith answered. "Well, hello, Blackie. Seems I owe you a heap of favors— No kidding. Twenty-seven? Well, hell, I guess it's a start. Read them off to me." He listened, nodding. "Sure enough." He hung up.

"Results?" she asked.

"Sort of." He pulled a legal pad near and jotted down names and numbers and addresses. "Twenty-seven Buicks in the Dallas–Fort Worth area with owners whose first, middle or last names are Rex. Information overload."

"We check them out?"

"Eventually. Grab something to eat while I call John and see how Piver is doing. Maybe John can give us some help on hunting down Rex. Then we'll feed your cats before heading down to Waxahatchie."

Kerry blew a long breath. "Will you think I'm a big chicken if I tell you that Randi Mae scares me?"

He tapped his fingers on the tabletop. "If it makes you feel better, she makes me nervous, too. I have a hunch that when we find Randi Mae, we aren't going to like her."

ROBERT MARSH SIPPED his Bloody Mary as he studied the financial pages. Oil futures dropped again. The cessation of conversation at the adjoining table caught his attention. He glanced up, then did a double take of the woman walking across the restaurant. Petite but rounded, her curvaceous figure was encased in a white Chanel suit. He preferred blondes, but he had to admit this woman was stunning despite her cloud of dark hair. Grinning to himself, he returned to his newspaper.

Chair legs slid on the carpet. Marsh stiffened as the woman took a chair across the table from him. The two men at the adjoining table gave him and her an admiring smile before turning back to their conversation. He almost rose and said, "Please, join me." Instead he lifted a finger to summon the waiter.

"Good morning," Marsh said to her, wishing she'd take off the sunglasses. He had a feeling her eyes were as beautiful as the rest of her. She was about thirty, he judged, and wealthy. It wasn't the clothes; it was how she wore them, with the same sleek assurance a leopard wore fur.

She accepted a menu and unfolded it. Studying it, she asked, "How is their brunch buffet, Robert?"

His left hand crunched the newspaper. He nearly dropped his drink. He opened his mouth to blurt her name, then caught himself. "What...? My God, what are— How did you find me?" He looked around the room to see if anyone he knew was having Sunday brunch.

She smiled, and that he recognized. "You're a creature of habit, Robert. Very predictable. What do you think?" She patted her hair.

The transformation was incredible. She had dark hair and rich, red lipstick and fingernails, and she'd padded her slender figure. She was a different woman. Robert blinked rapidly. "Have you gone crazy? Somebody might recognize you," he whispered.

"You didn't." The waiter appeared and she ordered a Bloody Mary. "I'm quite sick of hiding like some fugitive. And I need to speak to you. Would you prefer I make an appointment with your office?"

Marsh sipped his drink, barely tasting the tangy tomato juice. He forced calm, telling himself that her disguise was good. He doubted her own mother could recognize her. He folded the newspaper and set it aside. "I should have known this wasn't social. What do you need?"

She scraped the linen tablecloth with a bloodred fingernail. "Where is Tarkington Smith?"

Robert lifted his eyebrows and murmured, "How should I know?" He grinned.

"Taking pleasure when I'm concerned is a mistake," she said. "Where is he?"

"He'll show up. Relax. I'm telling you, there's nothing to worry about. Smith is talking to Ward, but Ward can't do anything without Lowell's okay. And Lowell—"

"Something funny is going on. I can feel it, and I don't like it. Nol—" Her head twitched just enough that Robert could tell she was worrying about being overheard. "My gentleman friend is getting nervous. He fired Kerry. I think he wants to protect her."

Marsh concentrated on the remains of his toast, wondering if he should inform her that Smith had made a connection with Nolan Piver. He chewed slowly, thoughtfully. Nolan Piver was a weak link. He could cause a lot of problems if he began talking to the wrong people. Marsh did a quick mental inventory of his own house and office, seeking evidence. There was nothing. He smiled. "I'm afraid your womanly intuition serves you well."

She sat back, and he felt the light brush of her foot against his leg. "Don't toy with me. I am not in the mood."

He watched her closely. "I'm afraid your gentleman friend is talking to the wrong people. Smith knows about him."

Calmly, she said, "How much does he know?"

"That I can't tell you. I only know his name has been mentioned a few times."

The waiter brought her drink. Marsh ordered another for himself. She toyed with the celery stalk in her glass. "What happens if Kerry recants her testimony?" she asked.

"Probably nothing."

"You better find out how Smith connected Nolan," she growled, her voice taking on a furious East Texas twang. She sounded as though she'd come straight out of the boondocks.

The slip from her cultured tones startled him. He gulped the remains of his drink.

"Perhaps Nolan spoke to the wrong people?"

To his surprise, she smiled. In a smooth, even voice,

she said, "I hope not. I'm rather fond of him you know."

Marsh's gut turned gelid. She frightened him. In his years as a prosecutor, he'd run across some very unsavory characters, but this woman was somehow worse. Once he'd imagined that they were equals, but now he realized she was extremely dangerous to everyone she touched, himself included.

She slid a slip of paper across the table. There was a phone number on it. "You find out how much Smith knows and where he is. Call me." She rose and gathered her lizard clutch. Looking down at him, she added, "I've come too far. I'm not about to give up now." She started to turn, then stopped. Very soft, very low, she said, "Everyone loves a dirty politician, but nobody votes for him."

He watched her walk away and then watched other men watching the graceful swing of her hips. *Beware of that one. She's a real man-eater.* He dabbed his lips with a napkin. A spot of bloody red on the white linen made his heart skip a beat. It was tomato juice. He chuckled at himself.

Still, he *had* been wondering where Smith was getting his information. It might be a good idea to find out just in case Smith's sources led too close to home. He snapped open his newspaper and resumed reading.

Chapter Eleven

Kerry fiddled with the radio tuner, trying to find something other than gospel music or Sunday-morning fire-and-brimstone preaching. She found a rock-and-roll station, but it faded in and out. She caught Smith frowning at the rearview mirror.

"What's the matter?" she asked, looking behind them. Few cars were traveling Interstate 35 on the way to Waxahatchie.

"We picked up some company," he said. He scooted forward. "Pull the seat and get my rifle."

"Rifle?" She gawked, certain he'd finally snapped. "This isn't funny."

"I noticed him doing some fancy shuffling downtown. He keeps passing other cars, but he's making a point to stay behind us."

"John said Piver's at home—"

"I'm thinking about Rex. Maybe we won't have to find him. Maybe he's found us."

Kerry unbuckled her seat belt and turned around to reach behind the seat. "How?"

Smith made a musing noise. "When we fed the cats possibly." He slowed the truck. A Cadillac with Arizona plates passed them. "Can you reach it?"

"This thing in the yellow case?" She strained, closing her fingers over the leather.

"You know how to load it?"

She shook her head, sheepishly. "Daddy always said he'd take me out to the rifle range someday, but Mom never allowed it." She rebuckled her seat belt, then unzipped the rifle case. The .30-30's walnut stock gleamed darkly, beautifully...and deadly. It smelled of metallic oil. She looked behind them again. "The yellow car? Is it a Buick?"

"It's a Toyota or a Honda. He's hanging back too far for me to tell. There's a box of shells in the glove department. We'll get off on 77, and see if he follows— Don't point that at me, sugar."

Kerry tried to match Smith's calm, but she dropped the box of ammunition on the floor and knocked the window with the rifle barrel. He grinned at her. She muttered, "Oh, boy, cowboys and Indians. I'll probably shoot off my toe."

"What's that, sugar?"

"Nothing. Is he still following us? I haven't the faintest idea what to do with this thing."

Smith put on the turn signal. He picked up 77 south toward Waxahatchie. The yellow car followed, but lengthened the distance. Smith picked up speed.

"What are you doing?" Kerry demanded, looking through the back window. The yellow car fell farther and farther behind.

"Looking for a farm road. Switch seats with me."

"While you're driving?"

"Don't tell me you're so pure you never did it as a kid?"

She didn't like the look in those sparkling, midnight blue eyes. She unbuckled her seat belt as he eased up on the gas. She unbuckled his seat belt, then maneuvered to put her right foot on the gas pedal. She ootched and scootched, wondering if her mother wasn't right about her being too broad in the beam as she worked her way under him. He was heavier than he looked. The truck bounced and he squashed her into the seat.

"I kind of like this," he said with a snicker before he relinquished the gas pedal completely.

"I have the wheel," she growled. "Move over."

"There's a sign for Garrett. There should be a turn-off. Take it. It doesn't matter which direction. He's catching up. Maybe he doesn't want us to get to Waxahatchie." Smith pulled back the bolt handle and slipped shells into the chamber with smooth expertise.

"Fasten my seat belt please."

"Relax, you're doing fine." He fastened her seat belt, then patted her cheek and winked.

"I'd like this better if you didn't like it so much. He probably has a gun."

"This ain't chicken livers, sugar," he said as he shot the bolt with an oily click. "There's the exit. When you get on the farm road, slow down. Let him know we know he's there."

With both hands on the wheel, Kerry concentrated on the road. She adjusted the rearview mirror and gasped when she saw that the yellow car was just a few lengths behind them.

"Hit the brakes."

She stomped on the pedal, crying out as the truck's tires squealed and the rear end slewed. She yelled a warning as the yellow car veered widely to the right then to the left. It missed the truck's bumper by inches. The car, a Honda, shot past them.

Rolling down the window, Smith said, "Catch him." He poked the rifle barrel out the window.

Kerry stomped on the gas. The big engine roared; the speedometer climbed quickly. The Honda braked, then made a sharp turn onto a dirt road. Kerry chased the cloud of dust, concentrating on the rutted road.

"Get up beside him," Smith yelled. She imagined him adding a whoop of glee.

"He's rolling down his window!" she cried.

"I see him. Duck down as low as you can."

Kerry heard a sharp report. She muttered, "It's just a backfire...."

Flat farm country, dotted with windswept houses and oil donkeys, flew past. Wind whistled through the open window, chilling Kerry. She wished she'd worn a coat, then wished she were at home, cleaning her apartment or reading a novel. She eased the truck up beside the Honda and saw the driver reach over, with a gun in his right hand.

Smith hung out the window, the rifle barrel between the bars that supported the side-view mirror. "Slow down, sugar," he said, calmly.

She eased up on the gas pedal, praying nobody decided to come down the road from the opposite direction. She heard that terrible cracking again and saw the Honda driver's hand jerk. Then a thunderclap punched Kerry's ears. She rocked on the seat, instinctively hitting the brake. Smith caught himself before he tumbled out the window.

"Sorry," she whispered.

The Honda slewed, the rear end fishtailing dangerously and spewing gravel.

She breathed, "What the—"

"Bingo," Smith said. "Got the tire. Now ease on

down the road. He can't get far." To Kerry's wondering awe he said, "Chuck Connors as the Rifleman was my hero when I was a kid. Not bad shooting, if I do say so myself. There he is. Stay down. Stop here."

She stopped, her hands aching from clutching the steering wheel. Her heart fluttered, and her chest felt too small for her lungs. She put the transmission in Park, muttering. "This isn't worth one fifty a day."

"Okay, one seventy-five, and you can drive. Get your head down." Smith leaned out the window and propped the rifle against his shoulder. He shouted, "Throw out the gun and get out of the car!"

Kerry peeked over the dashboard. She saw a stealthy movement and opened her mouth to warn Smith, but that thunderclap sounded again. She ducked, clapping her hands over her ears.

Smith shouted. "Next one is in your gas tank!"

The Honda's door opened. A handgun skittered across the gravel. A man emerged slowly, his hands held high. Kerry recognized the man from the Sheraton hotel's hallway. He still wore the cheap brown suit.

Smith left the truck, his rifle held at waist level. To Kerry he said, "There's a set of handcuffs in the glove compartment." He advanced on the man, ordered him to turn around, then he picked up the pistol and stuck it in his belt.

Keeping a wary eye on the man, Kerry gave Smith the handcuffs. She didn't breathe until the man's hands were cuffed securely behind him.

She noticed the Honda's side mirror in the dust. The .30-30 bullet had ripped it off the car. The left rear tire was completely flat, trailing strips of dusty rubber and spikes of steel belting. Smith was a good shot, indeed.

"How you doing?" Smith asked pleasantly. "Buick

in the shop?'' He pushed the man to a sitting position on the side of the road, flipping the rifle over his forearm in a casually deadly manner. The man cursed. ''You got a dirty mouth in front of a lady, boy.'' Smith said. ''Want me to clean it out for you?''

The man glared murderously. He had pale blue eyes, cold and flat as a doll's glass eyes. ''What are you going to do, cowboy? Call the cops? It's my word against yours. You're the one who shot up my car. I was just protecting myself against a nut.''

''I'm not interested in dealing with the Waxahatchie Police Department. I figure that might spoil an otherwise lovely Sunday afternoon.'' Smith beckoned Kerry with a curt nod. She edged behind him, gasping when he gave her the rifle; its weight made her lurch. ''Keep an eye on him, sugar. If he moves, shoot him.'' Smith was wearing that devilish smile, but it didn't touch his eyes. ''And make it a clean kill. Don't gut shoot him like you did the last one.''

Avoiding the trigger, Kerry clamped her grip on the rifle. She spread her legs in a tough stance and flipped her hair. She scowled at the man.

Smith whistled while he searched the Honda. Kerry thought the tune was ''Crazy'' by Willie Nelson. He emerged from the front seat with a gun in a case. He said, ''You going to war?''

''I have permits for those. You ain't got no warrant. That's illegal.''

''I'm not a cop.'' Smith opened the trunk. ''Now I wonder which one of these, the .38 or the 9 mm, matches up to the gun that killed a certain Thomas Nordoff back in June? Inquiring cops want to know.''

''I don't know what you're talking about.'' Sweat beaded on the man's forehead and upper lip.

"That little freak you sent to hurt my lady friend has been doing a lot of talking about you. Want to hear what he has to say?"

"You're blowing air, cowboy."

"We're talking conspiracy to commit murder. Who are you willing to take a fall for?" Smith pulled back the carpet that lined the trunk. "Randi Mae Firkins? Nolan Piver?"

"Never heard of them. You got nothing."

"What about this?" T.K. held out a Ziploc bag full of white powder.

"You ain't got a warrant to search my car. You just made that inadmissible, stupid."

T.K. stuck a moistened finger in the bag. He touched his tongue to his whitened finger, then spit, grimacing. He zipped the bag shut. "This crap will fry your brain. But you're too smart to indulge, aren't you? You just give it away."

"What is that?" Kerry asked.

"Cocaine," Smith replied. He knelt in front of the man, pulled back the brown jacket and slipped the bag into the breast pocket. "That's yours I believe. Now let's talk. Tell me about the Abernathy murder. Who killed Louise Abernathy? Did Thomas Nordoff pull the trigger? Who killed Nordoff?"

"I don't know nothing about it."

"Want to hear what I think? I think when I turn you in, there's going to be some warrants issued to search your place of residence. I think the police are going to turn up a snow storm in Dallas, and I bet there're a few more pistols where these two came from. I bet at least one them, if not one of these, matches up to a bullet in the back of the head of a cocaine dealer."

"Go to—"

Smith lifted an eyebrow, looking dangerous.

"You ain't got nothing on me."

"Let's take a little ride and find out. Kerry, drop the tailgate." He rummaged around behind the truck seat, coming up with a feed sack bearing the words Red Rose Seed and Feed. He slipped it over the man's head and secured it loosely with a length of baling twine. He wrestled the man into the back of the truck. "Enjoy the ride, partner," he said, slamming the tailgate.

"Where are we taking him?" Kerry whispered.

"I don't know yet. I have to make some phone calls first."

She settled herself in the truck and looked back at their prisoner. There was something horribly funny about the sight of the man on his side with a feed sack over his head. "You're crazy, do you know that?"

"That's why you love me."

She shot Smith a how-do-you-know look, but his attention was elsewhere. Another smart-aleck remark, she told herself. She pushed it from mind.

He handed her the man's wallet. "Go through there and see if you find anything."

She pulled out his driver's license. "Martin Rex Sondervon."

Smith laughed.

"What's funny?"

"Number sixteen on the Buick list. That rocket scientist just saved us a few days of looking."

Smith stopped at a gas station. While Kerry gassed up the truck, watching Rex all the while, Smith went to a pay phone. Kerry smiled at a carload of teenagers and tried to act nonchalant about the hooded man in the truck bed. Smith came back smiling and gave her a thumbs-up.

"Bob Ward and Ed Shanlin will meet us in Plano."

"Did you tell him about the guy who looks like Abernathy?"

"He said he'll make some phone calls."

They made good time to Plano. Sunday traffic was light. It struck Kerry as funny that Smith pulled into the Plano Place shopping center and parked in front of Copy Copy. She didn't know why it was funny. Was Smith's craziness infectious? Or was it nervous exhaustion? Maybe she was plain cracking up.

Bob Ward and Detective Shanlin were waiting for them.

Smith dropped the tailgate. "I made a citizen's arrest, Ward. This jerk was talking foul in front of the lady." He handed over the two guns. "You might turn up some interesting ballistics out of these."

Ward jerked a gnarled thumb at Shanlin. "Another believer for you, Smith."

Shanlin was a slope-shouldered bear of a man. Kerry remembered him from the original investigation. He looked as stone faced as she remembered. Shanlin did an admirable job of hiding his snickers as he took the hood off Rex's head. Rex's skin had a sickly green tinge under a coating of yellowish powder. The detective placed him under arrest and read him rights. Rex was stonily silent when frisked. When Shanlin found the cocaine, Rex's only comment was to demand a lawyer.

Kerry leaned against the truck and told Ward, "When T.K. showed me that picture of the cocaine dealer, I saw Abernathy. I know it's a coincidence, but it seems too weird. I honestly believe somebody used me as a witness in a setup. That makes me as guilty as they are for ruining William Abernathy's life."

Ward made a noncommittal noise. "Now what is this about ballistics?"

Smith explained that the bullets in the Nova might match those in Thomas Nordoff's body.

"Possible, but not likely. Still, I can get that checked for you."

Smith blew out a long breath and jammed his hands in his jeans pockets. "Well, at least we've got one part of the conspiracy solved. When that kid gets finished IDing Rex, Rex will probably have all—"

Ward shook his head and lit a cigarette, cupping his hand around a match to keep out the wind. He blew a big cloud of smoke. "The kid is in bad shape, Smith. He's in the hospital now. Detox. He can't point out his own face in a mirror, much less give us a positive on Rex."

"As long as Rex doesn't know that, then you can use what the kid has said already."

"Figger it," Ward said with a snort. "Rex knows more than we do what happens to a dope head in a detox ward. I bet he's counting on it. But we can hold Rex on possession with intent to deal. I can talk the judge into setting a high bail. I reckon if Rex sits around in lockup long enough, he'll get to thinking about the basic unfairness of life. He might decide to do a little dealing."

"Some names in exchange for dropping the cocaine bust?" Smith asked.

Ward flicked his ashes. "That might happen. Then again, it might not. You're dealing with some smart folks."

"Nobody is that smart."

Kerry thought about Blackie and knew better.

Shanlin joined them. Ward exchanged a knowing

look with the detective, and said, "I got to warn you. Lowell's on the warpath, Smith. I tried out your conspiracy theory on him and he's taking it as a personal affront."

Kerry huffed at the unfairness. "Personal? What about the people who are trying to kill me?"

Ward dropped the cigarette and crushed it under his heel. "I ain't talking against you, miss. I'm just saying ain't nobody, especially people in elected office, likes to admit they slaughtered the wrong cow. So you two watch your step."

Kerry signed a statement giving Detective Shanlin permission to search her Nova for bullets. After Ward and the detective left, Kerry muttered, "I can't believe this. I thought the police and everybody in the Justice department were devoted to the pursuit of truth and justice. That shows how stupid I am."

"They're just people, sugar. No different than anyone else trying to do a job." Smith draped an arm over her shoulders. "We just have to try harder to find some evidence. We have two believers, though. Ward's a good man, and so is Shanlin. Shanlin did a good job in the initial investigation, and now that he realizes he might have screwed up, he'll do his best to fix things. We can't ask for anything better. Want a frozen yogurt?"

SMITH CALLED JOHN FROM the phone outside the yogurt shop. Concentrating on events and trying to make connections, Kerry leaned against the wall, half listening to him talk. Then he reeled off a familiar phone number and she snapped to attention. Smith hung up.

"Why did you give him Copy Copy's number?"

"Because Piver is at the Lambeck Quality Care nursing home, and John is watching him. Let's go on over to Copy Copy.''

"That's breaking and entering.''

"You have the key and there's nothing to worry about. John has his car phone. The minute Piver gets in his car, John'll call us.'' He took her hand. "Come on, sugar. These are desperate times that call for desperate measures. We've got less than three days before Bill's sentencing date. After that, he goes to prison.''

Wishing Smith hadn't said that, Kerry protested. "I think we'll make more progress trying to find Randi Mae.''

"We'll find her. But—'' Smith gave her a far-too-innocent look "—as long as we're here, let's see what old Nolan is hiding in his closets.''

He led her around the corner.

Kerry tried to justify her actions as she unlocked the door to Copy Copy. She looked right and left to make sure the coast was clear, then slipped inside. She winced as the doorbell tinkled. Smith locked the door behind them and urged her to open Piver's office. Kerry tried her key, but it didn't fit. She muttered a curse. "He changed the lock.''

Smith pulled out a folding pocket knife. He crouched before the door. Kerry gawked as he hummed and picked the lock. Once the door was open, they shut themselves in the office and turned on the light.

"What are we looking for?'' she whispered.

"Whatever we can find. What does he keep in there?'' he pointed to a four-drawer, metal filing cabinet.

"Equipment brochures, contracts and customer credit forms. Our regular customers are billed monthly. He keeps it locked." She arched an eyebrow. "I don't have the key."

Smith took out the knife again and unfolded a very thin blade. He jimmied open the cabinet's lock.

She was amused despite the circumstances. "Where did you learn how to do that?"

"Boy Scouts." He rummaged through the top drawer.

Kerry turned to Piver's desk. She groaned. Next to the telephone was the business card that Smith had left. It had the Sheraton hotel's phone number inked on it. That explained how Rex had found them. In the middle drawer, she found a jewelry box. She opened it and gasped. "Look."

In turn, they studied a set of wedding rings. A carved gold wedding band and a large marquis diamond in a matching setting.

"That's at least two full carats. Maybe two and a half." She whistled her appreciation. "Or three carats. That's a big rock."

"At least they aren't married yet."

"Why does that bother you? What difference does it make?" she asked.

Smith turned back to the filing cabinet. "What bothers me is that Piver isn't running. He's got to stick around because of the person in the nursing home. But what's holding Randi Mae?"

"Piver."

"Right. And the fact that all that cash is flowing into his bank accounts. It's money she can't touch until she's Mrs. Piver." Smith leaned his elbow against the cabinet. "Or better yet, what happens if Randi Mae turns out to be the Widow Piver?"

"You think she's going to kill him?" Kerry looked at the diamond ring in a fresh, horrific light.

"It wouldn't surprise me, especially since the longer she sticks around and the closer we get, the greater her chances are of losing everything. You called Piver a wheeler-dealer, penny ante. Maybe you were right when you said he isn't a murderer. He's an extortionist, definitely willing to defraud the IRS, but maybe he isn't a murderer. That leaves Randi Mae."

He opened the second file drawer. "Bingo."

Kerry breathed out, "Wow." The leather cases held bound stacks of twenty- fifty- and hundred-dollar bills. She said, "Do you think Mr. Ward will mind coming back down here?"

"After what he said about Lowell? We can't call him in on this. This is only proof of our suspicions. Like he said, we can't prove this came out of Louise Abernathy's purse."

"So we leave it here?"

"At the rate Piver's going, it will take about a year to squirrel this into his bank accounts." Smith paused, chewing his lower lip.

Kerry stared at the money. The longer she stared, the angrier she grew. All her life she'd tried to do the right things. Her dad had taught her that. He had said the best people were honest when they didn't have to be. They did the right thing even if it hurt them. Kerry believed him then, and she believed him now.

Piver and Randi Mae had used her. Piver knew Kerry never tried to cover up her mistakes, but instead explained them to customers and made things right. He knew she never played hooky, and that she pointed out errors on her paycheck, even when they were in her favor. He had known that when she saw a man running out of the Abernathy house, she would get involved.

"Righteous indignation," she muttered.

"What's that?"

"You know how you can go your whole life hearing something, even saying it, and not know what it means? I just figured out what 'righteous indignation' means. Grab that other bag and see if there's any more money. I know how to stop Piver and Randi Mae from running." The other bag was as full of money as the first.

Kerry urged Smith to follow her into the back room. She closed the door, then turned on the lights. Her drawing table was exactly as she'd left it. Everything was exactly as she'd left it. That fueled her anger. Piver didn't care about her; he didn't care about his customers.

She pointed to a tall stack of cardboard boxes. Each box held ten reams of copier paper. As she and Smith moved boxes, she explained, "If—and that's a big if— we're wrong, I don't want Piver arresting me for theft. But if we hide the money…"

"Panic. Mayhem. I like the way you think."

Kerry carefully worked the shipping straps off the fifth box from the top of the stack. She mingled the reams of paper with the open inventory on the wooden shelves near the door. She said, "Piver always left this back room to me. I hope he's as unobservant as I accuse him of being."

They placed the money into the box, then worked the nylon shipping straps back into place, then restacked the boxes until everything looked as it had before.

"Too bad the whole shebang isn't in cash," Smith said. "This stops Randi Mae, but we could still lose Piver. Let's go see what else he's hiding in the office."

The resumed search was fruitless. They found no guns or incriminating photographs. Even Piver's books were missing. Kerry did find a floppy disk holder with eight disks inside. She puzzled over them. She'd taught Piver the rudiments of how to use a word processor, a basic spreadsheet and a data-base program. He kept the inventory on computer and also generated the monthly billing. Those files were with the rest in the back room. It seemed out of place for him to keep floppy disks in his desk.

"What do you have?" Smith asked as he scratched his head and studied a cardboard box full of advertising flyers.

"Disks. I don't dare fire up the computer. Mall security might see us through the window." She held out the orange box. "Do you think it's safe to go to my apartment? I doubt very much this is anything, but who knows? Maybe Piver wrote letters to Randi Mae."

"Or something even stupider. We can risk it. We'll swing by later and put them back."

AT HER APARTMENT surrounded by ecstatic and loudly complaining cats, Kerry turned on her computer. Smith rummaged in the kitchen for something to eat. Kerry called up a utilities program, then inserted a floppy disk, and asked for a directory of files. "Not so dumb after all," she said with a disgusted snort. "He's locked the files."

"What does that mean?"

"He's encrypted those files. I need a password in order to run them." She read the remaining seven disks. The majority were spreadsheet files, a few were word-processor files. All were encrypted. "It was stupid of me to teach him about that."

"Do you know how to find a password?"

"It can be anything. A word, a number, a string of nonsense. Maybe Blackie knows how to bypass the file encryption."

She went to the phone. Her answering machine blinked. She pushed the playback button. Her mother had left two messages. Someone had called three times and hung up without leaving a message. That gave her the creeps, but she told herself it was probably telephone solicitors. She started to dial Blackie's number, then stopped and hung up. She clapped her hands.

"Idea?" Smith asked.

"You bet. Write down all of Piver's bank account numbers for me—I know you remember them. I think there might be a way to keep Piver from running. If nothing else, we can slow him down."

Smith wrote down a string of bank names and account numbers. When Kerry reached Blackie, she said, "Hey, two big favors. This one you're really going to like. Remember when you asked if I wanted you to clean out Piver's hard disks? Want to go one better?"

Blackie chortled. "I think this new friend of yours is a bad influence, Kerry. What do you want?"

"Can you lock somebody's bank accounts? You know, freeze them, zero them out. One of those I'm-so-sorry-but-the-computer-made-a-mistake things?"

"It's possible."

"How possible?"

"Remember who you're talking to. Of course, you realize that banks don't rely solely on computer records. They back everything up."

"I only need to foul things up until Wednesday. I have all his account numbers. Got a pencil?" She gave him the information. "Now, the next favor. I have some of Piver's files, but they're encrypted. How do I bypass the password protection?''

"What kind of files?''

"Spreadsheet, word-processor and commercial programs.''

"You don't. I can if you want me to modify the original programs.''

"I don't have the time. So how do I find the password?''

Blackie chewed loudly on something. He finally said, "Smart people use nonsense, a string of meaningless letters and numbers. Ninety-nine point nine percent of people don't. They use something they can remember because they're scared to death they can't get back into their files. Most just use the word *password.*''

Kerry laughed softly.

"Try his name, his birthday, his Social Security number. Find something Piver will remember. If you get stuck, call me back. I can set up a random computer check for you. You probably won't need it. Think simple.''

"Thanks. You're a lifesaver.''

"You owe me some groceries.''

Kerry hung up and grinned smugly at Smith. He pushed a ham sandwich and a glass of Coke in front of her.

"Can Blackie freeze the accounts?''

"If anyone can.''

"Remind me to never get on that boy's bad side.'' He leaned on the counter and took her hand, entwining her slim fingers with his. "I couldn't have done this without you.''

"Piver is doing it to himself. We're just nudging

him." It grew impossible to look at his face. She dropped her gaze.

She studied his hand. A heavy callous rimmed the web between his thumb and forefinger. She remembered he had said he owned horses, and she wondered if the callouses came from holding the reins. She envisioned him riding the range, his cowboy hat pulled low… She was riding behind him, off into the sunset.

"Can I ask you a personal question? Do you come on to every girl you meet?"

"Only the pretty ones."

She shot him a hard look.

He tapped her chin lightly with a finger. "Want the truth, Kerry? When I saw you that first time in the shop, you looked so prim and pretty. Then you smiled, and you were beautiful. This old heart did a flip-flop." He kissed her hand. "It hasn't done that since I was thirteen and fell in love with Miss Carter, my English teacher. She married a truck driver and broke my heart."

"What are you saying?" *Too good to be true. Too good to be true.* The words played over and over in her head.

"That I'm looking to shake up your life and see what happens. I'm not toying with your affections, if that's what bothers you."

"We barely know each other." Oh, God, she thought frantically, how long *had* she known him? It felt like forever. "I admit that you are a very attractive man, and I like you…" The words trailed away. Caught in the spell of his hypnotic gaze, she could almost hear the wall of reluctance falling away, brick by brick. Eyelids lowered, she cocked her head slightly, desiring the feel of his lips against hers.

The phone startled her. She jumped, pulling away.

Breathlessly, she said, "It's Mom, probably. Oh, I don't want to talk to her right now."

The answering machine activated. Kerry's voice said, "Hi, this is Kerry. I'm busy right now, but if you'll leave your name and number, I'll get back to you as soon as possible." The beep sounded.

"Are you there? Please pick up the phone.... Damn it," a woman said. Then the connection broke.

Chapter Twelve

"That wasn't Mom," Kerry said, and played back the tape. The soft, "Damn it," spoke volumes of frustration.

"Recognize her?"

Kerry's stomach knotted at the sound of that cool, silky voice. She took a deep breath. "Piver's mystery woman." She loosed a nervous chuckle. "Randi Mae."

"She's getting panicky. Rex was probably supposed to check in." He gestured at the sandwich. "Eat up. She doesn't know where Rex is, and she doesn't know where we are. We have time to see what Piver has to hide."

Kerry locked the front door before she sat down at the computer. When she opened her word-processing program and inserted Piver's disk, the first word she tried was *password*. An error message appeared. She tried Nolan's first name, last name, middle name and then various combinations.

Error.

"Why does it show up as asterisks?" Smith asked.

"So no one can read over my shoulder." He took an automatic step backward, and she giggled. "All of them do that. Give me his Social Security number."

She tried every number Smith knew. Piver's driver's license, car tags, business license, bank-account numbers, phone numbers, addresses and birthday.

"Do you ever forget anything?" she asked as she stared at the latest error message.

"Nope. Not even when I try. Fortunately, it seems I have unlimited storage space."

"How do you keep it straight?" She tried *Copy Copy*. Error.

"I don't know exactly."

Smith looked as though he had a story to tell. She urged him to speak. "I took part in a research study at MIT one summer. I learned I can recall numbers faster than words, and that I'm not infallible. Sometimes names transpose with the wrong events. Sometimes I move chunks of lists or a stanza of a poem into the wrong place. I don't forget the words, just the proper order. It's sort of a breakdown in the cross-reference files.

"I also learned that memory and intelligence don't mean the same thing. Just like that computer, I can take in the data, but then it takes thinking to figure out how to use it."

"Amazing. Sometimes I forget my own birthday."

"That's what calendars are for. Sometimes I rely too much on memory and it makes me dumb. I forget to think." He chewed his lower lip, then said, "Try *Eustis*."

She typed in the word, chuckling when Smith told her it was Piver's mother's maiden name. Then she tried his ex-wife's name. They tried *Texas* and *Plano* and *Dallas*. The names of football teams, the makes of cars, the brand names of copiers and computers. She tried words like *yuppie, wheeler-dealer, money, blue chip, stock, bonds* and *millionaire.* Kerry growled each time the error message mocked her. She glanced at her watch. It was nearly nine o'clock. She wondered where the day had gone.

"Try *Randi Mae.*"

She did, trying every possible combination, including typing the name backward. Error. Frustrated, she typed in one more name, then reached for the escape key in anticipation of the next error message. The file directory opened.

"What worked?" Smith asked, sounding as surprised as she felt.

"You aren't going to believe this. *Louise.*"

"Isn't it funny what guilt will do to a man," Smith said, shaking his shaggy head.

Kerry opened the first file. It was a letter to an insurance agent, requesting increased life insurance. Piver wanted the beneficiary changed from April Eustis Piver to the Lambeck Quality Care nursing home. Guilt tweaked Kerry. It was his mother, after all. Another letter to the same agent asked about the possibility of reducing his car-insurance rates. Kerry went quickly to the next file.

"He's a crappy typist," Kerry muttered as they went through all the letters, finding nothing incriminating. "I told him if he'd take the time to proofread, he could correct his typos. That's all the letter files, T.K. We bombed on this one."

"Check the others."

She exited the word-processing program, then called up her spreadsheet. She inserted a file disk. The password *Louise* gained them entry.

"Here's how he's trying to launder the cash," she said. "I can't believe how blatant this is. I know for a fact Copy Copy can't bring in that kind of money on daily cash receipts. It isn't physically possible. He's stupid.''

"Maybe not, look there." There was a slight static crackle as Smith touched the screen with his fingertip. "He's covering his tail with the IRS by increasing his estimated corporate taxes. And he's calling these entries business loans. It'll take a full audit to disclose that this is phony. Still, it doesn't connect him to the murder. Try another file."

Most of the files were simple checkbook ledgers. They read each one carefully, but didn't find anything. Frustrated, Kerry printed a hard copy of all the files, then slipped the disks back into the orange plastic case. "Now what?"

"We still have a report to finish for Bob Ward. Let me check in with John. We'll put those disks back before we go back to the hotel."

Smith called John. From his facial expression, Kerry guessed he'd learned something interesting. After hanging up, he said, "Piver is over at Copy Copy."

Kerry dropped the box of computer disks onto the countertop and stared at them in guilty horror. "What if he calls the police about the missing money? Or these? He knows I have keys to the shop."

"I doubt he wants the police involved." Smith rubbed his chin, thoughtfully. "It might not hurt to put some pressure on the two of them. I figure he doesn't trust Randi Mae. His first thought is going to be that she ripped him off. Of course, she's going to think the same thing about him. We'll just hold—" The devilish grin appeared. "How long before Blackie locks those bank accounts?" Kerry shook her head. "Find out, sugar. Then you can get even with Piver for firing you."

"How?"

"We know Piver didn't pull the trigger. That's a physical fact. He might be willing to cut a deal if we give him immunity from the IRS."

"I don't get it."

"We know Piver is laundering money. Maybe he can make it look good on the surface, but he knows it'll never stand up. And any wheeler-dealer worth his name knows you don't mess around with the IRS. If we convince Piver you've gone to the IRS already, maybe he'll start talking about Randi Mae in order to cut a deal."

"Will the IRS make a deal like that? Immunity from prosecution in exchange for information about a murder?"

"Nope, but I bet Piver doesn't know that."

She giggled and covered her mouth. "That's cheating, T.K."

"That's right." He looked at the phone. "Find out how Blackie is doing. Then we'll give Piver a little nudge."

She called Blackie. He said, "That was too easy. Ah, the wonders of modern banking."

"I don't want to hear how you did it. But it's done? You've frozen all his bank accounts?"

"I even canceled his credit cards for him."

She laughed so hard—whether from humor or nervousness she wasn't sure—she nearly dropped the phone. "Are you certain nobody can trace this stuff back to you?"

"Sure I'm sure. Want anything else? Ruining Piver's day is getting to be a pleasant habit. I never liked that bozo."

"You never met him."

"You told me enough about him. Oh, by the way,

you're overdrawn on your checking account. Did you remember to deduct your service charges?''

She huffed in exasperation. "You aren't supposed to be looking at mine, Blackie."

"Want me to do a little fund transfer for you?"

"Don't you dare. Thanks for everything. And by the way, we found the password. I thought simple, just like you said. Talk to you later." She hung up. "It's done."

"Now leave a message on Piver's answering machine." Smith coached her on what to say.

Mustering a vindictive tone was easy. At the beep she said, "Mr. Piver, firing me was a mean thing to do. You know I never stole anything from you. Besides, you're the thief. As soon as I get through talking to the tax guys, you're in a lot of trouble. You shouldn't have fired me." She slammed down the handset. "Think that will panic him?" she asked.

"I'm counting on it."

On the way out, Kerry asked her neighbors to take care of her cats for a few days. Eyeing Smith wistfully, Becky Sind said she'd love to do it.

Kerry checked her mailbox. On the ride to the hotel she leafed through a bundle of advertising circulars, an invitation to buy a series of books about computer programming, and a notice that her driver's license was about to expire.

"Big deal," she snorted. "My car is full of holes and I don't have any checks to cash anyway. Who needs a driver's license?" She glared balefully at Smith. "I used to have a simple life."

"How about a change of venue, sugar? Ever been to Houston?"

She slouched on the seat. "Home, Smith. We have work to do."

KERRY BLINKED BLEARILY AT the clock next to the bed—7:30 a.m. Habits were hard to break even when she was exhausted. Her fingers and wrists ached. Smith's report had run to seventeen pages, and the typewriter had a harder touch than a computer keyboard. She lay quietly, staring at the ceiling, hoping Becky remembered her promise to feed the cats this morning.

Kerry's thoughts drifted to last night and the way Smith had massaged her stiff neck and shoulders as she hunched over the typewriter. His invitation was unspoken, but clear. She wondered if she was an idiot for not going to bed with him. *What are you doing to me, you crazy person,* she thought as she stretched. Actually, she knew what he was doing. He was making her rethink her reluctance to involve herself.

Other than deciding on the spur of the moment to take in an occasional movie, she'd never done anything really impulsive in her life. When she was a kid, she'd planned to go to college, and when her family settled in Texas, she'd carefully researched the local colleges and universities. Her search had been methodical. She'd known her major, computer sciences, before she'd graduated from high school. She'd selected her apartment for price and location. She made grocery lists and stuck to them.

Kerry's thoughts drifted to Mike. Even that had been planned, a perfect romance full of the best restaurants, weekend trips to the trendiest ski resorts, evenings at the most exclusive clubs and fraternity parties where Mike passed out his business cards and networked with all the right people.

Yes, care and planning equaled perfection. Mike and Kerry, a fairy tale. They'd never fought, never disagreed. Even their intimacy had been carefully staged and was always romantic, according to the latest issue of *Cosmopolitan* magazine. Mike had been comfortable and predictable, and a romance made college seem easier. Looking back, she realized she'd cared for him, but had never loved him. She'd never felt that spark of anticipation before seeing him or felt jangled up inside when he touched her. Looking into his eyes had been…just looking. Perhaps he never loved her, either. Maybe that was why it had been easy to go their separate ways.

Smith rapped on the door, calling, "Rise and shine, sugar. We've got work to do."

"I'm awake."

She sat up. A flash of color caught her eye. On the double bed's other pillow lay a single, perfect red rose. And a pink paper packet of sugar. An image of Smith watching her sleep crystallized in her mind. A rush of pure, smoking sexual desire surged through her body.

She held the rose to her lips, amused, bemused and completely befuddled that he could make her crazy without even touching her. As she passed the bathroom mirror, she caught her smile. It made her look like an idiot.

After she showered and dressed in a pair of jeans and a purplish-gray sweater, she joined him in the suite's sitting room. Glasses on, he was reading the business section of the newspaper while he ate breakfast. A blue-plaid flannel shirt brought out the lights in his eyes. Kerry drank in the details. The veins on the back of his hands, the way he piled eggs on a piece of toast, the sprinkling of sugar packets across the table, and how he used a knuckle to nudge his glasses higher. In passing, she kissed his cheek, warmed by the spicy scent of his after-shave.

"What was that for?" he asked. He removed his glasses and stuck them in his pocket.

"I'm starting to like you." She sat and looked with interest at the breakfast he'd ordered through room service.

"I knew you would." He poured fresh coffee into his cup and filled hers. "I hope that report is enough to get Ward into Piver's house. I called John already. He said Piver left Copy Copy in a big hurry last night. Smoking tires and all."

"Where did he go?"

Smith made a disgusted face. "Straight home. Where do you think Randi Mae is hiding herself?"

"It didn't sound long distance when she called last night."

"Eat up. Maybe we can catch her today in Waxahatchie."

Kerry ate heartily, enjoying a Spanish omelet and biscuits. Smith made small talk about an article he'd read in the paper. Had she, she wondered, thought Mike comfortable? This was comfortable: great food and that warm, Texan drawl caressing her ears.

She smacked her forehead with the heel of a hand. "I better call Mom. Otherwise she'll be calling Copy Copy. There's no telling what Piver will say to her."

Angela immediately scolded Kerry for her lack of concern. Didn't she know how much her poor, lonely mother cherished their long Sunday afternoon chats?

Kerry interrupted, "I was with T.K., Mom. Sorry. I lost track of time."

"Oh, that's different. Really, darling, where did you find him? He's what I wanted to talk to you about anyway. He's divine."

"He's not too bad." She mouthed, "Mom thinks

you're divine." Smith chortled, nearly choking on his coffee. Then to her mother, she said, "Look, I've got to go to work, but I promise to call you later."

"I want you to do better, darling. I want you to bring T.K. over to the house for dinner. It's very informal, just the three of us. I had so little time to get to know him. I'm dying for details."

"Uh, that's not really possible. T.K. is tied up until Thursday at least—"

"Thursday evening then. I'm writing you down in my book right now. How about something simple? Steak and baked potatoes? Belinda has this heavenly new recipe. Triple-baked potatoes instead of boring old double-baked."

"Can I call you back on this?"

"If you promise to call. Really! Even your friends are calling here looking for you. That answering machine of yours is no excuse for rudeness. I taught you better manners."

"Who called?" Kerry caught Smith's attention.

She had to wait for Angela to call Belinda to fetch the messages. She held her hand over the mouthpiece and whispered, "Somebody's been calling my mother— Yes, I'm still here."

"A woman named Jane called. She said you know the number. And Mr. Piver called, too. What a strange man. How you can stand to work for him is beyond me."

"When did Piver call?"

"Last night about—oh, dear, about eleven-thirty or so. He was rather rude."

Kerry thought fast. "I'm working on this huge account, Mom. He's worried about it. Thanks. Now I'm running late."

"Call me."

"Yes, ma'am. Love you, bye." She hung up, saying, "Jane? I don't know anybody named Jane. Randi Mae?" Kerry jumped to her feet, pacing. "Oh, God, if Mom finds out what's going on, I'll never hear the end of it." She clutched her elbows, bubbling with impotent anger, but uncertain where to direct it. "I know with everything else that's going on, this is a stupid thing to worry about, but, jeez, T.K., you don't know Mom. If she gets a whiff that I'm in trouble, she'll be on the phone to the governor. Do you know that after the trial she wrote a formal letter of complaint to Mr. Quintas? Because he was rude to me!"

To her annoyance, Smith laughed.

"It isn't funny," she muttered. "She treats me like a little kid. Worse, I act like a little kid."

"Bad news, sugar, it doesn't get any better. I'm thirty-two, and all my mother has to do is look over the tops of her eyeglasses and I'm nine years old again and wondering what I did wrong this time."

"Thanks a lot." Kerry slumped in her chair and rested her forearms on the table. "I'll be ninety years old and she'll still be trying to run my life."

He shrugged. "We just need to wait until we have kids, then get even by messing up their lives." He folded the newspaper and put it aside. "Eat up. We have a report to deliver."

She picked up the fork absently, trying to quell the hopeful fluttering of her heart. *Until* we *have kids?* Rationally, she knew he meant "when you have kids and I have other kids," but rational thinking had very little to do with anything where Tarkington Smith was concerned. She thought of the perfect red rose she'd found on her pillow. He wanted to shake up her life? He was doing an excellent job.

THROUGH A CLOUD OF cigarette smoke, Bob Ward drawled, "Got you some bad news and some bad news. What do you want first?"

"Bad," Smith said. He sat on a leather office chair, his Stetson on his lap.

Kerry was too edgy to sit. This office, with its shelves of legal volumes and legalese papering the walls, reminded her too much of Quintas and his pack of pitbull defense lawyers. The door to an inner office stood open. A television set hummed. A picture of Bob Ward in an army captain's uniform reminded her of her father. She relaxed a little.

Ward said, "The kid died of a heart attack. He went into arrest about midnight."

The news sickened Kerry. He might have been a cocaine addict and a would-be murderer, but he was only a kid.

"So connecting him and Rex is out of the question," Smith said dryly. "What's the other bad news?"

"Martin Rex Sondervon has a rap sheet only a mother could love. The night-court judge set his bail at two hundred fifty grand. That old boy ain't going anywhere soon." Ward stubbed his cigarette into an overflowing ashtray. He glanced at the door. "I'm not supposed to smoke in here. New antismoking reg." He lit another cigarette.

"Rex isn't talking though. He brought in a lawyer and nixed all interviews. That's the bad news. We have Rex on narcotics, but I don't think we can connect him to the Abernathy murder."

"What about ballistics?"

"Rex had in his possession a .38 and a 9 mm. Another .38 was found in his apartment. That murder back in June came out of a .32."

"What about the Nova?"

"Possible. That was a .32." Ward held up a hand. "Don't go losing your britches, boy. Ballistics isn't back in with a report. They're backlogged to last Christmas. Even if I can nudge the lab boys, there're still no guarantees. Making a match is going to be harder than the dickens."

"Why?" Kerry asked.

"Shooting into a body does different things to a bullet than shooting into metal. Those slugs we pulled out of the Nova were pretty chewed up. The very best you can hope for is a partial match. That won't stand up in court. Get me that .32 and it'll be a different tune."

Kerry asked, "What about a bullet shot into the ground? Remember, T.K.? He shot the ground over at the Abernathy house."

Smith slammed a fist into his palm. "That's right. Sugar, you're brilliant." He grabbed a pen from a desk holder and made a quick sketch of the Abernathy side yard, circling where he thought the bullet might have entered the ground.

"It'd still be best to find the .32," Ward said.

"If you can get those search warrants, you have a better chance than me."

Ward leaned back on his chair. His smile revealed nicotine-stained teeth. "Tell me something, Smith. What was your conviction rate for the Houston D.A.?"

"Ninety-three percent."

Ward cocked his pale eyebrows. "And how many times did some judge throw you out of his courtroom?"

"Forever? Or just temporarily?"

Ward snorted. "I should have figured. Go on, you all." He patted the report. "I have work to do, as if I ain't got enough already."

As she and T.K. left the office, Kerry said, "Did you hear that? A .32 and a .32. We're going to get them, T.K."

"Miss Byfield?"

Kerry winced at the familiar voice. She forced a smile as she turned around. "Good morning, Mr. Marsh."

Smith's eyes narrowed to slits. His shoulders seemed to swell, but his expression was neutral. Marsh made no such efforts. Hostility showed in his scowl and stiff posture.

"What are you doing here?" Marsh demanded.

"Public building," Smith said.

Marsh did a quick shuffle, his eyes darting at the doorways in the long hallway. Then he smiled. Kerry felt her hackles wanting to rise. Marsh was so phony that she thought he ought to wear a warning label. "Been in to see Ward?" Marsh asked.

"Uh-huh," Kerry said.

"I hear you brought in a suspect yesterday."

Smith rubbed the back of his neck, his jaw working. He shook his head. "Can't seem to recall that."

Marsh pursed his lips and clenched his fingers. "Cut the crap, Smith. If you're ferreting out information about any case in Collin County, it's my business."

"It was your business. It's mine now." Smith took Kerry's arm. "Come on, sugar. We've got work to do."

Marsh clamped a hand on Smith's shoulder. Smith swung his head around, his brow thunderous. He and Marsh were close to the same height, a little over six feet, but Smith suddenly seemed taller and more dangerous. His eyes glittered like a pair of diamonds.

Marsh dropped his hold, lurched backward, har-rumphed, and said, "Maybe you can get away with your cowboy tactics down in Houston, but not here."

Smith headed for the double doors. A red Exit sign glowed over the lintel.

"Watch your step, Kerry," Marsh said harshly. "Running with that hotshot will cost you more than your job."

She cast Marsh a disgusted sneer and hurried after Smith. When she caught up to him, she said, "You should have punched him in the nose. I never liked him."

He grinned at her, surprisingly calm. "If I went around bending every nose that deserved it, I wouldn't have time for anything else. Forget it."

"Why are you smiling? I thought you were angry."

He draped an arm over her shoulders as they crossed the parking lot. "Why waste good anger on a stiff-neck?" He opened the truck door for her.

As she buckled her seat belt, what Robert Marsh had said hit her. "T.K., how in the world does Marsh know I lost my job?"

For once Smith looked surprised.

"Did you hear what he said to me? He said hanging around with you will cost me more than my job. How did he know Piver fired me?"

"Now that's a real good question." Smith looked back across the parking lot, his eyes narrow and thoughtful. "Piver have any political connections?"

"I've learned more about Piver in the past five days than I've known in the past two years—" she held out her hands in a helpless gesture "—but I don't know."

"When we get back from Waxahatchie, we'll give Blackie a call. Think he's up to one more favor?"

"He hates politicians."

"My kind of man."

Chapter Thirteen

"Did that man at the gas station give us the right directions?" Kerry asked. She stared at the Red Pine mobile home community in Waxahatchie. It spread haphazardly over a large, flat lot. Trucks and cars rumbled past on Highway 77. Treeless, dusty and littered with children's toys and blowing paper, it looked like a ghetto.

"This is Garvey Road." Smith turned the pickup into the trailer court and drove slowly over the crumbling speed bumps. He followed the trailers' house numbers toward the end of the road. There, the trailers looked better kept. Many had gardens or tiny autumn-browned yards. Some had picket fences and ceramic ducks or donkeys standing silent guard.

"There it is, number 1173. I don't see the Mercedes."

Kerry doubted they'd find the Mercedes in Waxahatchie, especially not in this trailer court. The mailbox was fixed up to look like a red barn, complete with chickens painted along the edges. It read: W. Firkins.

Smith pulled into the empty parking spot next to the trailer. "I saw a curtain drop. Someone's home."

"You don't think Randi Mae will come out shooting,

do you?'' Kerry had meant it as a joke, but the words emerged strained.

"I doubt she's here. Stay in the truck while I find out." Smith sauntered up the metal stoop and rapped on the door. An older woman answered. Smith waved for Kerry. She joined him on the stoop.

"Ma'am, I hate to bother you, but I need some information on Miss Randi Mae Firkins," Smith said.

The woman was birdlike, very thin and bony. Her cheeks formed hollows between her square jaw and knobby cheekbones. Her yellow-gray hair hung thin and straight. Her eyes glistened with tears. "You brung bad news about my baby, didn't you?" Her voice was nasal and twangy, but soft.

"Uh—no, ma'am. At least, I don't think so." Smith introduced himself and Kerry. "You're her mother?"

The woman nodded. She stepped back and beckoned. "Come on in. It's too cold to stand around out there." She clutched the front of a faded cardigan. "Every time someone comes to the door, I think it's the police."

Smith scraped his boots on a sisal mat and removed his hat. Kerry followed suit. A spindly chihuahua yipped once, then streaked under a couch.

"Why is that, ma'am?" Smith asked.

Mrs. Firkins wiped her eyes with the back of a hand. "Don't you know? My baby run off." She urged them to sit. "I got a report filed with the police." She pronounced it "poh-leece." "Don't do no good. Said she's a grown-up. She can run off if she has a mind to. It ain't right, though. A mother knows when something's wrong and I know. I feel it." She rolled her eyes. "Oh, Lord. It's that Ella Louise. I know she has my Randi Mac—"

"Ella Louise?" Kerry interrupted. Her eyes felt

funny. She wiped them with a furtive gesture, wishing Mrs. Firkins wouldn't cry.

The woman nodded, her face suddenly hard and bitter. "I hate to call that one blood, but I've got no choice. That one, it pains me to say, is just like Charlie, her daddy. Tramps, the both of them. But Randi Mae's my baby. She's a good girl." The woman nodded. "She gets a wild hare every once in a while to take off, but only for a day or two. Then she comes on home. She's responsible." Her eyes teared again.

Kerry focused her attention elsewhere. She'd always been a sympathy crier. What would Smith say if he had two women blubbering all over him?

Mrs. Firkins said, "They miss her down at the truck stop. She's a good waitress. They like her. All them folks is just like a second family, and her regulars miss her. Why, Randi Mae brung home twenty or thirty dollars a day in tips."

"Have you any idea where Randi Mae might have gone?" Smith asked.

Bitterness flattened the woman's eyes. "Dallas!" She spat the word like a curse. "She's gone to see that tramp. I don't know what I did wrong with Ella Louise. Bad blood, maybe. Maybe she's just plain evil. There's devils in this world."

Kerry listened, but rather than look at Mrs. Firkins, she studied the room. There was blond, plastic-looking paneling on the walls, and blue-green shag carpeting on the floor. Pine shelving held cheap figurines of elves and puppies. A large white Bible with gold lettering, the edges stained by handling, covered a small coffee table. The mobile home was shabby, but very clean and neat. Compulsively neat.

Figures were lined up like soldiers. The Bible sat so

squarely on the table that it looked as though it had been measured from the edges. Coffee cups were on hooks, arranged by color. The same creepy feeling she'd had in the Abernathy house gripped Kerry now. She wondered if Smith noticed the similarity.

"Do you know where in Dallas?" he asked. His voice was gentle, his drawl pronounced.

"That's one thing Randi Mae doesn't ever tell me. She knows how I feel about Ella Louise. Of course, I always know when that tramp's come around. Randi Mae'll come strutting in with a fancy new hairdo and some geegaw or another. Then she'll pine around here and mope and talk about leaving. She'll talk about money and big cars."

"A new hairdo?" Kerry asked, remembering Louise Abernathy's bankrupt beauty shop.

"Oh, yeah. You ought to see what that child comes up with. It's that tramp doing it. Now me, I think my baby looks just fine. She's a plain sort, but honest looking. She doesn't need any poof-poofs to make her pretty." She swiped at her eyes with an impatient gesture. Kerry fumbled through her purse, looking for a tissue.

Mrs. Firkins jumped up. From a box, she extracted a cigarette and a book of matches. "The worst thing is how long Ella Louise stays away." Mrs. Firkins went to the door, propped it open, then lit the cigarette. She blew the smoke outdoors. "Not a peep out of her for a year, two years, then she pops in at the truck stop, showing off. She fills up Randi Mae's head, spins her around, then runs off again. My baby doesn't know what a good girl she is. We're poor people, I know that. But we're good people."

She waved at the curls of smoke, sending them outside. "She takes care of her mamma. She's not a drinker, and she's no tramp. She doesn't belong in Dallas. She don't know how to get along up there. It's that tramp. She let something happen to my baby."

"When did Randi Mae leave?" Smith asked.

Kerry stared at the cigarette. Something about it nagged her.

Mrs. Firkins said, "June 4. I've been saying my prayers for her ever since. The police won't help me. I keep asking, but they keep on saying she's grown." She smiled wanly. "Can I get you folks something to drink? I've got some coffee."

Smith told her he'd appreciate a cup. Kerry declined. Mrs. Firkins stubbed out the cigarette on the edge of the metal stoop, then flicked the butt into a trash can. Kerry chewed her lower lip. She felt bothered, but was unsure why.

"Has Ella Louise written to you? Or called?" Smith asked.

Mrs. Firkins barked out a laugh. "I ain't heard from her since the day I threw her out of this house. Caught her and some boy together, shaming themselves and drinking whiskey. It wasn't the first time, but it sure was the last."

She set down a tin tray. It held a coffee mug, bowl of sugar and a pot of milk. Everything perched neatly on coasters.

"Oh, but Lordy, I hear about her. Randi Mae thinks the world of her. I've never figured that out. Ella Louise is a devil."

"Have you any pictures of Randi Mae, ma'am?"

Mrs. Firkins brightened. "Oh, Lord, yes." She flitted like a wren to the bookshelf and produced a photo album with a plastic laminated cover. "You going to find my baby, Mr. Smith?"

"I'm working on it, ma'am." He opened the album.

Except for a few odd shots of blooming roses or flower beds, the pictures were of Randi Mae. A scrawny, petulant-looking baby, a gawky child, a skinny teenager who looked sideways at the camera. A school portrait showed a narrow-faced girl with small, flat eyes and her mother's knobby cheekbones. Her only exceptional feature was her hair. She had a cloud of lovely flaxen blond hair. Kerry noted the neat alignment of pictures. As far as she could tell, they were in perfect chronological order.

"Who's that?" Kerry asked, pointing to a picture of Randi Mae standing arm in arm with another blond girl. They were the same size and looked about fifteen.

Mrs. Firkins's eyes went hard. "I ought to throw that one out or cut it. That's Ella Louise. I made those dresses. Ain't they pretty?" She stroked her finger over the picture of Randi Mae's dress. "Randi Mae made good grades in school, has beautiful handwriting, and is as pretty as a picture."

Kerry perused the picture. Randi Mae looked clumsy, but Ella Louise looked as cool, elegant and beautiful as a young Grace Kelly.

Mrs. Firkins acquired a dreamy look. "That baby of mine, looks just like me. She has real pretty hands. A feller once told her she should put her hands on television. You know, use them for commercials where they show how washing dishes makes your hands pretty?" Her voice caught. She fussed with the chihua-hua, trying to coax him from under the couch with baby talk. She gave up and flitted to the cigarette box.

Kerry blurted out, "Does Randi Mae smoke?" Smith eyed her strangely.

Mrs. Firkins looked at the cigarette and loosed a rueful laugh. She said, "All of us have one vice. This is ours." She coughed delicately. "It's gonna be the death of me." She indicated the box with a jut of her chin. "Help yourself, honey."

Kerry remembered the crumpled cigarette package in the Abernathy house now. It had been so strangely out of place.

"Ma'am, have you a recent picture of Randi Mae that I can borrow?" Smith asked. "I promise to mail it back to you in a day or two."

"You going to help me find her? Send her on home?" The woman sniffed, keeping her head down. "Maybe she got mad at me. Maybe you can tell her that her mamma loves her? You don't think she's mad at me?" Tears rolled and perched on her knobby cheekbones.

Kerry's heart squeezed. She breathed deeply and sternly told herself, *No tears.*

"I'll do my best, ma'am." Smith pulled out one of his business cards. "This number is for a friend of mine, a Mr. Ward. If Randi Mae comes home or calls you, you call him. Can you do that?" He wrote Ward's number on the back of his card.

Mrs. Firkins leafed back to the end of the album. She pulled out a picture of Randi Mae wearing a waitress's uniform. Randi Mae was laughing; her hands hovered above a birthday cake that was ablaze with candles. "She looks real pretty in that one."

Smith murmured in agreement.

"Her friends at the truck stop gave her a surprise birthday party last year." The words had an undertone that said "Please believe me, she's such a good girl." Her tears fell freely now.

"You've been a lot of help, ma'am." Smith rose.

Kerry felt terrible as she left the trailer. Yet she couldn't stop watching Mrs. Firkins as they backed out of the driveway. She stood on the stoop, a hunched, hopeless, brokenhearted little woman. Her tears glistened in the bright autumn sunshine.

Smith drove to the end of Garvey Road. He stopped at the stop sign and stared at the photograph. "So, Louise Abernathy was really Ella Louise Firkins," he said. "And her 'distant relative,' Randi Mae, is really her sister."

His statement only made Kerry feel worse. In the past few days, they had found out more than had come out at the trial. The trail of lies and half-truths grew longer and more twisted. Now Randi Mae's lies to her mother added to them. Kerry thought of Mrs. Firkins's tears and she dabbed her eyes with a tissue. What was going to happen to Mrs. Firkins when her "good" daughter was charged with murdering her "evil" sister?

Smith started to drive again, shaking Kerry from her reverie. "I don't know if I can stand this," she murmured. "That poor woman—her heart is broken." A tear dribbled down her cheek. "We lied to her." Kerry wiped her face and the tissue disintegrated. She dug into her purse for another. "What's going to happen to her?"

"Ah, sugar, don't...."

Kerry's tears refused to stop, "I lie to Mom all the time. Does that make me like Randi Mae?" She tore through her purse in search of yet another tissue. "Of course, I haven't murdered anybody. Besides, Randi Mae's mother doesn't care about Louise. So maybe it was okay for her to murder her own sister—*her own sister!*" Kerry turned a helpless face to Smith. "What kind of monster is she? How could she do that, kill Louise? How could she do that to her own mother?"

Smith turned onto a side road, parked on the shoulder and turned off the engine. The dirt road was surrounded by flat, brown fields. The few trees in sight were stunted, warped by the constant wind. The truck sat in the shadow of a bobbing oil donkey. The grinding gears had a metallic rhythm. Smith unbuckled his seat belt, then Kerry's, then pulled Kerry close. "Things happen. The best we can do is try to clean up the mess. Try not to personalize this." Gone was the teasing drawl as his voice acquired a cautionary note.

Kerry strove for control. "I'm sorry. I don't mean to be such a big baby." Embarrassment crept through her. She blew her nose. "If I hadn't been so sure, so absolutely positive about Abernathy, none of this would have happened. I can't believe my conceit and self-righteousness. This is all my fault."

"Hush, don't say that. Remember when I told you why I quit the D.A.'s office? If I learned anything, I learned that if you take other people's doings too close to heart, you lose your perspective. Don't do that to yourself. It isn't worth it."

His arms felt strong, safe and comforting. She leaned against his shoulder and rubbed at her eyes with her knuckles. She whispered, "It's one thing to see evidence of this on the computer. That's just numbers…but that poor woman. Did you see her face?"

"I know. I'm not feeling so good myself, but, sugar, we can't right all the world's wrongs. We have to concentrate on righting the ones we can. Okay?"

She nodded. "I'm sorry."

He smiled and shook his head. "No need for sorry."
He stroked her hair. She sighed as he brushed his lips
across her forehead. He tipped her chin and gazed into
her eyes. "Do you trust me?"

"Yes," she said without hesitation.

"Then trust me on this one. It isn't your fault."

He separated strands of her hair with his fingers. His
words made sense. They were necessary if she was going to keep her wits and sanity. His heartbeat soothed
her, but his eyes, smoky and warm and understanding,
undid her. Her frazzled emotions bunched in her breast
and rebounded. Weird mindlessness compelled her toward drowning in his midnight eyes and moving toward
the scent of spice and maleness.

She pressed her lips to his, finding rising heat to
match her own. She wrapped her arms around him and
clutched his back, reveling in the strength of taut muscle
and heavy bone. A tiny animal moan escaped her throat
as the kiss deepened. It evolved from gentle exploration
to the provocatively erotic. Her skin greedily clamored
for his touch. He ran his fingers through her hair, then
down her throat and over her shoulder. His touch seared
through her sweater until her skin seemed to scream
demands.

She sighed deep in her throat when he brushed the
side of her breast, then tentatively cupped and fondled
her soft weight through the fabric. Her nipples strained
against her bra, and he brushed them with his thumb.
A deep-seated shudder coursed through her body, leaving tingling weakness in its wake. She left his mouth,
tasted the rough texture of his cheek and nuzzled the
heavy coarseness of his hair.

His kisses ranged over her cheek and along the tender
line of her jaw. She stiffened at the onslaught of desire

as he worked a hand under her sweater. His hand was hot and gentle as he searched her back, lingering over the shallow cleft of her spine. Her breasts ached with longing.

The rhythm of the oil donkey echoed the thud of her heart. The truck seat groaned under their shifting weight. Under his after-shave, another scent wafted. It was faintly musky, infinitely masculine, teasing, and stealthily invading her mind. She nibbled his earlobe as his hair tickled her nose and cheeks.

Aching to comply with the way he urged her to lean back, she twisted on the seat. He whispered against her throat, his breath swirling across her flesh. The unintelligible words wove a spell of rapturous wanting around her heart.

The rumble of a heavy truck startled her. Her eyelids flew wide open and heat blossomed across her cheeks. Were they really doing this in full daylight? In a truck? On a public road? She stared aghast as an oil tanker loomed behind them, raising a billowing storm of dust.

Torn between embarrassment and the deliciousness of Smith nuzzling her neck, she whispered, "T.K.? Quit."

"Hmm?" he murmured. He pressed kisses to the tender hollow at the base of her throat and rubbed slow circles on her back, inching her sweater higher and higher. Cool air brushed the small of her back, raising gooseflesh. Kerry's throat closed, and all that emerged was a low moan as he pressed her tighter against his body. She arched her back and clutched his shoulders, enamored by the quickened urgency of his mouth against her skin. The oil tanker, diesel engine growling, veered to give the pickup wide berth. A harsh blast reverberated when the driver blew his horn. Smith lifted his head, looking startled as the tanker roared past, enveloping the pickup in a cloud of reddish dust.

Kerry pushed away and tugged at the edge of her sweater. She panted in thwarted frustration. She'd felt a rainstorm after a drought. Smith was feast after famine. Sexual desire had shaken off its coat of rust and made her nerves sing. She whispered, "I can't believe I'm doing this." She cleared her hoarse throat. A deep-seated ache made her squirm.

He turned to her with that devilish grin. His face was flushed, his eyes dark pools. Catching the back of her neck, he pulled her close. Noses touching, he whispered, "We passed a Motel 6 coming into Waxahatchie."

Catching herself in midmelt, Kerry cried, "T.K.!" She shoved at his chest and ducked under his hand. She plucked at her sweater and crossed her ankles. "We don't have time for this. We have an investigation to…investigate."

"Just a suggestion, sugar." He shifted uncomfortably and plucked at his trouser legs.

The fit of his jeans told her he was affected, too. She'd never wanted anything in her life the way she wanted this man right now. *Where's your terrific sense of timing now, Byfield?*

Smith raked his hair from his face with his fingers. "You sure put my thermostat out of whack."

She gulped air, then said, "I just got…carried away. I don't do this sort of thing."

She wanted assurance. She wanted him to say that he understood and that he didn't do things like this, either. She needed him to say she wasn't a passing fancy or an afternoon quickie. If he said "Maybe," she determined she was getting out of the truck and walking home.

Staring straight ahead, his chest rising and falling in heavy breaths, Smith said, ''Let's go get a cheeseburger.''

ROBERT MARSH'S WORDS echoed in her mind. ''Smith knows everything. He left a report with Bob Ward. Names, dates, facts, figures. It's all there in black-and-white. Ward is trying to get warrants right now. It's safe to say he'll get them. Ditch the Mercedes. It's hot.''

How? Tarkington Smith and Kerry Byfield. Just as certainly, they had something to do with the missing money. Her fingers drummed a nervous tattoo on the desktop. ''Damn you,'' she muttered. ''That money's mine. I worked hard for it.''

She called Nolan. The naked terror in his voice made her smile. He deserved a good scare. He deserved it for letting her down and disappointing her. ''You're being watched and followed, darling,'' she said.

There was a sharp intake of breath on the other end. ''It's too late,'' he said, bleakly. ''It's over.''

''It isn't over until I say it's over. Now you listen to me, and you listen well. Get to the bank. I want my money and—''

''Too late.'' He sounded drunk.

''Now is not the time to—''

''The IRS has frozen my accounts.''

The handset slipped in her fingers. What? Years of planning so the IRS could steal her money? All her patience, her suffering with smiles and covering tracks...wasted? Slowly shaking her head, she lifted the handset. Very calmly, she asked, ''What are you talking about?''

"I tried to get the cash you needed. My account is locked. It's the IRS. They did it." He rambled on about missing accounting files and Kerry calling his house and threatening to call the tax men. His words slurred, and he hiccoughed.

During a lull she said, "Never mind. Go about your business. And Nolan, listen carefully. Remember that I have many friends in high places. If you go to the police—if you go to a priest—I'll kill you. You won't last twenty-four hours. Do you understand?" She took the silence to mean he understood. "I'll get the money from Kerry's apartment. It must be there. Then you and I will leave town for a few days. Okay?"

"The IRS—"

"Don't worry about them. By the time they get around to actually doing anything, we'll be out of the country. Trust me to take care of the details." She hung up, then stared at the ceiling, considering her options. The future loomed gray and bleak.

Details. She was good with details. Still, it gnawed at her that things were going badly. Once again, it wasn't her fault. She'd planned out every step and executed every detail. She'd done her part, but everyone had let her down, just like Daddy had let her down when he'd walked out. He'd said he loved her, but he'd walked away and never looked back. And her Mamma had let her down with her hatred, crying and going on about how blessed it was to be poor.

How she hated all the fine families of Dallas with their fake smiles, good names and big money. They'd snubbed her and whispered, "White trash," behind her back. A ping of pain shot up her hand. She'd tapped the desk hard enough to break a nail. She sucked the wounded finger.

The IRS? She scrunched her lips, knowing damned well that Piver's stupidity had caused Kerry Byfield to call the IRS. "Idiot," she muttered. She placed her hand on the phone, wondering if Robert could help her. Her hand slid off and rested on the desk. He meant to let her down, too. She'd heard it in his voice. Was he gloating, glad to see her in trouble? He was probably sitting there in his Bill Blass suit, in his fancy office with the leather-bound books, pleased as could be that she had got herself caught.

She jerked open a drawer and drew out an envelope. She counted through the cash it contained. It was less than five thousand. Should she go away? Start over? Cut her losses and start fresh in a new place? New York? Denver? Los Angeles? She pulled out another envelope and rubbed her fingers over the micro-cassette tape and photographs it contained. The tape contained a very interesting conversation between herself and Robert. He knew so many interesting people and loved to boast about the favors they owed him. She examined one photograph. It was a telephoto shot. Robert Marsh's face was barely recognizable. What was extremely clear was the face of the other man in the picture and the cash that he was slipping into Marsh's hand. Robert Marsh was very clever, but not clever enough. He shouldn't have let her down.

She slid the photograph back into the envelope then licked the adhesive delicately. She sealed it, then printed District Attorney Bradford Lowell's address on the front.

She pulled out the .32 and hefted its weight. Why bother getting angry when it was so damned easy to get even?

Chapter Fourteen

Smith pulled the key from the ignition and said, "I wish there was a way to put Randi Mae in the Abernathy house on the night of the murder." He wore a distant expression.

They had ridden to the West 77 truck stop in silence. All during the ride, Kerry had been searching for some way to apologize about rejecting his lovemaking and to explain that she wanted to develop this relationship, but they had to slow down. She needed time, needed room to think. Now it miffed her to realize all he cared about was the murder.

She raked her fingers rapidly through her hair. Once this was over, he'd go back to Houston and she'd go home to her apartment, and they'd never see each other again. It was better to just put her feelings on hold until he was out of sight and firmly out of mind. Maybe her hormones were taking over and she'd misread his every word, look and gesture. Suppose he was just stringing her along because he needed her help to break this case? Sure, he was attracted, but maybe it was simple lust. He probably had dozens of girlfriends.

Dejected, she looked at the truck stop. It had a vast, sprawling, semitrailer-truck parking lot and a smaller car parking lot that was marked by white lines on the asphalt. The main building held a restaurant, a gasoline-sales office, a gift shop and, according to the advertisement on the wall, free Showers With Fill-up. Business appeared light. The parking lots were dotted sparsely by cars and trucks. Few people were noticeable behind the tinted glass of the restaurant and gift shop.

Kerry sighed. Smith needed her help and she'd promised it. She reached for her purse, and Smith put his hand on top of hers.

"I'm sorry, sugar."

"For what?" Her confusion doubled when she saw how uncertain he looked.

He lifted his shoulders in a quick shrug. "You're special to me. I don't have a right to treat you like that. I embarrassed you. There's no excuse for acting like some randy stud without manners. I'm sorry." He squeezed her fingers, then released them. "I'd like to say it's because you're so beautiful that I lose my head, but that's not a good excuse."

A slow melt started in her toes and worked its insidious way upward. Smiling, she lowered her head, her hands fluttering on her lap. "Forget it. I mean, don't forget it...no, I mean..." Not knowing anything anymore, she whispered, "I have never in my life necked in a car with a guy. Never. You're just so..." His silence unnerved her. She blurted out, "You're the sexiest man I've ever—" Her cheeks burned.

Smith placed two fingers under her chin and gently lifted her face. He said, "I've been running all over you. I get caught up in what I'm doing and don't think about your feelings. And I'm sorry. So I'll tell you what. We'll just think about business until we clear Bill. Then afterward—'' He made a face that said, ''Whatever you want.''

''You mean it?'' Her heart was doing a dance.

''Ever caught me in a lie?''

All doubts wisped away, Kerry chuckled. She leaned back, then thrust out her right hand. ''Okay, it's a deal, then. Business first.''

''Then pleasure.'' He shook her hand and winked.

They walked hand in hand to the restaurant. When they pushed through the double glass doors, Kerry noticed a cigarette machine. She pushed his shoulder and cried, ''See! You get me all flustered and I can't think. The cigarettes.''

Realization dawned on his face. He patted his shirt pocket absently, as if seeking the cigarette pack they'd found in the Abernathy house. ''Circumstantial at best, but maybe we can come up with something to give it beef. Maybe Shanlin can find out if Randi Mae's fingerprints are on file somewhere.'' He gave Kerry a smile so full of approval, she practically floated into the truck stop.

The restaurant was uninteresting. Everything from the light fixtures to the floor tile to the plants were of heavy-duty plastic. The place smelled of cooking grease and diesel fuel. Ketchup and mustard, in respective red and yellow plastic squeeze bottles, sat on every table along with stainless-steel napkin dispensers. The waitresses wore white uniforms and pink aprons, their hair under spidery nets. It looked like a million other truck-stop restaurants that dotted America's highways.

They sat at the counter. Kerry picked up a one-page, laminated menu. It was greasy. She said in an aside, ''Are you sure you want to eat here?''

''How bad can it be?'' he replied with a chuckle.

A waitress who was about fifty and who had her puffy, teased hair under a silvery net, set two red plastic tumblers filled with ice water in front of them. She stood poised with a green order pad. Her name tag said, "Roxanne." She asked, "What can I get you folks today?"

"I'll have a cheeseburger and fries," Smith said, then looked expectantly at Kerry. She nodded. He added, "Same for the lady. And coffee." He paused. "If you have a few minutes, I'd like to ask you some questions about Randi Mae Firkins."

Roxanne looked from Smith to Kerry, then over her shoulder at the rectangular window between dining room and kitchen. Then she shrugged. "Be right with you."

Kerry said, "For such a close family, she doesn't seem terribly interested."

A red-haired girl with tiny features and gray eyes so pale they seemed silver, appeared. "I'm Lisa. Roxie said you were asking about Randi Mae. How come?" She chomped a piece of gum.

"Were you friends?"

"Sure. You a cop? Did Welladine send you looking?"

"Mrs. Firkins? No. I'm trying to find Randi Mae in order to help out a friend. Do you happen to know where she is? Does she call you?"

Roxanne joined Lisa. The waitresses exchanged a look. Both of them sniffed. Roxanne said, "Are you kidding? She always said once she was out of here, she was never coming back." She laughed softly. Her hair net bobbed. "It just surprises me it took so long."

"Why?" Kerry asked. If the police had talked to

these two, then no wonder they'd disregarded Mrs. Firkins's tearful pleas.

Lisa answered, "Because she hated it here." She made a face as if it were a stupid question. "I don't blame her. Her mother is crazy. I mean, Welladine's okay I guess. But living with her? All that Bible thumping and always cleaning everything. She came in here one time, and while Randi got her dinner, Welladine started straightening the chairs!" She nudged Roxanne's ribs. "Remember that? What an old fussbudget."

"Yeah," Roxanne drawled. "Poor Randi. She was such a pretty thing, but she always had to scrub off her makeup before going home. She didn't want Welladine getting on her about tramping around."

Smith said, "So you're saying she was talking about leaving long before she actually left."

"Oh, yeah," Roxanne said. "Course, it was sort of odd that she left without collecting her last week's pay and all. She left her stuff in her locker—"

"I'd have left it, too. That junk," Lisa interrupted.

"Why did she leave?" Smith asked.

"'Cause her and Louise found an apartment. She got new clothes and furniture and all that, you know."

"You know Louise?"

Roxanne snorted and strolled away to bellow at the cook. Lisa's face grew wistful, her eyes dreamy. She flicked at the countertop with a cloth. "That Louise is something. Man oh, man, you ain't never seen such a beautiful lady. It's hard to believe her and Randi are sisters. I mean they have the same color hair and all, but Louise looks like a movie star." Lisa nodded earnestly. "She was a model in New York and played a part in a movie once. She even had her own beauty shop and did hairdos for rich women.'' Lisa touched her carroty curls. "She used to fix my hair for me. She said—"

"A troublemaker," Roxanne spat. "Nothing but a big la-dee-da show-off. She came in here, showing off to Randi and giving her money. I never believed her stories." She made a dismissive gesture. "I told you and told you, Louise was too short for modeling. I read it in *Redbook* magazine. Models have to be as tall as me or more. A model! That's a bunch of horse puckey."

A bell pinged and a man called something unintelligible. Roxanne held up a finger for Smith and Kerry to wait, then went to fetch their cheeseburgers.

When Roxanne returned, Kerry saw, to her surprise, that the burgers were made of fresh beef and that they weren't too greasy. She put mustard on hers.

"Then Louise and Randi Mae got along well?" Smith asked.

Roxanne said, "Randi was jealous as could be. She always said she admired Louise, but it was envy. I could tell. She believed every one of those big stories about the money, the cars and the rich men."

A couple with three small children entered. Lisa hurried to wait on them. Roxanne jutted her chin at the redhead. "Girls like that. They always believe everything they hear. Louise came in here and acted just like a queen. Randi and the other airheads fluttered around her, kissing her feet." She shook her head in disgust. "It kind of made me sad. Randi believed you had to be Louise to get along in this world. I'd tell her, 'Honey, you got brains and you know how to work hard. That's all a person needs.' But, nope. Sometimes I think she'd make a pact with the devil to trade places with Louise."

Kerry exchanged a look with Smith, wondering if he

was thinking the same thing she was thinking. He asked, "How often did Louise visit?"

"Used to be all the time. I guess whenever she got tired of the high-and-mighty life." Roxanne threw back her head and roared with laughter. She brought herself under control and wiped her eyes with the back of her hand. "Sorry. I ain't seen her since Randi took off. I shouldn't speak ill of her. She never did anything to me." She leaned on the counter and looked conspiratorial. "But you know how to tell true class, don't you? Real class doesn't need to shove it in your face. Know what I mean?"

"Did Randi visit Louise often?" Kerry asked.

Roxanne nodded. "Every time she had it out with Welladine. That means a lot of times. She'd get mad and take off to Dallas. Or she'd call Louise and Louise would drive down and pick her up. Those two are close. The city mouse and the country mouse. That's what I call them." Roxanne made a wait-a-minute gesture. "I don't see why you're talking to me. If you want to know where Randi is, give Louise a call—hold on a second." She disappeared before Smith or Kerry had a chance to say anything.

Kerry whispered, "Don't they read the newspapers here? They don't know Louise is dead." He shrugged.

Roxanne returned with a phone number on an order form. "I had to call sometimes 'cause Randi always filled in for anyone who was sick. Louise can tell you where Randi is."

Smith nodded as he stuck the paper into his shirt pocket. He asked, "Did Louise ever say anything about Bill?"

"Bill who?"

Smith and Kerry exchanged glances.

Roxanne clucked. "That girl had so many boyfriends, she needed a book to keep them straight. Of course, if I looked like that, I might have the same problem."

"William Abernathy?"

Roxanne thought for a moment, then slowly shook her head. "Name doesn't ring a bell."

"What about Randi? Did she have any boyfriends? Maybe somebody named Nolan Piver?" Kerry asked.

Roxanne didn't hesitate. "Randi didn't have no boyfriends."

"Are you sure? Perhaps a man she met in Dallas?"

Roxanne waved both hands, as if to banish the idea. "She had this thing about men." Solemnly and with utmost seriousness, she added, "Randi couldn't even look at a fella unless it was over an order pad. If a trucker flirted with her, she'd break out in a rash. That's Welladine's doing. All that nonsense about tramps and going to hell. If you ask me, Welladine just stays mad because of Charlie. I can't say I blame him for leaving."

Kerry chewed her cheeseburger, listening to Roxanne grouse about Welladine and her Bible thumping. Randi Mae's motive crystallized. A life of oppression under a stern, man-hating mother; a sister who had it all. Envy, greed and escape. It made chilling sense.

"Might it be possible, ma'am, to have a peek in Randi's locker?" Smith asked.

Roxanne shook her head. "Cleaned it out for the new girl." She pushed her pencil under her hair net and scratched her scalp. "Oh, I know where it is. Her stuff's in a box in the back, I think. Let me ask Marty."

Kerry said, "Randi snapped. All those years of wishing she was Louise...and she snapped."

Frowning, Smith ate the rest of his cheeseburger. He

sipped his coffee. As he added more sugar, he said softly, "Whatever happened in the Abernathy house had nothing to do with anybody snapping. It was cold-blooded and premeditated."

"Randi Mae had to be crazy to kill her own sister." He shook his head. "The murder isn't the work of an insane person. A psychopath maybe, or a sociopath, or maybe someone who is just downright evil, but not someone who snapped."

"But—"

"Trust me. I've been up against enough insanity pleas to know that true criminal insanity is as rare as snow in August. Louise's murder was staged to look like an act of passion, but there's nothing passionate about it. It's pure cold-bloodedness."

Roxanne beckoned them. Once in the back room, Kerry regretted having eaten the cheeseburger. The storeroom was so filthy that the walls were shiny from grease. She was glad she didn't have to look at the kitchen.

Roxanne pointed out the cardboard box that sat on top of a stack of pork-and-beans cans.

Smith lifted a faded cardigan sweater with white yarn patches and mismatched buttons from the box. Tubes of lipstick, vials of perfume, small plastic cases of dime-store cosmetics, a hairbrush with flaxen hairs caught in the bristles and a pair of white, rubber-soled shoes followed.

"Do you happen to remember what Randi was wearing the last time you saw her?" When Roxanne rolled her eyes, Kerry pressed, "Maybe a denim skirt and a cotton blouse?"

"She dressed pretty plain."

Smith held up half a pack of unfiltered Camel cigarettes. "These were Randi's?"

"Oh, honey, those are stale." Roxanne snapped her fingers. "Oh, yeah, her dress. I didn't want it to wrinkle." She went behind the door and took a dress off a hook. "Her church dress for when she had to work all night on Saturday. We're open twenty-four hours."

It was dusty blue, of summer-weight cotton, with a Peter Pan collar. Kerry peered at the tag. It was size five. "The clothes in the hamper, T.K. I bet Mrs. Firkins can identify them."

"I was thinking the same thing." He made a gallant gesture at Roxanne. "Ma'am, I appreciate your help. I'd like to ask you one more favor. It's a big one. Some people in Dallas are going to be interested in this box. If you'll keep it safe for them? I'd appreciate it."

"Is Randi in some sort of trouble?"

"Possibly. But let's keep that between you and me."

WHEN THEY PICKED UP Interstate 35 toward Dallas, Kerry exclaimed, "We did it! Physical evidence, motive and I bet once we find Randi Mae, the murder weapon. Both murder weapons. The gun that killed the cocaine dealer who actually killed Louise and the shotgun." She clapped her hands and bounced on the seat.

"The cigarettes and the clothes put Randi Mae in the house. We did it, T.K. Hard evidence. And just wait until the police talk to Mrs. Firkins and those waitresses. They'll have so many motives, they won't know what to do with them all." Kerry beamed at him.

"Maybe."

Kerry stopped bouncing. "I hate it when you do that."

"Do what, sugar?" He put on the turn signal and changed lanes.

"That! *Maybe*. I know what that means. So what's wrong?"

"Inconsistency. If Randi Mae is the murderess, who is Piver's mystery woman?"

"Randi Mae."

"The same Randi Mae who breaks out in a rash when a trucker flirts with her? I'm no criminal psychologist, but one thing I've picked up over the years is the knowledge that people—good, bad or indifferent—tend to be consistent. Now what is consistent about living with your mother for all those years, basically being a mouse, then suddenly masterminding what might be a perfect murder?"

"You heard how envious she is. Maybe she's been planning this for years. Maybe she's been waiting until she had something on Louise." Kerry glared at the passing scenery. "Louise could have told Randi Mae she had a boyfriend. Maybe Randi Mae was holding on to those love letters and using them as blackmail." She threw up her hands. "Or what if Piver was the mastermind and Randi Mae was only caught up in events?"

Smith shrugged. "Something doesn't make sense, but I haven't figured it out yet." He checked his watch. "If we don't get caught in traffic, we can get to Copy Copy before it closes. It's time we talked to Piver. We haven't got enough evidence to hit the D.A., but we have enough for Piver."

Traffic proved horrendous. A tractor trailer that had overturned on Thornton freeway snarled traffic to a crawl. They didn't reach Plano until nearly six-thirty. Smith pulled into a gas station to make phone calls.

He beckoned Kerry to the phone booth. "No answer

at Copy Copy or at Piver's house. I left a message on Ward's machine to check out that phone number Roxanne gave—''

"It isn't the Abernathy house?"

"No. It might be Randi Mae's current place. I want you to leave a message on Piver's machine. Tell him if he wants to stay out of prison, the two of you have some talking to do.''

Kerry eyed the phone mistrustfully. "Where do we meet?''

"Copy Copy. Tomorrow morning at ten o'clock. With any luck, Bob Ward will have decided we have enough evidence for an investigation. If not, then it's too close to home for Piver to do anything stupid.''

Kerry left the message. She tried not to reveal how frightened she felt knowing she would soon confront Piver. "Now what?''

"Now we go throw you into a hot bubble bath so you'll quit sulking.'' He chucked her chin.

"I'm not sulking. You just hate to admit that I might be right and your so-called hunches wrong.'' She shook her head in exasperation. "You're the one who started this. What we found confirms what you suspected all along. Why the doubts?''

"Inconsistency.'' He reached for the phone and dropped another quarter into the slot.

"Now who are you calling?''

"John.''

Kerry shivered, rubbing her arms. The sun had set. It was cold and growing colder as the wind gathered force. She headed for the warmth of the truck. Within minutes, Smith hurried after her. He started the engine, then slammed the heel of his hand against the steering wheel.

"What is it?'' Kerry asked.

"John lost Piver. Damn!"

"Oh, no. Did Piver know he was being watched? Is he running?"

"I don't know. John said Piver left the shop at five minutes after six, but when he pulled out of the parking lot, John got stuck behind a stalled car. He figured Piver went home, but he didn't. He's checking out some places now."

AT THE EMBASSY HOTEL suite, Smith sat on the floor with the police reports, investigative reports and computer printouts that concerned Louise, Piver and Randi Mae. The radio emitted a soft country-and-western tune. He hummed along with the music and he shuffled the papers, using a red pencil to make notes. As a prosecuting attorney, he'd had the ability to put himself in a criminal's shoes and lose himself in another's way of thinking. Frustration gnawed at him now. He couldn't glimpse into Randi Mae Firkins's mind. He picked up the police report on her. It was standard procedure in a murder case to investigate everyone who might have gained from the victim's death. The investigators hadn't looked far into Randi Mae. One note said, "Distant relation—no lead."

He stared at the photocopied report. The police hadn't found out that the two women were sisters. There was no notation as to who talked to Randi Mae, or even when. He considered calling Shanlin to find out who had spoken to her, then decided it was too late in the evening. Besides, Shanlin had enough to do. Smith made a mental note to find out later.

Kerry muttered. He glanced up. She was scowling as she held her checkbook in one hand and tapped a pencil against her chin. With her long legs curled kittenlike on the chair and her lower lip pooched out, she looked beautiful. He studied the way the lamplight reflected on her shiny hair.

Smith lived a busy life. If he wasn't working on a case, then there was fishing or tooling around on his boat or working his horses. There were plenty of pretty women to squire around to concerts or out to dinner; his friends were more than happy to while away a Sunday at a football game; his family was insistent about filling gaps in his social life. He rarely felt lonely. Yet Kerry made him see the hole in his life. His life was full, but basically pointless. He had money, but no one to spend it on. He had plans, but no one to share them with. *I'm going to marry her,* he thought, feeling satisfied. He looked down at the paper in his hand and struggled to shift gears back to business.

"T.K.?"

"Uh-huh," he murmured absently.

"This is really embarrassing, but I need some money. I bounced a check. Piver owes me two weeks' pay, and I'm overdrawn." She rolled her eyes. "I know I've been letting you pick up all the checks, and usually... well...I don't know what else to do but ask you."

Touched by her embarrassment, he grinned. She could have anything her sweet heart desired. Then the checkbook caught his attention. The great state of Texas had an interesting way of dealing with people who wrote rubber checks. Bad-check complaints went to the Department of Motor Vehicles, and unless a person made good on the charges, there was no license renewal. Without a license, no one could cash a check, use a charge card or open a bank account.

"Uh—I guess I can ask Mom. Never mind. It's just,

if I don't clear this bad check, then I can't renew my driver's license...."

"Sure, sugar. We can stop by your bank on the way to Plano in the morning.

She glanced at her checkbook. "I don't need much. I'll pay you back."

"I hired you, remember? Don't worry about it." He rifled through a stack of paper and extracted a sheet. Randi Mae Firkins had a driver's license, so why hadn't she opened her own bank account? But she'd never had a bank account. Consistency. She broke out in a rash when truckers flirted with her. But she was Piver's girlfriend?

"I hear that little clicking noise that means you're thinking. What is it?"

"I don't know. I keep trying to draw a mental picture of Randi Mae and keep coming up blank. It's like we're dealing with two different women."

"A split personality?"

He lifted his arms high over his head and stretched. He removed his glasses and rubbed the bridge of his nose. "Thinking that just confuses the issue. The answer is here, but I can't see it. There are too many questions. The police cleared Randi Mae in the initial investigation, so why is she hiding?"

He blew out a long breath and dangled his hands over his knees. Bill had been railroaded. That hunch was so strong it was a fact as far as Smith was concerned. But how? By Robert Marsh? Everything Smith had seen revealed that Marsh was an arrogant, overbearing stiffneck who didn't give a damn about people, but he was still a good prosecutor. Nothing in the police or D.A. investigations revealed flaws. There were no signs of tampering with evidence or of making shady deals in court. The case had gone through unusually fast, but by the book. So how had Marsh known that Piver had fired Kerry?

Smith managed a wan smile and motioned with his chin toward her bedroom. "You look tired. Go on to bed. We have a lot to do tomorrow." He watched her, feeling a pang of shame about this afternoon. Her sense of humor and earthy sweetness aside, she was a lady to the core. Patience, he counseled. All he had to do was keep them alive for the next few days and then he had the rest of his life to make love to her.

Kerry reached the bedroom door and turned, giving him a somewhat puzzled gaze. Her big eyes were soft, green pools, and he caught himself mentally urging her to say she wanted him, to say she loved him and wanted him in her bed and in her arms. She entered the bedroom and softly shut the door.

Kerry leaned her back against the door and mentally kicked herself. All it would take was a look or a soft-spoken word and he would join her. The thought made her weak-kneed. Then what? A one-night stand? A two- or three-night stand? Emotions tore her. The logical part of her brain told her that he was too cocky, too light-hearted and too fast. But her soft and womanly part believed every word he said. She stared at the bed. Mints in gold foil dotted the center of each pillow. "Get a grip, Byfield," she muttered. "The plain fact is you're a chicken. What's the worst that can happen?"

That he'd think her cheap? That they'd make love and he wouldn't like it? That he'd prove her instincts correct and she'd spend the rest of her life loving him? *Oh, I'm in love with him.* She didn't know how it had happened or when, but in spite of the big red letters in her sensibility saying, *There is no such thing as love at first sight,* she was madly, hopelessly and irrevocably in love with Tarkington Smith. She jerked the door open and went back out into the sitting room.

Smith eyed her strangely as she grabbed her purse. "Forget something, sugar?"

She dumped the contents of her purse onto a table and sifted through the bits of paper, rumpled tissues, pens and pencils and lipsticks. Unable to look at him, she mumbled, "Whenever I date a man, Mom manages to slip me a present. She's really hopeful, but she thinks I'm an awful prude." She opened her wallet and searched the pockets. "Ah, she didn't let me down." She enclosed a small foil square in her fingers. *Live a little, Byfield, take a chance.* She steeled herself and held up the condom. "Do these things offend you?"

His smile turned bone-melting warm. "No."

"I've never used one." Heat blossomed on her face. Emotions romped in crazed acrobatics, and her chest felt so tight, she thought she might pass out from lack of air. "I thought I was happy...then you came along...."

"You want to talk about it?"

"Oh, God, no."

He set his glasses and the paperwork aside, then rose in one lithe movement. He hooked his arm around her neck, pulling her close. He took the condom from her fingers and murmured, "You're worth waiting for, sugar. You want to take it slow, that's okay. We made a deal, remember?"

She plunged her fingers into the heavy softness of his hair. "I take everything slow. I put everything in order and think everything through, and damn it, T.K., nothing ever happens. I talk myself out of everything. Until I met you, I don't think I ever did anything spontaneously. Never…I've never followed a hunch." She was babbling and she knew it, but she couldn't stop. "I go to work and I go home and I have my little routines. Oh, T.K., you make me feel so crazy and so good."

"Want to hear how you make me feel?"

She shook her head. "Show me."

She met his kiss, and all her senses joined in a happy *thank you.* She groped at his back and clutched his shirt, pulling it free of his jeans. His skin was warm, supple and smooth. His back muscles undulated in a tantalizing dance as he pressed her against his lean body. Urgency maddened her as she touched her tongue to his, inflamed by the erotic slipperiness and passionate strength.

Her body sang with life. His belt buckle ground against her belly and his thighs rubbed hers with quivering tension. She felt the hard wanting as his hand caressed her arm, then her waist. She moaned her yearning as he slid his hands under her sweater, and her skin tingled with heat.

He broke the kiss and she gasped for air. He nibbled her lower lip, her cheek, her chin and the sensitive spot under her jaw. He murmured, "Kerry…oh, sugar, let me pull off my boots." He stepped back, his hands lingering across her back and shoulders as if he could not bear to let her go.

Balancing on one leg, never taking his eyes from hers, he pulled off one boot, then the other. Mesmerized, she lifted a foot, untied her sneaker and worked it off her foot. His smile enchanted her.

So did his body as he popped pearly snaps one by one then shed his shirt. His collarbones jutted in heavy ridges and his chest was chiseled from stone. Grown giddy with boldness, Kerry kicked off her other sneaker.

I love him... The movement of his large, muscular hands distracted her, and she watched his fingers slip under her sweater then slowly slide the soft wool upward. Lifting her arms, she shivered as he pulled the sweater over her head. Smiling, his face gentle yet dark with passion, Smith traced the lacy edging on her brassiere. Her knees turned to water.

She closed her eyes as his tanned flesh seemed to melt against her paleness. He kissed her, gently, softly, and his scent invaded her brain, blotting out the world as he worked a hand over her back and finally reached her bra hooks and undid them. She fondled his shoulders, felt the knots and the faint shivers, and she wondered if he, like her, wanted to rip off their clothing and fall to the floor. As he eased her bra off her arms, then lightly stroked her breast, she bit her lip to stop a cry of ecstasy. His hand grew bolder, firmer, weakening her with rising passion.

Smith pulled back, then lightly touched her cheek with the foil packet. "If you only have one, then we best make sure we use it well." He caught the back of her knees. She gasped to find herself in his arms. "Your bedroom or mine?"

"Surprise me."

He kissed her all the way to his bedroom door. She groped, found the knob and turned it. He shouldered the door open.

"T.K.?"

"Yes, darlin'?"

"Tell me this ain't some casual affair."

He looked her straight in the eye, and she knew her instinct was right. He was hers and she was his, and nothing else in the world mattered.

"There's some things I don't take lightly, sugar," he

whispered. "You're at the top of the list." Then he carried her into the bedroom and closed the door with his foot.

SMITH PLANTED TEASING kisses on Kerry's bare back. Her skin was warm. He tasted it and found it sweetly salty. Her flowery perfume had acquired a darker, more sensual scent. It made blood pound in his ears. She was more than beautiful, she was right. She fit him as if custom made. She lay on her belly with one arm under her head; her silky hair covered her face. All he could see was the gentle curve of her smile.

She giggled. "I have the most awful urge to call Mom."

"Tell her I say hello." He cupped her buttock in his hand; it was a perfect fit. He opened his mouth to tell he loved her—hell, he wanted to sing it, throw open the windows and shout it at the top of his lungs—but he bit back the urge. Reason reined him in, telling him to slow down and not scare her off. He felt too good to say something hasty and put that startled look back in her eyes.

She propped herself on her forearms and looked over her shoulder. "Don't you take anything seriously?"

"You." He caressed the soft mound of her buttocks and kissed the small of her back. "I think—" He kissed her again "—you're the most serious—" his lips trailed downward "—thing I've ever run across."

A burst of laughter escaped her. "That tickles." She rolled to her side.

Smith reeled at the sight of her, and his heart felt six times too big for his chest. Her pale skin glowed by the light of a small bedside lamp. Her round breasts were tipped with honey. He was surprised that he didn't feel in the least sleepy; what he felt was sixteen years old again, randy and raring to go. He cupped one of her breasts and thumbed the nipple. His grin widened at her response. Making love to her could easily grow into one of his favorite pastimes.

"You better stop," Kerry whispered, but she didn't look as if she wanted him to stop at all. "We don't have any more of those—"

Wishing he was sixteen and still carrying that two-year-old condom in his wallet, he laughed. "Condoms?"

"Don't laugh at me."

"You're a priss."

"I am not." She shrugged. "Okay, so I'm a priss. We still don't have any more." She sat up and stretched, and he clenched his fists to keep from grabbing her.

Groaning at the rising ache of his desire, he swung his legs off the bed and searched the carpet for his underwear. He found them and pulled them on. She sat with her arms around her knees, her face soft and dreamy. *I love you.* The words pushed at the back of his throat. He scooped up her panties and took a moment to study them. Apricot silk with lace on the front. Prim, but sexy, just like her. He tossed them onto the bed. "Come on, sugar. Can't make love to you, may as well get something to eat."

"What…?" she murmured.

He asked, "Aren't you hungry? Let's go to the grocery store." He found their jeans. Her sleepy, satisfied smile made him feel twenty feet tall and able to conquer the world.

She said, "We could order in a pizza."

"I'm thinking about dessert."

Chapter Fifteen

"Last chance, Nolan. Did you take my money?"

She pressed the barrel of the .32 pistol behind his ear. Nolan Piver quivered. A stink as rank as battery acid rose off his body, and dark circles appeared under his armpits and across his shoulders. She had caught him in an awkward, hunched over position as he had searched a clothes hamper. He kept jerking as if his knees were going to collapse. She wondered if perhaps she needn't shoot at all, but merely wait for him to have a heart attack. She repeated the question.

"No, God, no. I swear I didn't take your money." The words dribbled out of his mouth as erratically as the drops of sweat that fell off his nose.

"I believe you," she said with calm resignation. She pulled the trigger.

The pistol report made her jump, and her shoulder protested against the kick. She flinched, grimacing as Nolan pitched forward onto the hamper, then crumpled and rolled. She shuddered once, then looked away. This was Kerry's fault. Kerry took the money.

She peeled off the bathrobe she'd worn to protect her clothing from blood, then tossed it onto the bed. She looked around at the bedroom, disgusted by the mess.

Dresser drawers were upturned, the bedding stripped and the closet emptied. It was a stupid room anyway, with the flowered bedspread and rosy curtains. Kerry probably thought she had plenty of cash for redecorating now. *We shall see about that,* the woman thought.

Photographs in frames on the dresser top caught her eye. She picked up a portrait of a man in an army uniform. He was a good-looking man, about forty-five or so, his sandy hair cut close to his skull. His mouth was stern, but his eyes were smiling. Silver eagles decorated his shoulders; four rows of medals decorated his chest. It reminded the woman of her daddy with his tales about Korea and the war. She laid the portrait down, then smashed the glass with the pistol butt.

That small violence did nothing to soothe her rage or change the fact that the money wasn't in Kerry Byfield's apartment. Clutching the gun in her gloved hand, she stalked out. She stood in the middle of the ruined living room and caught herself breathing hard. She swallowed, nudging down the panic. She glared at the smashed computer screen, then at the little orange plastic box of disks that had so panicked Nolan. Somehow Kerry had used it to find out about her. What had Nolan called Kerry? A glorified typist? Well, even if she didn't have the money, she was going to pay.

A blinking red light drew the woman's attention. She gazed down at the answering machine, then pressed the Playback button. Nothing but Mom's increasingly snotty demands that Kerry return her calls.

Thoughtful, the woman left the apartment.

STARING DREAMILY OFF INTO space, Kerry rested her chin in her palm. She was cold this morning, and the air and the pickup's door chilled her arm, but she barely felt it.

Smith glanced at his watch. He said, "It's 10:10. He isn't going to show."

Kerry tried not to look at him. All it took was a glance to melt her bones and muddle her with memories of last night. Merely thinking about his big, sleek body and the way he had murmured loving words in her ear set her trembling. She mused over his lazy satisfaction and the slow warmth of his hands after their lovemaking. How long had they talked? Hours it seemed. About what? It didn't matter. She yawned widely. They'd caught a few hours of sleep, but not much. Who needed sleep? She had him.

A giggle escaped when she remembered them in the all-night supermarket. They were like a couple of randy teenagers. Prowling for sexual protection turned out to be exciting instead of embarrassing. Especially with their other purchases—canned oysters, cream-filled donuts, bananas, candy bars and whatever else she or Smith had deemed tempting. Smith's antics had given her such a bad case of giggles, she'd thought the store manager was going to throw them out.

Sex, Kerry decided, did odd things to her appetite. Smith definitely did odd things to her libido. She marveled yet again at how the pair of them had ended up at two o'clock in the morning in a bubble bath, wearing their Stetson hats and feeding each other smoked oysters out of the can. God, he was fun.

She shook her head to clear it. Briskly rubbing her cold arms, she paced next to the pickup. *Get a grip, Byfield,* she told herself firmly. Think about business. She eyed Detective Shanlin, and that sobered her. This was supposed to be his day off. If he took this seriously enough to use his free time, then the least she could do was get her mind out of the bedroom.

The three of them waited in front of Copy Copy. The store's windows were dark. The parking lot was three-quarters full. Pedestrians strolled along the covered walkway. A woman tried Copy Copy's door, peered closely at the posted hours, then shook her head disgustedly and stomped away.

Shanlin sipped coffee from a disposable cup. He looked from Kerry to Smith, then shook his bearish head. "Looks like you spooked him, Smith."

Smith grunted, his arms folded across his chest. There were brownish circles under his eyes. He put a fist to his mouth and fought a yawn. "How long before the boys in the ballistics lab have anything?"

Shanlin held out his hands. "Whenever. I almost have the chief talked into reopening this case, but until then, the lab can't give this much—" An imperious squeal made the detective scowl. He reached under his coat for his beeper. He eyed the strip that displayed a phone number. "Back in a minute," he said, and ambled toward a pay phone.

"This is so frustrating," Kerry said.

"Imagine what Bill feels like." Smith tapped his fingers on the truck. "Quintas asked the judge for a delay in sentencing, but Lowell is putting on the heat from the other side. Deadlock."

Kerry was fed up with the justice system. "You don't think Piver found the money, do you?"

Smith jerked a thumb at Copy Copy. "Let's find out."

"More illegal entry?" Kerry loosed a nervous giggle. "Not with Shanlin here."

Shanlin reappeared, moving quickly. He looked

pointedly at Smith. "We have another body." He looked at Kerry, then half turned. She stood taller to try and see his face. "Over at Parkway Manor. Apartment 111."

The news hit Kerry like a fist in the belly. "That's my apartment!" she cried. She thought of Becky and Sharon, feeling sick and dizzy. One of them may have been attacked while feeding the cats. She clung to Smith's arm, staring up at his face. "The girls. Oh, my God—one of the girls?"

Shanlin trotted to his car, calling over his shoulder, "Victim's a man, Miss Byfield."

KERRY TOOK A DEEP BREATH and walked into her apartment. Disbelief and a wavering rise of unreality washed over her. She shook her head in denial. This wasn't her apartment. Her apartment was clean and cheerful, with chatty cats and yesterday's newspaper on the coffee table. This strange place had tipped over bookshelves and a computer monitor lying smashed on the floor. Couch and chair cushions were slashed apart, the stuffing littering the floor like dirty clumps of snow. Tables were upended, rugs torn back and plant pots emptied. In the kitchen, the refrigerator was open. Water dripped from the defrosting freezer. All the cabinets stood open. Glass covered the floor.

A police officer brushed her arm in passing and Kerry jumped. Smith placed steadying hands on her shoulders.

"I need you to look at the body, Miss Byfield," Shanlin said.

Kerry shook her head and felt her mouth turn stubborn. This was some sort of bad dream. If she just stood here, eventually she'd awaken. A black shadow streaked past. She cringed and tried to scream. All that came out was a whispery, "Wheep!" Smith scooped up Midnight. The kitten meowed piteously and tried to burrow under his hair.

Beckoning from the hallway, Shanlin asked, "Any idea what someone was looking for?"

Kerry nodded, dumbly, thinking about two bags of money and a box of computer disks. She followed the detective to the bedroom.

The corpse was curled on his side, one arm next to the clothes hamper. Technicians with badges flopping on their jacket pockets snapped photographs and took measurements. Kerry didn't need to see the face; she recognized the suit. "Nolan Piver," she said.

Shanlin, his face bland, scribbled the name in his notebook. "You sure?"

"I'd know that back anywhere."

"You have to do better, Miss Byfield." Shanlin asked a technician to turn the body.

Piver's eyes were open, cloudy and staring. His mouth, too, was open, as if he were about to shout. Kerry nodded affirmation. A surprisingly small bloodstain marred the carpet. She quickly averted her eyes.

Smith touched her cheek. "You okay?"

She sighed, afraid that if she opened her mouth, a scream would emerge.

A miserable yowl came from under the bed. Kerry lifted the dust ruffle. Keystone and Lucy were huddled together. Their eyes were wide and their ears laid back.

"Don't touch anything, miss," a technician said.

"My cats."

Shanlin gave her the okay. She and Smith coaxed the two cats from under the bed, then carried them and Midnight next door to Becky and Sharon's apartment. They found the girls in a semihysterical state. Becky had gone to feed the cats, found the apartment trashed, then she called the police, who found the body.

"I have to find Dash," Kerry muttered. She rushed out of the apartment, past the police officers who were taping yellow strips around her apartment. She passed the reporters who were shouting questions. It was unreal.

Smith caught her arm and she jumped again, her heart pounding. "Hey, sugar, it's okay. Come on, let's go sit someplace. Your face is dead white. You look about to pass out on me."

"No," she said firmly. "No, I won't sit down. I can't. I just can't." She twisted away from him and forced herself to look under cars and behind bushes for the missing cat. Feeling Smith on her heels, she said, "If I sit down, I'm going to start thinking about things I don't want to think about. Okay?" Her voice rose, high-pitched and cracking. She stopped and planted her fists on her hips. She breathed very deeply, surprised to find a reserve of calmness deep inside. "I think I'm freaking a little, but I'll be all right. I promise." She groped blindly for Smith's hand, found it and squeezed. "Just help me find my cat. Once I find her, everything will be okay, okay?"

They continued to search for the missing cat. Ignoring reporters, policemen and gawking passersby, Kerry looked under more cars and ran her hands into wheel wells.

"Here she is," Smith said.

Dash crouched, every hair on end, in the mouth of a drain pipe. Fortunately, a metal grating had prevented her from going too deeply into the hole. As he hauled the terrified cat into the open, Smith suffered a few nasty scratches and bites.

Kerry brushed a bead of blood from his hand. "She's had her shots. I'm so sorry."

He eyed his bloodied hand good-humoredly. "This should be the least of my problems. You feeling better?"

Hating herself for putting the anxious lines in his brow, she stood on tiptoe and kissed his lips. "I'm going to be okay." It was the truth. "Funny, a few days ago I would have gotten mad at you for staying calm. But you just get used to it, don't you? I mean, I feel lousy, but I don't think I'm going to lose it." As long as she didn't dwell on Nolan Piver's staring eyes, anyway. She took Dash, and the cat immediately bit her thumb, hard. Kerry yelped and caught the scruff of Dash's neck. In an odd way, the physical pain snapped her out of the grip of unreality. They took the cat to Becky's apartment.

To the accompaniment of whirring cameras and shouting reporters, the coroner carried the body out. Shanlin came out next. When he spotted Smith and Kerry, he made a gesture for them to meet him at Smith's pickup.

The detective held a notebook and pencil ready. He settled his stone-faced attention on Kerry. "I have to ask you where you were last night."

"Hold on a minute there, Shanlin," Smith said. His eyes became narrow and angry.

She hooked her arm with his and said, "It's okay, I understand." In a gruesome sort of way, being a suspect in Piver's murder was almost ironically funny. How many times had he made her so angry, she'd wanted to kill him? "I was with T.K. at his hotel."

"Can anyone confirm that?"

"I can," Smith said coldly.

Kerry thought about the grocery-store manager who'd witnessed their foolery around the aisles, the desk clerk who'd grinned at them departing and arriving and the man who'd caught them kissing in the elevator. "I think there are a lot of people who can tell you I wasn't here last night." She felt her cheeks burn.

"Had to ask."

Smith said, "Find Randi Mae Firkins. She probably killed Piver. I'll bet you a steak dinner she used a .32 pistol to do it."

Kerry told the detective about the money they'd found, how and why they'd hid it, and about threatening Piver with the IRS in hopes of a confession. She balked at telling him about Blackie, deciding that now was not the time. With luck, she need never mention his name at all.

Smith rubbed the back of his neck. His eyes had lost all trace of humor. He looked bleak and a little dangerous. "I'm betting you'll pull a .32 slug out of Piver that will match the slug taken out of Thomas Nordoff back in June. The important thing is getting hold of Randi Mae. Money or no money, she's going to run."

KERRY STRETCHED, listening to her aching neck creak. She smacked her lips and found them gummy. It took her a moment to remember where she was. Bob Ward's inner office. The tiny television set made crackling background noise. Beyond the door she could hear the murmur of male voices. She stretched again and glanced at her watch. It was seven in the morning. Yesterday was finally over; she wished she could block it forever from memory.

She swung her feet to the floor. She'd been up until nearly one in the morning, going over and over the Abernathy murder. A high-powered and almost obsessively dedicated group had gathered last night. Homicide detectives Shanlin and Ott, men who gave Kerry faith in the police again. They weren't getting paid for this. They did it because they wanted justice done. The same applied to the attorneys from the D.A., Bob Ward and a junior assistant named Babington. Quintas had joined them, bringing box loads of case information, his antagonism subdued as he worked with the prosecutors to clear William Abernathy.

Still, it had been a singularly disappointing night. Armed with all the computer printouts, Smith's report and statements from Smith and Kerry, they had all worked against the clock to compile a report for Bradford Lowell. But evidence was circumstantial; connections between Randi Mae, Piver, Thomas Nordoff and Louise Abernathy were coincidental. Every man, even Smith, agreed that finding Randi Mae was the only sure thing. Right after the murder, the police had investigated Nolan Piver's house in Richardson. They'd found the Mercedes, but no guns and no Randi Mae. The police had distributed her photograph, and airports, bus stations and car-rental places were being watched, but everyone doubted they'd find the woman. When Kerry finally gave in to exhaustion, the mood in Bob Ward's office was glum.

Ward had offered Kerry the couch in his inner office. The inner office was crowded by a couch, overflowing bookcases and a minuscule desk piled with paperwork. Kerry rubbed her stinging eyes. Her stomach growled. She blinked blearily at the outer office where Ward's cigarette smoke made a blue haze.

Quintas was saying, "Go over the chart once more. Pretend I'm the judge."

That had been Quintas's favorite phrase throughout the night. "Pretend I'm the judge." *Pompous ass,* Kerry thought. Even with them on the same side, she didn't like him. She went to the door and eyed one of the charts. It was a time-flow chart showing her exact actions on the night of Louise Abernathy's murder and how the murderer must have waited for Kerry to appear, to make sure he ran past her in a way that she had to see his face.

Smith spotted her. His eyes glittered from the coffee he'd been drinking all night long. He grinned triumphantly.

"You geniuses figured it out yet?" Kerry asked.

There was a knock on the door, then a man poked his head inside. He had messy black hair and aviator glasses. He thrust forth a sheaf of papers. Ward immediately arose and held out a hand. He introduced the man as Frank from the police lab.

Frank shook his head. "By golly, Ward, you owe me at least a case of beer for this one. I don't get overtime for this. And my wife isn't none too happy about me coming in at 4:00 a.m., either."

"What have you got?"

Frank absently pushed back his hair and it stood up on his head like a cock's comb. He glanced at the papers. "What we have is some partials. I can't do better than get thirty percent of the bullets from the bodies, but what I did get was a real good partial from the Nordoff body and the bullet out of the dirt. Ditto with the Piver bullet. Put 'em all together and I can say that it's, oh, seventy percent likely they match. I need the weapon to get you one hundred percent."

Kerry guessed from the smiles and table pounding that Frank bore good tidings. Ward threatened to kiss

Frank, and the man grimaced and scooted out of the office. Kerry hadn't understood a word. She leaned close to Smith's ear and asked, "What did he just say?"

"There's about a seventy percent chance that the same gun was used to shoot Nordoff, Piver and your Nova. Unfortunately, that isn't good enough for a jury. Fortunately, it ought to be good enough for the judge."

Searching his smiling face and bloodshot eyes, she absorbed the information. "You did it? You have enough to reopen the case and free Mr. Abernathy?" Relief weakened her knees, but she wanted to dance on the tabletop. She shrieked, grabbed his neck and pressed a jubilant kiss to his mouth. "You did it!"

Ward stretched back in his chair, arms high, reaching backward. "Lowell will be in around eight o'clock. If this ain't enough to convince him, I don't know what is." He yawned mightily, showing all his teeth. "Quintas, you better get your butt cleaned up. You have a court date in three hours. Babington, go rustle up a stenographer for Miss Byfield's deposition. If you sweet talk Mrs. Larson, she might come in early. Shanlin, see if you can rope some cooperation with the Waxahatchie Police Department. Miss, do me a favor and turn off that TV. Don't know why I run that thing all the time. It gives me a headache."

Kerry floated despite the discomfiture of knowing that grins were directed at her outburst. They had done it! It made the week worthwhile. And now? She could live again, free of fright, free of guilt. And there was Smith....

I'm going shopping, she thought firmly. *And I'm going to buy the first pretty, sexy thing that catches my eye. I'm going to make him dinner—fried chicken and mashed potatoes and a huge chocolate cake for dessert.*

If that wasn't sweet enough, they'd eat ice cream, too. They'd feed it to each other and make love, and their laughter wouldn't have anything to do with nervousness or close calls.

As she reached for the television knob, she froze and her eyes widened. The morning news showed a close-up of her apartment with the coroner's attendants carrying Piver's black-bagged body out her door. Her face showed on screen, blank eyed and slack mouthed as she walked out of Becky's apartment.

Mom. Angela ate breakfast every morning in the kitchen while the morning talk shows and news blared.

"Oh, my God. Mr. Ward, may I use the telephone in here?"

"Dial nine for an outside line."

Wondering how she was going to slither out of this one, she dialed her mother's number. Her mind whirled with explanations. To her surprise, she got the answering machine. She listened to her mother's chirpy message, waited for the beep, then said, "Mom, it's me. Sorry I haven't called. I need to—"

"It's about time you called."

Kerry's knees buckled. Her belly twisted so violently that she nearly doubled over. She whispered, "What are you doing at my mother's house?"

"Waiting for you. You ought to listen to your answering machine more often," the cold, elegant voice said. "Where's my money, Kerry?"

Kerry glanced at the door. The men were busy putting papers in order. She hissed. "Where's my mother?"

"I asked first."

"You want your money, then you let me speak to

my mother. Damn you, if you've harmed her, I swear I'll kill you.''

"Sure you will. Here she is.''

"Baby? Oh, God, what's—'' Angela's voice was strained and cracked with tears.

The woman's voice returned. "Happy? Now listen carefully, Kerry. I want my money. I want it now. No more games.''

Kerry blanked on ideas. She only knew that she dared not tell Randi Mae that the police knew about the money. "It's hidden. I'll have to show you where it is.''

"And I suppose you don't show me anything without seeing your mother, right?''

"That's right.'' Kerry chewed her lip, then blurted out, "I have it hidden. I'm the only one who knows where. Meet me at Copy Copy. I'll give you your money. And you leave my mother alone. Just leave her alone.''

There was a long, icy silence. "Fair enough. But I warn you, if you go to the police, well…the only thing you get out of me is the location of the ditch where I dumped your mother. Do you understand?''

"No cops,'' Kerry whispered.

"Bring that irritant Smith with you. I never liked him.''

Kerry's insides settled downward. She groped behind her, found the couch and sat, hard. Randi Mae wanted her dead, and Smith, too. "He doesn't know where the money is. I took it because Piver fired me. T.K. doesn't know about it.''

"You *and* Smith. Copy Copy. Thirty minutes.'' Randi Mae hung up with a soft, final click.

Icy calm settled over Kerry. Ruin her life, make her

a party to a conspiracy, victimize her? Murder Nolan Piver? Threaten her mother? *No.* With a tight smile plastered on her face, Kerry went to Smith and said, "Can I speak to you in the hallway for a minute?" He eyed her strangely and she dug her fingernails into his shoulder. "Now."

Once out of the room full of lawyers and policemen, she exclaimed, "Randi Mae has my mother!" Shaking gripped her head to toe, and Smith had to hold her to keep her from falling. In a harsh, shaky whisper, she told him everything, emphasizing over and over that Randi Mae had said to bring no cops.

"Let's go get your mother."

"Randi Mae means to kill you!"

"Means to is one thing, doing's another." He held her shoulders. Burning intensity darkened his face. He was thinking again. "If she wants that money, she'll have to bargain for it."

"It's my mother! What are we going to do? Oh, God, I'm so stupid. For all I know, the police are already picking up the money! She's going to hurt my mother!"

The darting of Smith's eyes warned her. Robert Marsh, his arms laden with legal volumes, came down the hallway. He glared at them, then glanced at Ward's office. The smokey haze and shirt-sleeved men made it look like a poker party. To Kerry's relief, Marsh kept walking.

With narrowed eyes and a tight expression, Smith watched the assistant D.A. Then he stuck his head into the office and said cheerfully, "I'm going to get some fresh air and breakfast. Any requests?"

There were calls for Danishes and more coffee. Shanlin asked for a heavy-duty fan to blow away the smoke. Ward growled at him.

Smith hustled Kerry down the hallway.

Chapter Sixteen

The parking lot at the Plano Place shopping center was mostly deserted. As Smith parked the truck in front of Copy Copy, Kerry studied the few cars. Most were parked in front of the dental offices. There was no sign of mall security. Copy Copy's windows were dark and blank.

Kerry whispered, "Do you think she's here?" Deep, hurting anger made her clothes seem too tight and her skin too hot. Randi Mae Firkins wasn't getting away with this. Her crimes had transcended excuse or reason. The woman was evil, and no motive could possibly make sense.

Smith slowly straightened and lifted his head. His lips parted, and he exhaled a barely discernible, "Well, hell."

Looking right and left, Kerry demanded, "Do you see her?"

He gave her a mirthless grin. "It just hit me. Copy copy. There's not one impersonator, but two. Motive, opportunity and consistency. That isn't Randi Mae Firkins. Randi Mae is dead."

"What? Then who—" Then it hit Kerry, too. Randi Mae and Louise were the same size, with the same color hair. The dead woman's face had been destroyed. Kerry had seen a man who looked like Abernathy running from Abernathy's house, and she had believed she saw Abernathy. Why not go one step further? "Oh, my God, it's Louise."

"Bingo."

"What do we do? She has my mother."

"Don't panic, sugar. We can handle her. I'll bet that getting away with it means as much to her as doing it. We have to get her talking, Kerry. She'll want to talk. Distract her. Louise is a little woman. If we can keep our heads, we can take her. Understand?"

Uncertain if she wanted to understand, Kerry nodded.

"She's only going to do what she can get away with. If we or the police can trap her, she'll give up. We have to stall her. It won't take Shanlin long to connect you making a phone call to our not returning to the office."

Smith didn't add "I hope," and Kerry was grateful. Taking a deep breath, she put her hand on the door handle, then paused. A whirl of emotions and desperation caused a succession of lumps to fall inside her chest. She said in a rush, "I love you, T.K."

He reared back, blinking.

Realizing her blunder, Kerry felt her face grow warm. She opened the door. "It doesn't matter. I figure we're going to die, so you might as well know it. I'm not sorry I said that. I'm just sorry I didn't say it sooner. I do love you."

He caught her arm. "I knew it the minute I saw you."

"That I love you?" she asked, confused.

"That I love you." He leaned across the short span between them and pressed a gentle kiss to her mouth. "And, sweet thing, we aren't going to die. Give me the shop key." He raked back his chestnut hair, then held out his hand.

His words gave her strength. His eyes filled her with courage. Love was her talisman. No harm could touch her with him at her side.

The bell sounded as loud as the Westminster Cathedral Chimes as they opened the door to Copy Copy. Aching with tension, Kerry called, "Hello?" The place felt empty and deserted, like an old warehouse, and it smelled dusty. Piver had forgotten to leave the fan running.

"Close the door and lock it," a soft voice said.

Hating the way Smith used his body to shield hers, Kerry locked the door. Then, peering through the gloom, seeking the source of the voice, she said, "Where's my mother?"

"Safe."

"If you want your money, do better."

"Nolan's office. Hold your hands where I can see them. Get in there, both of you." With a slight movement, Louise revealed herself. She stood in the doorway to the back room, where there were no lights or windows. She was a shadow. Her voice was as anonymous now as when she had spoken on the phone. But she was no longer anonymous. It was Louise Abernathy, evil and murderous. "Get into the office. No tricks, Smith. I'll blow your brains out." She punctuated the words with a metallic click.

As Kerry eased past the woman, she caught a whiff of Chanel No 5. Smith touched her back lightly.

Kerry entered the office and relief flooded through her. Angela was alive. Bound and gagged, seated awkwardly in a corner of Piver's office, but alive. Her blouse was buttoned crookedly and it didn't match her slacks. Her face was blotchy without cosmetics, and her tearful eyes rolled. But she was alive. Smith looked at Kerry as he moved away from her. She took her cue and took a sideways step. *Distract her, stall.* Kerry turned to the door. Surprise took her off guard. It wasn't Louise Abernathy.

The woman had dark hair, cut just above her jawline and styled softly and fully. Her figure, encased in a white linen suit, was anything but petite. She could enter a Dolly Parton lookalike contest and stand a chance of winning. She held a pistol in one gloved hand. Gradient sunglasses hid her eyes and kept Kerry from telling who she was looking at.

Smith said, "Hello, Louise. Gained a little weight I see."

Bloodred lips curved in a feline smile. "Always the charmer. You don't sound surprised to see me, Tarkington," Louise said.

"I've had this figured out for a while. Truth is, though, you looked better as a blonde." The pistol bore pointed at his belly, but he jammed his hands into his pockets and rocked nonchalantly on his heels. "I knew at the wedding Bill had found himself a smart one. I just didn't know how smart. So how'd you do it? Style Randi Mae's hair so it looked like yours? Say, 'Here, try on my dress? And wouldn't these rings look pretty on you?'" He lifted his shoulders in a lazy shrug. "Then obliterate her face. Easy. Where'd you find Nordoff? Lucky chance, or did you audition several candidates?"

"My goodness, aren't you the clever fellow? You figured that out all by yourself?" Louise gestured with the pistol. "Tie him up, Kerry. Now." She pointed the gun at Angela.

Smith turned around, putting his arms behind his back. His hands were in fists. Kerry picked up the ball of heavy shipping twine Louise had placed on the desk. Surprisingly steady, she tied his hands. His fingers twitched, giving her a glimpse of his pocket knife. She glanced at Louise. The woman still smiled.

Smith said, "One thing puzzles me. Why set up Bill? If you wanted to fake your own death, that's one thing. But why Bill?"

"Nothing personal. But a murder victim must have a murderer or else the police keep digging and digging." An amused, almost boastful edge gave a lilt to her voice. "It would surprise you how much I've learned about police investigations. I had quite an instructor."

He chuckled. "Won't say I agree, but I have to admit I admire you, Louise. You've got guts. But tell me, how did you manage to get the mortuary to cremate Randi Mae's body?"

Louise's laughter sounded high and sweet. "I wish I could take credit for that, but it was just a lucky mishap that happened to work out very well. Tell me, Tarkington, who else knows who I am?"

Kerry's skin felt as though it were crawling with ants. She finished tying Smith and stepped back.

He lifted a shoulder. "Everyone. Sorry about that, Louise. Your cover is blown."

"Pity. I really do love Dallas. There's so much life here. You know, I never realized how difficult it is to become someone else. Everyone is so insistent about digging up the past." Louise pursed her lips in a rueful gesture. "It really isn't my fault. If anyone is to blame, it's Bill. All I wanted was the money and a fresh start. But Bill is funny about owning things…owning me. He would have found me eventually, if I'd just run. I wanted to stay here. I like Dallas. You cannot know how disappointing it is to have to leave. This is my home, where I belong.''

"Haven't you ever heard of divorce?'' Kerry asked.

Louise chuckled. "I've been divorced. It's ugly— In the corner, Tarkington. His ankles, too, Kerry. Come on, I haven't got all day. I plan to be sipping margaritas in Acapulco by six.''

Kerry tied Smith's feet together, all the while searching his eyes for a clue as to what to do next. He mouthed, "Keep stalling.'' Kerry spun around. "Okay, he's tied up. Now let my mother go. She doesn't know anything.''

"Where's my money?'' The pistol was pointed at Kerry's forehead.

Kerry glanced at her mother's sickly white face. Her eyes were stripped of color, blank and terrified. Keep Louise talking? They were running out of friendly subjects far too fast. Kerry clamped her arms over her chest and lifted her chin. "I'm really sick of this!'' she shouted.

Louise flinched.

"Do you know what kind of rotten week I've had because of you? Have you any idea? I've been shot at and I lost my job. My former boss was bleeding all over my apartment! I've had it!''

"Kerry—'' Louise growled in warning, but she tensed her shoulders and swayed as if debating escape.

"So what are you going to do? Shoot me? Fine, just fine! My damned cat bit me because of you!'' She thrust out her wounded thumb. "See that? So you just go ahead and top off a really terrific week, Louise. Just go ahead.'' Shouting gave Kerry strength, and Louise's wary uncertainty gave her courage. A giddy sense of power lightened her head. "Yeah, shoot me. Then walk out of here broke. Because I'm the only one who knows where that money is. You'll never find it! So shoot my mother, go ahead. Shoot T.K.! Then you know what I'm going to do? I'm going to go absolutely crazy. I'm going to scream and throw things and you won't have any choice except to shoot me! Fine! It's just fine!"

Louise pulled the trigger.

Kerry's eardrums reverberated; ringing filled her head. She staggered backward and knocked her buttocks against the desk. She looked down, seeking blood, her nostrils flared in protest against the cordite stink. From far away she heard pitiful whimpering and it took a few seconds to realize that it was her mother.

"That was a deliberate miss, Kerry," Louise said. "The next one will be right on target." She swung the pistol at Angela.

Kerry swallowed hard, not daring to look at Smith; too much fear possessed her. Then she couldn't help it. She looked. He sat rigid, cords standing out on his neck, but he was unharmed. He shook his head just enough to let her know this was definitely the wrong thing to do.

Mustering calm, she said, "Uh-uh. If you hurt her, I'll never give you the money. Never. Ask Quintas if I'm stubborn; he'll tell you. Hurt my mother or T.K. and that's two big bags of cash you'll never see again." She glared directly into Louise's eyes. Steeliness she never knew she possessed locked her spine. Shouting had been a desperate ruse, but these words she believed with all her heart. Louise Abernathy could go straight to hell.

"All right, Kerry." Louise stepped backward, her high heels clicking. "All I ever wanted was the money.

Nothing else. I didn't want to hurt anybody. I won't hurt anybody unless you give me no choice. Now, follow me.''

Kerry looked at Smith. His shoulder muscles flexed and worked. His eyes told her to keep stalling. She followed Louise from the office, knowing the woman lied, but not knowing what else to do. Closing the door, Kerry locked it. She was dismayed when Louise ordered her to leave the key in the lock. Louise was too smart. They'd made a terrible mistake.

"The back room," Kerry muttered. Louise turned on the overhead lights. The back room had been searched, but the stack of cardboard boxes was untouched. Kerry asked, "Why Piver?" Did Louise only want money? No way. Something else drove her, and Kerry's life depended on finding out what it was.

Louise snorted softly, impatiently.

Kerry remembered that flashing diamond ring. "You made him fall in love with you, so he could launder the money." She smiled mirthlessly. "You didn't know about his mother, did you?"

The slight twitch of arched eyebrows said perhaps Louise didn't know everything. "The money—now."

"He double-crossed you." Kerry searched for a weapon. "He always was a wheeler-dealer. I guess he figured he could put you off long enough to use the money himself. He was stealing from you." Her gaze lit on her drafting table and the long, metal straightedge.

"Have you ever been shot in the leg? I understand it hurts...a lot." Louise acquired a nasal tone, and the words were spoken through clenched teeth. Her finger tightened on the trigger.

Out of ideas, Kerry jerked a thumb at the stack of boxes. She said, "Up there."

"Get it."

With the unwavering pistol pointed at her head, Kerry pulled the step stool to the stack of boxes, climbed up and tugged at the top box. It was very heavy, but as if reading her thoughts, Louise stood far enough away so throwing it at her was impossible. Kerry was sweating profusely by the time she reached the fifth box. She searched frantically through the files of her memory. What drove Louise? All those name changes, divorces, bankruptcies, expensive habits, showing off to Randi Mae and boasting about movie stars and modeling. That picture-perfect house…cosmetics lined up like soldiers in formation. Her compulsive neatness and control.

She dawdled, pretending weakness as she wrestled with the box. Was Louise obsessed? A compulsive manipulator? "Too bad you don't have more time," she said. "I know how to get the rest of your money."

Louise said, "Sure you do."

Watching the woman's reaction, Kerry said, "I can. The same way I locked Piver's accounts and canceled his charge cards."

Louise drew her head up and to the side. She looked surprised, but interested.

"I'm a computer hacker. That's how I found out that you signed over your car to Randi Mae and how I found your mother in Waxahatchie. I know a lot of things about you."

"Impossible."

A prickle of intuition told Kerry she was right. Louise wanted control; she was phobic about losing control. "I froze Piver's accounts. It was easy. I can do anything with a computer. I can control *anything*." She lifted a shoulder. "I can even open accounts and transfer all the funds from Piver's accounts into yours."

"You're lying. The IRS—"

"Piver thought it was the IRS, but *I* did it. On the computer at my house. The one you broke."

"You're lying. You'd say anything right now." The nasal quality was turning twangy. Was Louise frightened? Excited?

"Then how did I find out about the money? Or that you bought the shotgun?"

Louise sucked in a quick breath. She bowed her head and peered over the sunglasses. For a fleeting moment her eyes were wide and wondering.

Kerry forced a steady gaze. "You bought it at Sears. I didn't think you were the type to shop at Sears. I know all about you. You can't hide from a computer. No one can. Unless you're like me. I know how to handle them. I can make them do what I want. I have complete control."

Louise licked her lips. Kerry envisioned a vampire after a meal of blood. Kerry said, "Okay, fine, I'm lying. So leave your hard-earned cash in Piver's accounts. His mother can use it. That's what Piver wanted all along. She's in the Lambeck nursing home. It cost him more than four thousand dollars a month to keep her there. He *used* you." Kerry tore the shipping straps off the box. She took off the top and revealed the cases. Her back itched squarely between her shoulder blades. She wondered if a bullet hurt.

Gaze locked on Kerry, Louise crouched and fingered a bundle of twenty dollar bills. She said, "I worked hard for this. You don't understand. I worked very hard. If you and Tarkington hadn't interfered, no one would have gotten hurt. You just couldn't keep your noses out of my business. You have no one to blame but yourselves."

Kerry forced a smile. "If Piver hadn't acted so strangely, I never would've suspected him. Then he fired me. He called me a thief. That's why I hid the money and froze his accounts." She chuckled and shrugged. "Sort of ironic that he managed to get exactly what he wanted. Even if he can't enjoy it, his mother will."

Louise caressed the money as if it were a living thing. In a tone of careful nonchalance, she asked, "How long does it take? To do what you said with the computer?"

Shoving her hands into her pockets and ducking her head to hide her elation, Kerry shrugged. "A few hours." She grinned. "I get it. You don't have any identification. You can't open a bank account or cash checks. Randi Mae had everything you needed except a credit rating. That's why you needed Piver."

"I don't need anybody."

Wrong words. Kerry swallowed and eyed the raised gun. "But you can cash cashier's checks and money orders. Or traveler's checks. I can get those."

"You know a great deal." The words held an ominous ring.

Kerry said, "I never wanted to be involved in this thing in the first place. Marsh, the prosecutor, he forced me to testify. I never wanted in on it. Just let my mom go. Then you don't have to worry about me. I'm not going through that again—not the court or the testifying or the attacks on my character." Her throat grew dry and raw. She was doing too much talking, but she didn't dare stop. She pointed at the money. "I don't want to have to explain breaking and entering or computer hacking. That's against the law, you know. They're felonies. They can put me in prison for it. Just let my mother go and we'll be even."

"Even."

Something about the way Louise said that made Kerry's dry throat grow drier. "Do you want the rest of your money? The entire $432,900.00 you took from Bill? The insurance money?" It grew very quiet as Kerry tried to stare Louise down. She tried to believe she hadn't said too much or the wrong things, that her intuition was right, and that following it wasn't a deadly mistake.

Louise looked at the door. "Any slipups and I'll blow your brains out all over the floor. Then Smith, then your mother."

They went out front and Kerry booted the computer. She stared at the prompt in the upper left-hand corner of the screen. *I'm stalling. I'm stalling, T.K. Do something.* She looked at the office door, but in the dim light she couldn't tell if he had tried to pick the lock or not.

She typed in the commands to turn on PowerComm. She glanced at Louise. The woman stood behind the counter, the gun out of sight of anyone who might look in the windows. Kerry stared at the keyboard and wondered what to do now. Without telephone numbers and passwords, she couldn't even break into the local electronic bulletin board. She wiped her sweaty palms on her jeans, called herself an idiot bigmouth, then instructed the computer to dial Blackie's phone number. She had never called him via computer before and wasn't certain he would answer.

"What's it doing?" Louise asked, suspiciously.

"Waiting for its turn to break into the network," Kerry said. She lifted an eyebrow when Blackie answered the phone. What he would hear was her computer's electronic signal. *Hook in,* she prayed, *Answer.*

Words suddenly appeared on her screen. "Be good or be gone."

Kerry blanked. No names, no plain English. Chewing her lower lip, she typed, "Vampire Twinkie Time," and transmitted the message. *Please be as smart as you think you are,* Kerry urged.

"Go ahead."

Shaky with relief, Kerry typed. "Dit-dit-dit, dah-dah-dah, dit-dit-dit."

"What is this?" Louise demanded.

Darned good question. Kerry babbled, "It's encryption codes to make their network think I'm legit. Pretty soon it starts asking for passwords and authorization codes. That's the hard part. They change them a lot for security measures."

"Sam is home go ahead," Blackie transmitted. Kerry sagged with relief. Sam referred to Samuel Morse. Blackie had recognized the phonetic spelling of S.O.S. Then a new message appeared on the screen. "1984?" Kerry scowled, wondering what that meant.

"Is this some sort of trick?" Louise demanded.

Kerry sniffed derisively. "Don't you know anything about computers?" Louise's bristly flinch filled Kerry with elation. Obviously she knew nothing.

"1984?" appeared.

Kerry said, "It wants a confirmation code." She fought a whoop of elation. Blackie was referring to Orwell's novel about Big Brother. Was Big Brother watching? Kerry typed. "Confirm." She paused, needing to tell him who. She added, "Re: show the 486 turbo charge."

"Go ahead."

She typed, "Formatting initialize caterpillars often play saratoga."

"?"

Something cold and icy pressed against her skin just behind her ear. The cold sensation spread, chilling her bones. Kerry looked at Louise, and at the very edge of her vision she saw the faint gleam of steel. Louise said, "You're disappointing me, Kerry. I'm deeply disappointed."

SMITH WORKED HIS WRISTS against the twine. Kerry followed orders far too well. His fingers were numbing rapidly, dulling his grip on the pocket knife. Hot trickles of blood dribbled down his wrist, but he ignored them, concentrating on the twine, dreading the sound of a pistol shot. With a light *pop*, the twine gave. He jerked his arms. His flesh burned as he worked his hands free. He took a second to flex his fingers and get the blood moving again, then he sawed through the twine binding his feet.

He looked at Angela. She was in shock, her breathing barely discernible. "Everything is going to be all right, Angela," he whispered. "Angela?" He scooted to her and worked the gag off her face, then immediately clamped a hand over her rising scream. Her face was clammy under his hand, but her huffy breathing was hot.

"Hush, not a sound. Trust me. Can you do that? Trust me?" Angela quivered, but the blankness left her eyes and she nodded slowly. He hesitantly removed his hand. Though her throat worked and her cheeks puffed, she didn't scream.

He cut through her bonds. "Now you listen to me, and listen good. What I want you to do is scoot under that desk and stay there. Don't make a sound, don't move. No matter what happens. Okay?"

"Kerry," Angela said huskily. "My baby."

"She's going to be fine. I won't let anything happen to her." Locking his gaze with hers, Smith smiled. "I'm in love with her, and I'm going to marry her. I'm not about to let her get hurt. So you just do what I say and keep your head down."

It was strained, but she smiled, and he knew where Kerry got her strength. Angela was a tough lady. She scrambled on hands and knees under the desk and curled into a tight ball. He gave her a thumbs up, then stood. Always watching the door, he picked up the telephone handset. Instead of a dial tone, there was an odd electronic noise. He jiggled the plunger, but the sound wavered. It was out of order. He hung up and went to the door.

He wiped his bloody hands on his jeans, then placed a hand flat over the lock mechanism and very carefully turned the knob. It wouldn't budge. He jiggled it, tried it both ways, but nothing happened. Cursing softly, he knew the key was in the lock. He couldn't even pick it open. He eyed the hinges. He could jimmy them off and pull the door, but it would take too long and Louise would hear. He held onto the sight of pure determination he'd seen in Kerry's eyes. Her outburst had startled him, for a second giving him the impression that she'd cracked. But she hadn't cracked, and she wasn't going to. He held on to that with everything he possessed. His gaze swept the office. He glanced at the ceiling. Acoustical tiles.

Hunting had taught Smith that the best place for a blind was up a tree. Game didn't look up. People didn't, either. After a whispered assurance to Angela, he hopped onto the desk, then pushed at the tile overhead. It lifted easily.

Keep her talking, sugar. We have too great a future to blow this now. He groped and found a steel beam. He pulled himself through the ceiling.

KERRY PULLED HER HEAD AWAY from the gun, but Louise followed, holding it steady. "What are you doing? How am I supposed to think with that thing pointed at me?" Sweat had made her armpits clammy. She didn't want to die. "I won't remember the right password if you don't back off. I need to think."

The steel barrel dug against her flesh, then drew back. "If this is a trick…" Louise stepped back.

Wiping her brow with the back of a hand, Kerry thought hard. Blackie loved word games, didn't he? She typed, "Go back initialize formatting."

"Maybe."

Either you understand or you don't, Blackie. Wake up. Kerry chewed her lower lip, seeking some other way to tell Blackie that he had to call the cops.

Louise scowled at the screen. She asked, "What kind of machine answers, 'Maybe?'"

"AI," Kerry said, glibly. "Artificial intelligence. People hate talking to machines, so programmers make them sound human. Some even talk. I think it's stupid, but it doesn't matter. Please stop waving that gun at me. I need to remember the codes."

Then a sentence appeared in beautiful glowing green. "Re: castor oil and presidents sons, bullhorn."

God bless you, Blackie. She typed in, "Affirmative re: sam."

"Landline locked."

Kerry grinned at Louise. "We're in. It gets easier every time." Now to put the woman off until the cavalry arrived to the rescue. She typed, "Bank accounts realtime."

"?"

"I thought you were in?" Louise glared at a couple who strolled past the windows and stared in at the two women who were illuminated only by the glowing computer screen.

"It's their protection series. They build them in levels. Pass one, then find another. It's okay. As long as it keeps answering, we're okay. Let me think." She typed, "bank accounts on-line: transfer accounts and display."

A long moment passed. The gun moved closer to her face and Kerry gagged at the metallic stink of oil and gunpowder.

"Name name."

"Nolan Piver," Kerry typed. "On-screen display."

"Wait."

Satisfied that soon a jumble of numbers would fill her screen and throw off Louise, Kerry settled back and folded her arms. By not looking at the gun, she could at least pretend calmness. Maybe she'd inherited some of Angela's flair for dramatics after all. "Now we wait for miracles to happen. The wonders of modern banking." Louise looked skeptical, so Kerry added, "Of course, you realize this only messes with their computerized data banks. They back everything up with regular hard copies. Once this is done, you have to move fast or they'll catch the mistake."

"How fast?"

Kerry shrugged. "It depends on their auditing system. A week. Maybe less."

Louise smiled that evil, catlike smile. "I only need a few hours."

A scraping from above startled Kerry. Louise didn't

seem to notice. Kerry said, "So why Piver? You never told me why him. He doesn't seem your type."

"He's an idiot. All men are idiots, hence all are my type." Louise laughed lightly. "Don't feel sorry for him."

"You didn't have to kill him in my apartment."

The noise sounded again, directly overhead. Kerry wondered if it was her overwrought nerves amplifying natural sounds. She asked, loudly, "What I don't get are the love letters and gambling slips. Did you put them there for the police to find? That's pretty smart. It sure made you look bad, though. It's a shame about Bill. You know, he never believed any of the bad stuff anyone said about you. He really loved you. He still loves you."

"One must do what one must do."

Kerry thought the way Louise's voice remained cool was creepy. Had she no conscience at all? Louise gestured with the gun. "Isn't that thing taking a long time?"

"It has to search through a huge data base. Massive. This is central banking. It handles several banks. You want all the money, don't you? Patience."

"Oh," Louise said in the way people do who want to sound knowledgeable. "Find a way to speed it up."

"It's going fast already. You've stood in bank lines. That's what this is...sort of. I have to wait my turn—"

There was a tremendous ripping noise. Kerry jerked up her head in time to see the ceiling collapse.

Enveloped in a choking cloud of dust, insulation and acoustical tile board, Kerry shoved away from the computer desk. The wheels of the chair caught the edge of the carpet, flipping her backward. She hit with her shoulders first, then her head snapped onto the floor.

Bright lights exploded in front of her eyes. A noise like crackling television static filled her ears. From what seemed a long, long distance, a woman screamed. Kerry tried to move, but something fell over her legs. Her sense of up and down was turned around. She blinked away grit and sneezed.

"Sugar? You all right?"

Smith's voice drew Kerry out of the haze. She struggled to a sitting position and gingerly touched the goose egg growing on the back of her head. "Couldn't you have used the door?"

Chapter Seventeen

As Kerry handed the handcuffs to Smith, she surveyed the hole in the ceiling and the mess on the floor. Relief caused an urge to laugh; the feeling gripped her so tightly her stomach ached. The metallic snap of the handcuffs on Louise Abernathy's wrists was a beautiful noise. Kerry caught Smith's neck and hugged him tightly.

"The police will be here any minute, T.K. I don't know what's taking them so long. Oh, God, but I love you. Your hands are bleeding. Are you hurt? What—"

Smith glanced at Louise quickly, then kissed Kerry. He kept his eyes open and held a gun, but his kiss was wonderful anyway.

Then Kerry remembered Angela. She pushed away, mouthing, "Oh, my God," and hurried into the office. She reeled in confused circles, then a hesitant noise from under the desk made her bend over and look. "Mom, oh, Mom, everything is okay now." She helped Angela out, and they fell into each other's arms.

Smith called, "Everything all right in there?"

Walking out with her arm firmly around Angela's shoulders, Kerry nodded. "Uh-huh. You sure made a mess, though. The property managers are going to hate this.''

''I was listening to your voices and didn't watch where I was going. I slipped off the beam. You okay, Angela?''

''This is some man you've found, Kerry,'' Angela said. Her eyes were tearful, but her smile was genuine. With her usual aplomb, she recovered quickly from her ordeal and held her chin high as she combed her hair with her fingers.

Admiration warmed Kerry's breast. Suddenly she remembered her mother's unflappable courage when Kerry's father had served in Vietnam; her smooth efficiency when it was time to move, yet again, and she had to handle packers and movers and changing addresses and all the other details of uprooting their lives; how she had grieved when her husband died, but how it never broke her spirit. For the very first time, Kerry realized her mother wasn't a flake. She was strong. Quirky, unusual and demanding, but strong.

Kerry squeezed Angela's shoulders and murmured, ''I'm sorry I didn't tell you about this, Mom. I should have warned you. I should have realized you were in danger. I'm so sorry.''

Angela gave her a sour look.

''Well,'' Kerry mumbled defensively, ''I didn't want to worry you.''

''Worry me?'' Hurt colored Angela's face. ''I'm your mother. We share everything. Honestly, Kerry, when did you start keeping secrets?'' She clicked her tongue and looked away.

''I'm sorry, Mom, it's just that—'' Kerry noticed the computer screen. The word *wait* still glowed. ''Oh, no,

Blackie. Just a minute.'' She peeled away from her mother and typed, "Break break Blackie all is Okay."

"?"

"Good guys Won. You did call the police didn't you?"

"Not there?"

" "

"Where's a cop when you need one?"

"Try speeding through a school zone. Love you. Twinkies are on the way."

"When the cops get to your house, don't tell them I called. I prefer the persona-non-grata gig."

Louise gaped at the computer screen. Her lips tightened in a thin line.

Kerry groaned. Blackie had sent the police to her apartment. No wonder they hadn't arrived. She thanked the heavens above for Smith. She typed, "We need to work on our coding. I'm at Copy Copy not—"

The doorbell tinkled. Kerry jumped, her first thought that a customer had seen the lights and figured that the place was open for business. She turned, saying, "I'm sorry, but— Mr. Marsh?"

"Going for the glory at the head of the cavalry charge?" Smith asked.

Angela strode to the D.A., hand extended, crying, "It's about time the authorities arrived. Good heavens, but this horrible woman has put us through the most horrendous—"

Kerry caught Louise's triumphant smile and opened her mouth to shout a warning.

Marsh snatched Angela, spinning her about. Angela cried out in pain and fear. He held a very large, extremely ugly automatic pistol to Angela's head. He growled, "Drop it, Smith."

Holding Louise's gun in both hands, Smith hesitated. Marsh squeezed Angela's arm, making her squirm. Smith placed the gun on the floor and used his boot to nudge it toward Marsh. "Not a bad setup, Marsh. Stay in the background, give a little technical advice and manipulate the evidence."

"Shut up, cowboy. I'd prefer not to shoot you. But it is a possibility I am willing to explore."

Rattling the handcuffs, Louise ordered, "Get these things off me."

Marsh shoved Angela toward the counter, then he scooped up Louise's gun. "Where's the money, Louise?"

"You knew!" Kerry cried. "Damn it, you knew all along. We should have checked him out, T.K." She looked behind him for the police, but knew they weren't coming. She inched her fingers toward the Enter key. *Come on, Blackie, one more favor and I'll never ask you for anything again.*

"Don't move, Kerry," Marsh ordered and she froze. "The money."

Kerry grabbed the cases and plopped them on the countertop. Rage bubbled like lava in her belly. Now she knew why she'd never liked Robert Marsh. He was a slimy creep.

"Uncuff me," Louise ordered, giving the handcuffs a shake that set them rattling.

"Don't bother, Smith," Marsh said. "All four of you, into the office. Now."

"Robert?" Louise breathed. Her sunglasses had fallen off in the struggle; now her eyes were plainly frightened.

"You're no longer an asset, Louise. You're a liability. Ward knows all about you." Marsh herded the four of them into the office. The key turned in the lock with a clunking noise.

"Great," Kerry said, glaring at Louise. They had Louise, but now Marsh would be running for Mexico and they'd never catch him. "You sure can pick them, can't you? Why didn't you shoot him instead of Piver?"

"Shut up." Louise slumped against the desk and glumly regarded the hole where Smith had removed the acoustical tile. "You aren't the one going to prison. This whole thing was his idea. He's the one who found Nordoff, and he's the one who told me about planting evidence. It was him. I didn't do any of it. It isn't fair!"

Waving away her mother's warning to be careful, Kerry climbed up onto the desk. "T.K., can you get the door open? We have to catch him fast."

"It isn't my fault. I never hurt anybody. Robert did it. He did everything!" Louise began to cry.

Kerry wrinkled her nose. Louise had lapsed into an East Texas accent as twangy as guitar strings. With her lipstick smeared and her suit filthy, she looked pitiful, but Kerry couldn't muster an ounce of pity.

Smith pressed his ear against the door. He waved for silence. Angela snatched up the telephone, then huffed. "Out of order."

Kerry groaned at the sound of the computer tone. "It isn't out of order. That's the computer. Jeez, can't anything go right today?" She called Piver fifty types of idiot for being too cheap to install a second phone line. She reached for the ceiling, seeking a handhold.

"Hold on, sugar. He hasn't left yet."

"Maybe he went out the back door. What is he doing?"

"I don't know. I haven't heard the bell yet. There it is." Smith tried the lock, then muttered.

Kerry pulled herself into the ceiling, kicking her legs for impetus. She hooked one arm over a steel beam, then swinging her body, she found a firmer hold. An acrid chemical stench struck her nose. Her eyes burned and watered. Coughing, she dropped to the desk. "T.K.! The crawl space is full of smoke. My God, he set the shop on fire!"

The smoke alarm began to scream.

ROBERT MARSH GLANCED AT his watch. There was plenty of time to get back to the courthouse before ten o'clock. As he eased his Ferrari into the morning traffic, he caught himself smiling. There was no reason now to feel annoyed that Tarkington Smith managed to overturn Abernathy's conviction. It just didn't matter anymore. He guessed that when he finished counting the cash in those bags, not much of anything would matter anymore. He slipped into a pleasant daydream of giving his acceptance speech, shaking hands with the mayor as flashbulbs popped and cameras whirred....

A Chevette cut in close, in front of him. Marsh stomped on the brake, but only smiled at the other driver's inconsideration.

"You're a lucky boy, born under a lucky star," Marsh's grandfather had told him long ago. It was the truth. If he hadn't gone to the office early to catch up on paperwork and hadn't seen Smith and Kerry leaving Ward's office in a near panic, he never would have found out where Louise and her money were hiding. Now he had enough money for a last-minute push to oust Bradford Lowell and seat himself firmly in the District Attorney's office. Who knew how lucky he might get? Collin County this term, the entire state of Texas

the next. Perhaps a seat on the Texas Supreme Court?
He'd make an excellent judge.

"Thank you, Kerry and Smith," he said cheerfully.
"I couldn't have done this without you."

KERRY GRABBED SMITH before he could climb onto the
desk. She cried, "The chemicals! The place is full of
chemicals. The smoke will kill you!"

Bitter, chemical-tinged smoke curled down from the
ceiling and from under the door. The smoke detector
blared. Kerry quailed at the uselessness of it, knowing
that the back room, full of paper and highly flammable
chemicals, was an inferno by now.

Angela coughed, her eyes already red and tearing.
She clutched Kerry's sleeve. Louise looked terrified.
Kerry almost felt sorry for her.

Smith ripped open his shirt, all but tearing it off his
back. He said, "When we get out of here, will you
marry me?"

Kerry stared at him, incredulously. "What?"

"Marry me."

If there was a *Guinness Book of World Records* cat-
egory for craziness, this would fit right in. She gaped
at his grin. "I'll think about it."

"Don't argue with the man," Angela said.

"You're all crazy!" Louise screeched, tearing at the
handcuffs.

"Yes!" Kerry yelled. "Yes, I will marry you. Now
go!"

He wrapped his shirt around his lower face. Then he
jumped onto the desk and pulled himself through the
hole with lithe motion.

Kerry grabbed Louise's head and pushed her to the
floor, yelling, "Get down! Mom, get down." She lis-

tened for Smith, but all she heard was a steadily growing roar of flames.

A list of flammable items ticked through her mind in a macabre inventory. Copier toner, copier developer, liquid adhesive, spray paints, turpentine, rolls of plastic for the shrink-wrap machine, boxes of paper, chemically treated paper for carbonless copies. Warning labels: "Keep away from open flame."

The interior of the office turned blue with smoke. Kerry coughed, trying not to breathe the stinging fumes. Smoke inhalation killed more people than flames. She'd read that in the newspaper. How long did it take? How long before their lungs collapsed? How long could Smith hold his breath? One good lungful of that noxious atmosphere would surely knock him out. She pulled her sweater up over her mouth and nose, but it did no good. Her lungs screamed for fresh air. Her eyes watered, blinding her. She pressed her hand against the door. It was cool, but for how long?

The door shoved inward, knocking her off balance. Smoke and heat rushed into the office, fluming up to meet the roaring inferno in the ceiling. Dimly aware of her mother's hands clutching her sweater, Kerry crawled, guided by the tough, implacable hand that gripped her shoulder.

Her chest burned, seemed to swell and ached for air. Licks of flame curled from the back room. Incredible heat scorched through her jeans and sweater. Her body rebelled, but she forced herself to crawl and crawl, resisting the urge to stand up and run in the lethal smoke.

From faraway a bell tinkled. It sounded sweetly tinny under the screeching wail of the smoke alarm. Hands pulled. Her feet stumbled, hurrying away from the billowing smoke. Something hard and cold hit her face. It was a rush of pure oxygen that both elated and stung her tortured lungs. She heard voices and saw flashes of slick yellow. Sirens wailed. A static-charged crackle filled Kerry's ears. Blackness teased like a curtain on the edges of her sight. It was as though a naughty child were playing with the draw cords, closing the curtain, then opening it.

"Can you hear me, miss?" a concerned voice asked. "This is going to sting."

Kerry squinted through her tears, trying to find the source of the voice. Cold water struck her eyes and she gasped, but hands held her head still while the chemical-laden smoke was flushed from her eyes.

"T.K.?" she rasped, realizing that an oxygen mask had been placed over her face. She tried to tear it away, but a paramedic urged her to keep it on.

As her vision cleared, she saw her mother and Louise. They were also wearing oxygen masks and were seated in the parking lot, surrounded by paramedics. Blue-and-red emergency lights strobed through a blanket of black smoke. Men shouted. Sirens still wailed. People filled the parking lot. Policemen formed blockades.

Kerry struggled against the paramedic. She searched the crowd. Her heart swelled and seemed to burst with an unimaginable pain. She tore away the mask and croaked, "T.K.! T.K. is in the ceiling!" She clawed at the paramedics and scrambled away from their clutching hands. Asphalt scraped her palms and ripped her jeans. "T.K.!"

Metal slammed against metal, then a beloved drawl said, "Hey, sugar."

Blindly, she fell into his arms and buried her face against his smoky skin. A paramedic tried to fit the oxygen mask over her face again, but she didn't need it. Smith was safe, and she loved him. She didn't need anything else.

COLLIN COUNTY COURTROOM number three seemed cavernous in its emptiness. While the trial of William Abernathy had jammed the room with spectators, the sentencing drew only a few. The public wanted suspense, not certainty.

Judge MacElroy's round face was impassive. "I regret yet another denial, Mr. Quintas. But you have shown me no hard evidence to convince this court that your client deserves any delay in this matter."

Quintas said, "Thirty minutes, your honor. Just thirty minutes! Bob Ward is compiling the reports now. There are some problems. A witness is delayed, and I must beg the mercy of the court."

"You have known for many weeks about this court date, sir. No more delays."

Robert Marsh tapped a sheaf of papers on the prosecution's table. With all witnesses permanently delayed, he was feeling magnanimous. He glanced at William Abernathy. Marsh mustered pity. Abernathy was a born victim, the man had no class at all. The prosecutor smiled at Judge MacElroy. "Your honor, new information concerning this case has recently come to my attention. It is in the interest of the state for you to honor the defendant's request for delay."

"Can you explain, Mr. Marsh?" the judge asked.

The double doors slammed inward. Courtroom reporters lost their bored expressions and brightened as they turned toward the source of the interruption.

Tarkington Smith strode down the aisle, holding a disheveled Louise Abernathy with her arms handcuffed securely behind her. Close on their heels were Bob

Ward, Ed Shanlin and two uniformed police officers. Geoffrey Quintas jumped to his feet. William Abernathy arose more slowly, his shocked gaze locked on his wife.

The judge rapped his gavel. Marsh laid his papers neatly on the table. His smile was tight and fixed. His feet itched to run, but he resisted. Smith and Louise could babble until the next ice age and it was nothing but hearsay. Not one shred of physical evidence connected him to anything. Robert's secretary could testify he'd been in his office all morning. No one had seen him leave. No one had seen him return.

Judge MacElroy demanded, "What is the meaning of this? Mr. Ward, you'd better have a good explanation. Court is in session."

William Abernathy held out a hand and said, "Louise? My God, Louise."

Smith planted Louise before the judge. He drawled, "Louise Abernathy, your honor. Murder victim." He swiped at his soot-stained cheek and grinned at Bill.

William Abernathy stared at his wife. Reporters furiously wrote down every word.

Louise, her white suit streaked and reeking of smoke, held her head high and graced Robert Marsh with a smile. In an almost cheerful twang, she said, "I believe the proper phrase for this is 'gotcha, you son of a bitch.' No hard feelings."

Marsh ignored her. It was all hearsay. After this story broke and the extent of Louise's crimes was known, no one would believe her if she said the sky was blue. There was nothing to connect them, nothing at all. He cleared his throat, then looked at the judge. "As I said, your honor, it is in the interest of the state to delay this sentencing. With the help of Mr. Smith, it has come to our attention—"

The double doors opened again. District Attorney Bradford Lowell, his black suit severe and his expression befitting an avenging angel, strode down the aisle. He clutched a bulky manila envelope. He glanced at his watch, then nodded at the police officers. He looked at Ward and said, "Sorry it took me so long." He nodded a gracious apology to the judge.

Robert Marsh felt the first wave of panic as Ed Shanlin read him his rights.

KERRY LEANED against Smith. His arm rested comfortably over her shoulders, and his hand toyed under her hair. He'd scared her after the fire. After getting her and Angela out, he'd gone back for Louise, then the paramedics had placed him inside an ambulance to treat him for smoke inhalation. Kerry feared letting him go now. She never wanted to let him go. Her shakes had started in Bob Ward's office. It was a delayed reaction. *Get a grip, Byfield, it's finally over.*

Kerry held her mother's hand. Having taken the time to fix her hair and raid Kerry's purse for lipstick and blusher, Angela looked radiant. Belinda Forester stood behind them. The housekeeper's face was triumphantly vindictive. She'd signed her complaint against Louise Abernathy for knocking her on the head and then locking her in a pantry.

Bill Abernathy sat on a chair in Bob Ward's office. He looked baffled. Quintas kept pounding him on the shoulder, murmuring, "I told you we were going to beat this thing."

At the center of it all, Ward leaned back on his chair, hands locked behind his neck. He drawled, "You've left me with one hell of a mess to sort out, Smith. Corruption, conspiracy, murder, attempted murders. Even got good old Rex yelling about cutting a deal. He wants to give us Marsh in exchange for the cocaine bust. I'm going to be busier than a one-armed cowboy in a roping contest.'' He swung his head from side to side.

Smith lifted a shoulder. His finger tightened against Kerry's neck, and he flicked her earlobe with his thumb. ''Your problem, Ward. I did what I set out to do. Thanks for your help.''

''Nope. Thank you.'' Ward chuckled. ''I figure with Marsh going down, the press is going to look real hard at Bradford Lowell. From the looks of that little package he got in the mail, Marsh's corruption runs deep. Hell, this about stomps the crap out of Lowell's campaign for reelection. You know how the press thinks. Corruption always trickles down.'' He chuckled, his eyes glinting. ''It might be short notice, but who says I wouldn't fit the job just fine?'' He cocked his head. ''You wouldn't by any chance be looking for a job? I could use a man like you.''

Smith caressed Kerry with his eyes. ''No, thanks. I've got plenty to do.'' Smith made a hat-tipping gesture. ''If you're finished taking statements and affidavits, I have a dinner date with a trio of lovelies that I don't mean to miss.''

Bill Abernathy stood and shook hands with Ward. ''Thank you, sir.''

They all walked out into the glorious late-afternoon sunshine. Smith and Kerry walked hand in hand. In the parking lot, next to Quintas's Lincoln Continental, Smith turned to Bill Abernathy. ''That cut it pretty close, old buddy. Next time, don't be so shy about calling.''

Bill nodded. His eyes were moist. To see him, Kerry thought her heart would break. Her eyes burned, and she blinked back tears. In a few short months, he'd gone from being the happiest man in the world to being betrayed and heartbroken. Softly, she said, "Mr. Abernathy, I'm terribly sorry."

His head quivered in a barely perceptible motion. "You did what you had to do." He looked up at T.K. "Call me before you leave town. We can catch up on old times."

"Sure you won't join us?"

"Not tonight." Bill smiled in the way miserable people do. "Not tonight." He got into his attorney's car.

Watching them drive away, Kerry asked, "Will he be all right?"

"Eventually. He's pretty tough. He survived all them Yankees at Harvard." Smith squeezed her hand. His grin turned devilish. "You and I have some things to discuss. I remember you saying something about marrying me."

"T.K., not now." She looked at her mother.

"I heard you, darling," Angela said. "You can't back out of this one. I won't let you." She tucked her hand into Smith's free one. "I don't think I've ever seen a more perfect match."

Kerry rolled her eyes, wondering how to get out of this, or even if she wanted to. How long had she known him? It was unreal. Or had she been waiting for him forever? Her heart said yes. Still, she protested, "I've only known you a week, Tarkington Smith. I don't believe in whirlwind courtships."

Strolling through the parking lot, Smith looked at Angela. "What do you think, Angela—"

"Call me Mom, darling."

"What do you think, Mom? I take her on down south for a while? Maybe down to the Gulf for a few sunsets, watching dolphins in the surf, and some candlelit dinners?''

"Perhaps some scuba diving or horseback riding," Angela offered.

"We can do that."

"Mom…"

"Oh, hush, Kerry. You are such a fuddy-duddy. Your father and I only knew each other for three weeks before we were married. We had a perfectly wonderful life together." Angela giggled like a girl and swung Smith's hand. "This wedding is going to be so much fun! Oh, Kerry, I know the perfect couturier to design your gown. White is passé. We'll use that new shade of pink called wood rose…" She talked on and on, with Smith smiling approval at every word.

Kerry looked at Belinda and murmured, "Have you ever seen a more perfectly matched pair?" Her heart was doing that dance again. Was it possible to die of happiness?

Belinda merely smiled as she opened Angela's car door.

"We'll meet you ladies at the house about seven o'clock. Drive carefully, hear?"

As soon as they were seated in the truck and Smith closed his door, Kerry said, "You make a lot of assumptions, Tarkington Smith. We barely know each other. These things take time."

In reply, he pulled her close. His kiss reached down deep into her soul where it shredded all the little doubts. His hair smelled of smoke, but underneath was that scent of spicy maleness that set her blood afire. She clasped his back, never wanting to let him go. When they finally parted, his midnight blue eyes smiled at her.

He slowly stroked her back. "With those pretty green eyes looking at me, how can I go wrong?"

"Are you ever wrong?"

"Do you love me?"

"Crazy as it is, yes. With all my heart, yes, yes, yes." She placed a finger against his lips. "But this is so fast. I have to know you're sure and that we aren't making a mistake. This could be a mistake you know."

"Maybe," he said, and he kissed her again.

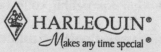

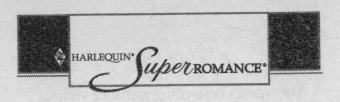

...there's more to the story!

Superromance.
A *big* satisfying read about unforgettable
characters. Each month we offer *six* very different
stories that range from family drama to adventure
and mystery, from highly emotional stories to
romantic comedies—and much more! Stories
about people you'll believe in and care about.
Stories too compelling to put down....

Our authors are among today's *best* romance
writers. You'll find familiar names and talented
newcomers. Many of them are award winners—
and you'll see why!

If you want the biggest and best
in romance fiction, you'll get it
from Superromance!

Emotional, Exciting, Unexpected...

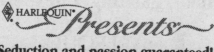

HARLEQUIN®
INTRIGUE

WE'LL LEAVE YOU BREATHLESS!

If you've been looking for thrilling tales of
contemporary passion and sensuous love stories
with taut, edge-of-the-seat suspense—then
you'll love Harlequin Intrigue!

Every month, you'll meet four new heroes
who are guaranteed to make your spine tingle
and your pulse pound. With them you'll enter
into the exciting world of Harlequin Intrigue—
where your life is on the line
and so is your heart!

THAT'S INTRIGUE—
ROMANTIC SUSPENSE
AT ITS BEST!

HARLEQUIN®
Makes any time special ®